THEM

THEM

JAMES WATTS

THEM

Published by Sinister Smile Press, LLC
A division of Crystal Lake Publishing
P.O. Box 637, Newberg, OR 97132

Copyright © 2022 by James Watts

Trade Paperback
ISBN: 978-1-964398-53-2

www.sinistersmilepress.com

CONTENTS

ACKNOWLEDGMENTS

Thank you to Chris Miller for the amazing foreword and for the support and friendship. You will never know how much it means to me.

I would like to dedicate this novel to my father, Charles Eugene Watts— Bud to those that knew him— who passed away on October 13th, 1997. Wish you were here. I miss you.

I also want to dedicate this book to my ex-wife, Andrea Renee May, who passed away on August 21st of 2006. I know sometimes we fought, but I'll always miss you.

Finally, I dedicate this work to my son, Bailey, whom I owe the courage to begin writing this book. I love you son, never forget that.

DO YOU LIKE SCARY BOOKS?
A FOREWORD BY CHRIS MILLER

You remember the 80s, right? It was a time when horror finally seemed to find some real acceptance in both film and print, a time when creatures found their way on the screen with terrific (and sometimes *not* so terrific) practical effects using corn syrup and hollowed out melons rather than CGI and green-screens. A time when slashers ruled the box-office and a whole host of new authors were being first discovered and old pros were coming into their own. Think of all the great movie posters and the great covers on books. We call them retro now, but at the time they were new, exciting, and chilling.

Well, whether or not you remember them, I do. I'm a *huge* fan of the horror wave of the 80s. I guess it technically started in the 70s, but it really came into its own in the next decade. Not that I was allowed to watch any of the films or read any of those books, but I remember them all the same. The movie trailers on the TV about Jason or Michael or Freddy, about monstrous parasites from outer space getting dug up in Antarctica. A thousand other awesome ideas.

While I wasn't allowed to watch them, I recall being enraptured by the trailers and by the covers I would see on the shelves at pharmacies, even Wal Mart on occasion. They were *so* scary looking and *so* cool in their presentation. In fact, I'd often sneak away from my mom when we were out shopping with her to go find the book aisle in the store so I could browse and sample snippets I wouldn't get to properly appreciate for another ten to fifteen years, all because I couldn't get my eyes to turn away from the amazing artwork that used to draw me in so much back in those days.

I mentioned I wasn't allowed to watch those movies or read those books, remember? Well, that's because I was raised in a very conservative, Christian home. My parents believed at the time that those movies and books would be harmful to my psyche and spiritual life. Or something. Anyway, if I wanted to see or read any of that stuff, it had to be done in secret, and always at a friend's house.

I think the first time I watched a real horror flick from that period wasn't until sometime in the 90s when I went to a girl's house I went to school with for her birthday party. She was a huge fan of all the horror I could only lust after, and at her party we watched the original 'Halloween'.

I was blown away. The only thing I'd seen before that which could be called a horror movie and approached the level of suspense I felt as I watched Michael Myers hack and slash his way through Haddonfield was the original 'Psycho'. And while I always adored that movie, this one seemed to have even more teeth. I was unnerved, fascinated, and relished every hammering heartbeat in my thundering chest. It was awesome.

I was hooked. I was old enough to be able to ignore my parent's hand-wringing objections to my consumption of the forbidden arts, and started haunting my local video store—yeah, yeah, I'm *that* old—and grabbing every classic and obscure release I could lay my hands on.

Over time, I eventually watched virtually everything on their shelves in the horror section of worth. And some that weren't (the 80s didn't exactly have a perfect track-record when it came to film). I was finally well-versed in the movies I'd been admiring from afar all those years, and I kept consuming more as more modern classics were released like 'Scream' and 'Event Horizon' (God, I fucking *love* that move!).

I've also always been a big reader. Like the movies I wasn't allowed to watch, my parents were likewise unwilling to allow me to consume horror in the written word. However, as the 90s drew to a close and I was ready for something more vicious than Tom Clancy's Jack Ryan novels (which I still am a big fan of), I decided to pick up my first Stephen King book. Because to someone who has never read horror, King is most often your first experience with the genre.

I picked up 'Black House', written by King along with Peter Straub. At the time I got the novel, I didn't realize it was a sequel. 'The Talisman' had never come across my radar, and I'd never seen it on the shelves at the stores. After reading all the 'about the book' sections on the back or inside flaps of the novels in the book aisle of Wal Mart, I decided 'Black House' was the right one for me. I got home and began reading, and it wasn't until I reached the end of the book that I realized I was reading a sequel to something else. But I adored the book (fuck ALL of you who deride it, you're fucking wrong and I'll never be convinced otherwise) and decided I had to have more.

Naturally, like any young, budding horror book lover, I got some more King initially. I still didn't find 'The Talisman' anywhere, but I did find 'Gerald's Game' and 'Rose

Madder'. Both of these are not often referred to fondly by either fans of the genre or King himself, but I devoured them both, reading into the wee hours of the morning for nights on end, and adored them both. Especially 'Gerald's Game', which still stands as one of my favorite King novels and one of my favorite horror novels ever. It's a suspense masterpiece.

Once those were done, I once more found myself on the book aisle of Wal Mart, reading the backs of books and the inside flaps of the hardcovers. There wasn't much in the way of King books that day, I remember, at least not ones I hadn't already read. But there were a handful of other horror books. I'd managed to read my fair share of 'Fear Street' and 'Goosebumps' books by R.L. Stine from my school library for Accelerated Reading (always hiding them from my parents), but I wanted more *adult* stuff like King's.

I settled on a title called 'Ghoul' by the now-legendary Brian Keene. At the time, he only had a couple of books out, but the cover caught my eye and the description on the back of the mass-market paperback drew me in and I took the dive.

One of the best books I've ever read to this day. It blew me away. And while King was (and still is) my favorite, that book opened a whole new world up to me in the genre of horror. Keene was a bit more *extreme* in his horror than King was, and I found that this characteristic was enthralling to me, how far he was willing to go with his characters (and in the instance of 'Ghoul', they were kids), and it was then I decided I *had* to write stories of my own, where before I'd only *wanted* to.

Fast forward a couple decades and I'm a published author of horror and suspense myself. Along with that comes meeting and getting to know other authors in the field, and one that kept popping up on my Facebook time-line over and over again was James Watts. He was advertising for his novel 'THEM', which you're holding in your hands now. I ignored it at first—*everyone is trying to pimp their wares on Facebook*—but it kept showing up in my feed over and over. Eventually, we became friends and I finally took the dive and read the novel.

I was pleasantly surprised. It had all the feel and grittiness of the 80s while having a modern setting. The gore wasn't over the top, but it was there when it needed to be to serve the plot. The characters were so real they seemed like actual people I'd met in my own life. It had creatures and human villains alike (oh, you are going to *love* Ol' Judd in this one!), and a terrific setting in a small southern town. All the elements were just right, and I devoured it in only a couple of days.

James and I became fast friends, sharing work back and forth for feedback, and then he went to the 2018 ScareFest in Lexington, Kentucky. ScareFest is a horror convention put on annually where authors, filmmakers, celebrities, artists, and myriad others associated with horror come and set up shop for a weekend full of cosplay and fun. Since we were Facebook buddies, I saw all his posts from the weekend where he sold all but one of the copies of 'THEM' he'd brought along to sell. He'd done well and told me and some other authors about how he was definitely going back the next year.

Fast forward with me once more to 2019 and James and I shared a table with Tony Evans (author of 'Sour' and 'Better You Believe') and Richard Rumple (author of 'Gabriella: Tales From a Demon Cat', 'Train of Blood', among others) at the 2019 ScareFest. It was really too many people for a single table, all selling our books, but the tables were expensive and we had a blast all the same. It was my first convention, actually, so I was looking to James and Richard (who'd both attended the year before) to get some pointers, along with getting some from my air B & B roommates for the trip, John Wayne Communale (author of 'Sinkhole' and 'As Seen on TV', among others) and Jarod Barbee (half-owner of Death's Head Press). They'd all been to more Cons than me, so I watched and learned the art of pimping your own books.

James is a short, stocky southern man. He chats with you in a very conversational, informal way. He isn't stuffy or full of himself at all. In fact, he's as regular and personable a guy as I've ever met. He'd had a lot of success the year before, so I paid particular attention to him.

James was situated at our table right at the corner of two perpendicular aisleways. We were right across from acting legends Lee Majors and Bruce Campbell, so the traffic was pretty heavy. Any time someone walked by our booth, whether they showed any interest at all or not, James was all over them.

"Do you like scary books?"

This question resounded every minute or two at the very least. Some folks would nod, purse their lips, and line up for the spiel, while others would either ignore him or just say, "no thanks" while they moved on. But it didn't stop James, not for a second.

I probably heard the question, "Do you like scary books?" in the neighborhood of five-thousand times during that weekend, James sitting there at his chair behind his mound of books, a perpetually grinning face and a twinkle in his eye as he engaged with potential readers and customers. At some point (don't ask me just when), he elevated his game by slapping the top of his book when he asked the now-famous question, which inevitably drew the eyes of whomever he was speaking to. This often led to them grabbing a copy, hefting it, turning it over in their hands. It's hard to tell if people are just being polite or if they're actually reading about your book on the back cover, but I think most of these folks were being genuine as they perused the description.

The rest of us—Tony, Richard, and I—were either trying to snag the attention of those James was engaging with or trying to catch folks coming from the other direction. But James's book-swatting question seemed to dominate the table.

2019 didn't prove as successful as 2018 had for James in terms of sales ScareFest, but it *did* serve as a helpful bit of instruction for selling a book to people who don't know who the fuck you are. He knew how to get your attention. The repeated question, the audible slapping on the stack of books that drew the eye, the practiced spiel of what the book was about and what his writing style was like. All of it came together to teach me—the 'new guy'— what it means to be an author. James had already written a great book, something you're about to discover shortly, but that isn't enough. It's fundamentally important, but far from all there is to success.

James just knows how to connect with people. Personalities may clash between certain people, and no everyone is going to like you or your work, but none of that stood in James's way when it came to trying to put the book in your hands into the hands of total strangers who had no intention of buying a book that day. And that's when—and *how*—I learned to reach out, grab hold of a strangers arm, and convince them they needed to read my books.

James knows how to engage with people, but more than that, he knows how to tell a *story* that engages people. Isn't that what all this writing thing is all about, anyway? Telling a story that draws people in, makes them forget all about their own lives and problems and allows them to escape for a while with total strangers they come to love by the book's end.

And this is what James Watts has accomplished, not only with 'THEM', but a host of short stories and coming novels I've had the privilege to sample being his friend. Slap the goddamned book. Make them look at it and take notice. Engage with them whether they want to or not. *THAT* is how you sell a story. Make it as good as possible, and put it their hands. Hell, I even watched James walk up to Bruce fucking Campbell and stick a signed copy of 'THEM' in his hand and make the 'Evil Dead' legend's eyebrows raise as his pearly whites made an obligatory appearance when he said, "A novel? I *love* novels!"

True story.

I'm going to stop rambling now and let you get on with what you came here to consume: James Watts's 'THEM'. It's a horror novel that captures all the energy and nostalgia of the 80s horror flicks and books we all grew up adoring, while updating it and keeping it relevant. The monsters within these pages are vicious and sly, but so is Watts's writing. It unfolds like an onion, a layer at a time, finally cumulating in a horror story that would be right at home along all the classics of the era we grew up in as Gen-Xers and Millennials. There's not a single drop of gore that doesn't serve the plot, not a single gratuitous scene, but all the same, it fits right it with intelligence and suspense and terrific characters. This is a book that belongs on the shelves of every horror aficionado in the country and beyond, and you'll soon see why. From the opening scene that grabs you and chills your bones, all the way through to the intense, horrifying ending, you'll be enthralled and curled into a defensive fetal position. And when you close that final page, though you'll be satisfied and shaking, you're going to want more.

Luckily for you, I happen to know more is coming.

So, I'll shut up now and let you get to the real reason you're here to begin with: to read James Watts's novel 'THEM'. I expect you'll be as enthralled as I was, but I hope you'll learn an important truth along the journey, the same as I have. And what's that lesson, you ask? Scary books are a lot of fucking fun.

Slap!

That's the sound your eyes are drawn to as you look down on the cover of this tome. James *makes* you take notice. Forces you to pay attention.

And then he scares the shit out of you.

Chris Miller—Author of THE DAMNED PLACE and THE HARD GOODBYE, 12—14—19

PROLOGUE

She found it hard to breathe as she ran; her nightgown soaked from the rain, clinging to her tiny frame the way a sheet of newspaper clings to the wet surface of a city street. Branches and thorns cut into her face, ankles, and arms as she trampled through the tangled undergrowth and sapling trees. Deviating from the red rock path, she had chosen thorn patches and prickly limbs over immediate death. She could hear them behind her, thrashing and cutting their way through the brush. Angry, bad-tempered, creatures of hate and darkness, they roared in fury at their prey's defiance against them. Their fury filled by giving chase to such a fragile old woman. That, however, would not change her course, nor would it instill in her the need to give in, to give up so that they could ravage and desecrate her remains. She may be old, perhaps, but weak-willed and subservient, no. If they were to overcome her and tear her apart, they would have to earn that right. Until that moment, she had no intention of stopping, no matter how bad it hurt to breathe or how treacherous the ground beneath her feet had become.

A fusillade of explosions tore across the heavens as flashes of light brighter than a midday sun illuminated the world around her. In those brief instances of light, she spied glimpses of the beasts hunting her. They were closer now, much closer than she had thought. The tangles of weeds and limbs had slowed them some, but apparently not enough as they were closing the distance at a fair speed. A tarnished silver pendant in the shape of a dolphin and affixed to a rusted chain dangled between the fingers of her right hand. She raised it to her lips, praying silently and reaching out her left hand to grab hold of a young oak. This was the point where the old road had cut through the property some one-hundred years before, the road that had led to the Atkins' home place. She cast a look over her shoulder as she ascended the small bank, holding onto the sapling oak with a firm grip and careful not to slip on the mud and dead leaves. They were still coming.

Forcing her way through an even denser thicket of blackberry bushes and pines, she pushed onward. The woods here had always been wild and untamed, at least as far back as she could remember, but never had she noticed so many of the smaller trees and bushes that were now causing her so much grief. If her husband were still alive, it would not be like this, he would have had it all cut back into neat little paths and trails. This had been his turf, out here amongst the trees, had been his Never Land, but that was no more. For almost eleven years now, and for eternity, he was gone, and she was alone.

She hated being alone. She hated having to face these devils. She hated not knowing what to do. Worst yet, she hated herself for being so weak. Her husband had been strong and always knew exactly how to handle things. Oh, how she missed him and wished that he were here now. He had always believed in her, believed in her strong will, even her tendency to be hardheaded at times. "Liz, you're the most pigheaded, stubborn woman I've ever laid eyes on," he used to say, "but by God, I wouldn't trade you for all the gold in Fort Knox." Oh, how she missed him.

She was reaching up to wipe a lock of gray hair from her eyes when she fell, slipping on a slick bed of pine needles, and landing on her back. For a moment, she lay there with the rain pecking her face; her back and legs quivering in pain, and then she slowly stood up, using the base of an aging poplar tree for support. A loud metallic shriek echoed around her, followed by another, then another, until the stormy night was alive with the twisting metal shrieks of them. You could hear the anger, the hunger, the frenzied longing for the kill in those mad cries. Leaning against the knotted old poplar in the pouring rain, hitching in breath after breath with the unholy wails of the damned skirting the shadows, a refreshed determination shone in her teary eyes.

"I am not weak," she sobbed and let go of the tree.

Taking a step forward, wincing from the pain in her legs, she cast one more glance behind her. "I am not weak!" she shouted into the darkness. "Do you hear that? I...am...not...WEAK!"

"Nor are we, bitch!" A thousand voices at once, discontent and irate, screaming at her in a thousand tongues. Thunder rolled and lightning struck across the night and she moved forward. Not yet defeated, and filled with anger of her own, she was unwavering in her decision to evade her hunters and make it to the safety of her house.

Slapping branches out of her way and mindful of the dead leaves, slick pine needle beds, the exposed roots of trees, and the not too distant memory of her spill to the sodden ground, she held high her goals to make it to her house and through the front door, shutting out the madness behind her. Her lungs were not used to such strains and her heart, lazy and frail thing that it was, was beating a bass drum solo in her chest. She hadn't had this much exercise in several long years, and on a normal day would have no exercise at all, other than tending her flower beds or weeding out the vegetable garden behind the

house. Lord lend me the strength to go on, she prayed silently. Lend me the will to survive this nightmare.

In the distance, dim amber light seeped through a break in the tree line. It was the floodlight at the end of her driveway. She was no more than twenty, maybe thirty feet at the most, from her front yard. Limping a little on her left leg, and gritting her teeth with each step, she hurried on, using the occasional oak or pine to keep from falling flat on her face. In her hurry to be free of her pursuers, she nearly tripped and fell over the rusted frame of a child's tricycle that jutted from the mulched woodland floor like the skeletal corpse of some tiny, discarded robot. A rotted old string hung from one mildewed white rubber handgrip with a tiny G.I. Joe action figure hanging on the end of it like an old west cowboy hanging from a noose. Unlike the tricycle and the string, the G.I. Joe seemed to be unaffected by age or the elements. How strange was that?

"Look at him go, Liz!" Her husband's voice, happy and content as they stood on their front porch watching their five-year-old son peddle his little trike across the yard, dodging and weaving between young dogwood trees like a test driver maneuvering through the orange rubber cones on a test track. "He'll be ridin' a regular-sized bike before long! Damn, look at him go!"

He had grabbed her around the waist and hugged her tight, then planted a kiss on her cheek. "That boy's growin' so damn fast." He had then turned and called out to their son. "Give it hell, boy! By God, give it all you got!" And he had laughed that deep, joyful laugh that had been an Earnest Sanders trademark.

Fresh tears mingled with the rain streaming over her cheeks and for a moment, she thought she would drop to her knees and weep. Then, to her left sounded a loud snap and pop of breaking limbs and a rustle of brush. As vivid and as pleasant as it was, the memory of her husband and son had lulled her into a false sense of well-being. They were almost right on top of her, and she could linger no longer, lest she meets her maker at the tips of their razor-sharp claws. Calling on what little strength she had left, she bolted through the last wall of vines and thorn bushes and out onto the red rocked driveway, refusing to let her aching legs buckle and send her sprawling to the ground.

She was running hard now, the tarnished dolphin pendant bouncing and swinging from her clenched fist and pushing her body as much as it would allow her to push it. The outside light above her front door became a beacon for her salvation and suddenly she felt no pain, only relief, and hope. Her nightgown was nothing more now than filthy, tattered rags and her arms, legs, and neck a network of bruises and cuts, but she took notice of none of this. She would soon be in her house with the doors locked and the furnace set as high as it would go. Then, nothing of this would truly matter, not in one little bit, and all her fears and regrets would smother underneath her pillow as she dozed off to sleep.

Behind her, they burst into the clearing, growling, and barking, filling the night with their inhuman rage. She wanted to look back, to see them, to see how far or close they might be, but she didn't dare; it would be like a person terrified of heights looking down from atop a very high place—it would heighten her fear and cause her to make a crucial mistake. "Don't let them get you, momma." It was her son's voice, not as he was now, a grown man, but the voice of her son as a scared six-year-old boy. "Them is mean old monsters hidin' in the woods. Don't let them get you, momma." Get you, not get me, which is what he had said back when. Back when he was so little and still needed his mother.

"Momma's comin', baby. I won't let them get at you," she said, breaking out of her dash to safety and falling into a lumbering stagger. "I promise."

"You ain't goin' much of anywhere, Lizzy," She looked up and saw his hulking shadow between two dogwood trees, as menacing a form as any horror story monster. "I'll tell you what, though. You gave us one hell of a run. By damn if you didn't. But it's all over, now, old girl. I reckon you ain't got nowhere else to run."

Slimy, rotting fingers wrapped around her arms, something cold and bristly nudged her neck, and she screamed. From the shadows, over the pouring rain and thunder, she heard them laughing.

The phone on his nightstand was ringing, but it was as far away to him as an uncharted galaxy. At last, he opened his eyes and looked over at his alarm clock. Bright yellow numbers stared back at him. *Who in the hell's calling at three in the damn morning,* he thought, fumbling for the phone and succeeding only in knocking it out of its base and onto the floor.

"Damn it!" He reached down and picked up the phone, thumbing the talk button and pressing it to his ear. "Hello?"

The voice on the other end was tired and frightened. "Ray, this is Roy. Hate to wake you, cuz, but it's about your mom! You need to come home just as soon as you can!"

"What about my mom?" Ray Sanders asked, sitting up and swinging his legs over the edge of the bed. Concern for his mother replaced all thoughts of returning to sleep. "What's happened, Roy?"

"I…damn, man, I hate to be the one to tell you this."

"Just say it," Ray shot back. "Just tell me what's happened."

"Your mom, she called us about two or three hours ago, said she had a really bad scare from a bad dream and that her chest was hurtin'. Me and dad went over and got her over to the hospital, but it was no good, Ray. We were too late…and…and…" There was crying on the other end of the line, then an older, deep baritone voice.

"You still there, Ray?" It was his uncle James, who sounded as if he had done his own share of crying.

"I'm here," Ray said, dreamy and far away, afraid of this conversation, praying that it would end, and afraid of where it was heading. He did not want to hear what his uncle was about to say, not in the least. *You're dreaming, you know that, don't you?* But he wasn't.

"Your mom, she passed, son. Was a heart attack, that's what Doc Holden says. I am so sorry, with your dad gone and all, I know this is…"

"I'll be home tomorrow. I'll tend to things."

"All right," his uncle replied. "That's best, I imagine, but you be careful on the drive up. If you're not going to be able to hold up to it, me or Roy could come down to Panama City and pick you up, or you could take a bus."

"No. No, I'll be okay. Be a waste of gas and time for one of you to drive down here. And buses take way too long."

"Well, okay, but mind me and be careful, now. Don't go speedin' down the interstate and get yourself killed. We'll hold things down here until you get here."

Ray started to say something about how ironic it would be if he were to die in a car wreck rushing home to bury his mother, but instead, he said, "Thank you, Uncle James. I'm glad you and Roy were with her. I feel better knowing someone in the family was there."

They said their goodbyes and Ray pressed the end button on his phone and tossed it across the room. There was a loud crash as it smashed against the wall and Ray dropped his face into his upturned palms. He stayed like that for several minutes before getting up and crossing over to the bathroom to get dressed. He made it as far as the bathroom door before he broke into tears.

CHAPTER ONE

The drive to Maple Grove, Alabama took about six hours, stopping once for a meal and restroom break. At the forefront of his mind during the trek to his old hometown was his mother: her smile, her laugh, her gentle nature that she mostly hid beneath a veil of sarcastic wit, and her ability to always give Ray comfort no matter the reason for his woe. Outside of the one stop he'd made to eat and pee, he had made a few more shorter stops alongside Highway 231 to force those images from his mind, so as not to lose control of his emotions and fall into a tirade of snivels and jerks, weeping uncontrollably when he desperately needed to be strong, to be a man.

What would it take?

Ray Sanders seemed to ask himself this question more and more every day. For the last seven months, he had been trying to come up with an answer and repeatedly he had found himself unable to do so. What would it take? He wondered again. The strange thing was that he felt like he knew the answer; it was just far away and on the tip of his mind at the same time. It was like when you lay awake at night trying to remember the name of an old acquaintance or a character on a television show you used to watch as a kid; you knew it but it was hidden away in your mind and odds were, you would not remember it until you really were not thinking about it. It would just pop up. It was so terribly frustrating. He did not know how to conjure up a response and all he could do was question it; question it until his head seemed ready to burst like an over-ripe melon on a firing range.

Life and all its little inconveniences were a trifle beyond what Ray had expected as a child growing up in rural Alabama. He had been born the son of a farmer-his father and a waitress-his mother. They had never been rich, by any means, but there had always been hot meals on the table and clothes on their backs. They had lived a good country life. The days Ray wasn't at school, he had helped his father work the land while his mom would drive the five miles of country back roads to Momma's *Kountry Kitchen* where she would wait tables for ten hours a day. The pay was not great but what little his mother had brought in and the money his dad had made at the Farmer's Market in Birmingham, and his full-time job at Omnifab Steel, they had been able to live comfortably. Not "high on the hog," as granddad would say, but comfortable. It wasn't until the year following Ray's graduation from Maple Grove High School, in 2006, that he had realized just how bad life could be; how monstrously cruel life could be.

That was the year his dad had died. Cancer had come and ushered Earnest Sanders into the misty realms of the afterlife as silently as it had come to infest his body, to begin with. Ray didn't believe in Heaven and Hell—well to a degree, he did believe—but mostly he believed there was another world; a world not unlike a large train depot where you would sit and wait until final judgment was passed down. A childhood fantasy he had always used, not so much to explain death, as to ignore it.

After four hours of driving and rehashing the past, Ray pulled to a stop in front of his old home, red rock crunching beneath the weight of his Tahoe. Ray shifted into park and stepped out onto the familiar ground of his childhood, a relief he hadn't expected. A cool breeze was blowing, and Ray temporarily escaped his thoughts. The world was so beautiful, the part of it that was not a tangle of concrete and asphalt, at least. To the left of the old Victorian house, about fifteen feet away, was a red rock path cut through the pines and maples. Ray knew it well and walked its half-mile length to the little clearing along Locust Fork River. Here was his dad's little slice of Heaven, his riverside cabin, and for most of his life, Ray had made it his, as well. Crossing the small clearing, Ray climbed the steps and turned to face the river, propping his forearms on the dusty porch banister and leaning forward, the cool breeze kissing his cheeks and ruffling his hair. The ankle-high grass around the cabin swayed lazily, and Ray realized, with more than a touch of affection, just how beautiful it was. The muddy waters of Locust Fork rolled along without haste, like a refined gentleman strolling through the park on a sun-soaked Sunday afternoon. The birds were singing, and the squirrels were playing, darting from tree to tree, or zipping through the grass. Somewhere a fish jumped, and Ray smiled; he was home, he was finally home, where, indeed, his heart was.

After a good ten minutes of reflecting on long days of fishing and fish fries, Ray stepped off the porch, inhaling deep the fresh country air. His father and Judd Atkins had cleared away all the trees around the small cabin some twenty years before, opening up the land clear to the river. The only trees left in the clearing were the small cropping of Dogwoods at the edge of the red rock path leading up to the main house and a few old sycamores along the bank of the river. For a moment, a crazy thought occurred to him (not too crazy, but crazy considering why he had come home in the first place), to grab his old rod and reel from the cabin and cast her out; *damn sure the fish are biting today.*

Not today and you know it, Ray thought and shook the idea away. *Maybe sometime later, after you got her in the ground, and only maybe.* All the smiles evicted from his heart then, and tears formed at the corners of his eyes. He was here, after all, to see to his mother's burial. It was the last thing on this Earth that he wanted to do; not wanting to believe his mother was dead, but knowing he had no choice but to accept it.

What would it take?

Ray turned back toward the river in time to see Jerry Collier trolling by in his little aluminum boat and Ray threw his hand up in a wave. Jerry waved back and went back to work on his trotlines. As painful, as it was, this trip home, he still felt the warmth of being—nothing more, just being. Another smile curved the corners of his mouth. No matter the reason, no matter when, what, where, or why; he was home, even if it was only for a short while. He planned to make the best of it, regardless of the circumstances. What was it Dorothy had said in *The Wizard of Oz? There's no place like home.* To Ray, there was no other statement in history to hold so much truth.

She was murdered, you know.

This thought hit him as he passed between the dogwoods and was heading up the sloping red rock road.

Why in the hell would he think something like that? Doctor Holden had told him his mother had died of a heart attack and as far as Ray knew, the doctor had no reason to lie about something like that. If that was true, then why was there a hint of doubt flickering in his mind? No, he would not let his imagination take over, not this time. There were no conspiracies; no vengeful malevolent forces in the shadows, there was only nature. A cardiac arrest and that is all it was. His mother had died of natural causes and nothing more.

"There's no place like home," he muttered and continued upward, along the half-mile-long road that would take him back to the main house.

The first thing Ray noticed as he topped the hill was the old gray Ford pickup parked next to his Chevy Tahoe in the driveway. He knew who owned that truck as well as he knew his mom kept a fifth of Jack Daniels under the sink in the kitchen. It was Judd Atkins's truck. Probably here to express his condolences, probably here to reclaim some tool or piece of lawn equipment Ray's father had borrowed God knows when, or maybe he was here to check and see if no one had left the stove on. Never had there been a time when Judd Atkins had stopped by without some underlying motive; he always wanted something and Ray figured the want, in this case, was a first bid at the Sanders land. Why his father had tolerated that man for all those years was beyond Ray, and his head hurt when he thought about it. However, Earnest Sanders had been, after all, one of the kindest people in Jefferson County. He would always lend a hand to someone in need; do what little he could afford to do. Even if the ones he helped seemed only to be taking advantage of his kindness.

Ray was halfway to the house when Judd Atkins stepped off the porch and lit a cigarette, meeting him with an outstretched hand and a crooked, tobacco-stained grin. Ray took the old man's hand and pumped it a few quick shakes. Judd's grip was every bit as firm as Ray imagined it had been when Judd was young. Judd was a large man, around 6"10", and he was a good 300lbs, at least. He was wearing his usual faded overalls, torn and ripped around the knees, with a white T-shirt underneath, large sweat stains visible underneath the arms. Cotton ball tufts of white hair poked out from under the old John Deere cap on his head. Although the shadow cast by his cap mostly hid Judd's eyes beneath the bill, Ray thought he saw a flare of scorn behind them; a blazing firelight of hatred the old man was doing his best to conceal. Too late for that, however, as he had let it slip, just a little, but just enough so that Ray had caught it.

"Welcome home, boy!" Judd said those yellowed teeth spread even wider and he took his hand back. "Hate like hell you had to come home for somethin' as bad as this. I sure do. She was a good woman, Ray. Folks around here are damn sure goin' to miss her."

"Thank you for coming by, Judd. I know mom would have been happy to know you came by to express your condolences." That was a lie Pinocchio would have been proud to claim. If there were any one person on this earth Elizabeth Sanders had hated, it would have been Judd Atkins. "It leaves a bad taste in my mouth just to talk to that man," his mother had once said to Ray, about a year or so before his dad had passed.

"Didn't expect you would be by so soon, to tell the truth. How did you know I was in town?"

"Saw you when you turned off the 78. Was havin' a bit of lunch over at the Kountry Kitchen. Figured I'd drop by and see how your trip was and see if you'd be able to get in the house okay."

"I appreciate it," Ray said. There were only a few roads into Maple Grove. If traveling west along Highway 78 you would turn onto Pine Lane about a mile past the Graysville exit, Pine Lane becoming Maple Grove's main street about three miles in. If you took the Graysville/West Jefferson exit and cut left on Flat Top road, then hooked a right on Wood Street three miles down, it was a five-mile jaunt into town. It was the longer of the two routes, but Ray wished like hell that he had taken it instead. He could have postponed this uncomfortable meeting with Judd Atkins, at least for a few hours, maybe even as long a day.

A large plume of smoke rolled from between Judd's cracked lips and he inconsiderately tossed his cigarette to the ground and squashed it out. The crunching of the red rock beneath that oil-stained work boot seemed to bore wormholes into Ray's brain. "No worrying about thankin' me, boy. Hell, you damn near family to me and with your folks gone, the least I can do is keep an eye out for you."

Come on, Ray! Get rid of this old fart, go, and see the ex. But she's just going to run you off. She hates you, loathes you, and right out despises you. Best to forget it. Love cannot be rekindled, no matter how many sappy ass movies they made to moot your point. Besides—you're here for a funeral—your MOTHER'S funeral. Prioritize, as your dad would say.

"You all right, boy?" For the first time, probably in all the man's life, Judd Atkins sounded sincerely concerned.

"I'm fine. Had a long drive, that's all. I'm just a little tired."

There was silence between them for a moment, then Judd said: "You look a bit pale. You sure you okay?"

"Yeah. Never been better. Say, would you like a cold glass of tea? Mom always keeps a pitcher in the fridge."

Judd made a passing glance at the old service-station-special wristwatch on his right wrist. "Well, it's going on 3:30, 'bout time I got along. I guess I could settle for a glass of tea, though. Would be a might refreshin', 'specially in this damn heat."

You just had to offer him a glass of tea. No need in slapping yourself over it now, the offer was out, and rudeness is not in your raising, and it would definitely be rude to retract the offer.

Ray asked Judd if he wanted to wait in the living room while he poured them a couple of glasses. Judd declined; said he would wait out on the porch if it was all the same to him.

"Going from the heat to the cool air'll make a man sicker than a dog," Judd said.

Ray nodded, thoughtfully, then unlocked the door and went inside.

About five minutes later Ray came back out on the porch, two glasses of iced tea in his hands with wedges of lemon floating in them. Judd was leaning against the banister and looking out across the big front yard, with its congregation of dogwoods and the circular drive, red-rocked, just like the road to the cabin. *No place like home,* Ray thought and fought back a gusher of tears. If he had to cry, he would wait until later, when he was alone. The idea of bursting into hysterics in front of this big, two-faced man was unbearable.

"Here you go, Judd," he said and handed him one of

the glasses as he turned around. "Mom must have made this pitcher of tea right before she…well, never mind that. It's still good and plenty sweet."

Judd nodded sympathetically. *I won't make you talk about it if you don't want to,* that nod indicated, and he gulped nearly half of his tea away in one long swallow. "Ah. Best damn iced tea around. Your momma sure knew what she was a doin' when it came to iced tea. Woman had God-given talent, and that's the truth." Judd set his glass on the porch railing with a little rattle of ice.

"'Can't call yourself a true Southerner if you don't know how to make decent iced tea', that's what mom used say. Her and dad —both—they loved their sweet iced tea. Going to be…damn, it's going be hard without her…was hard enough when dad died…but I don't know how…"Ray trailed off. On the verge of crying, his eyes flooded with tears. He held them back with a remarkable inner strength he was not aware he had. The last thing he needed, the last thing he *wanted,* was for Judd Atkins to mistake his emotional turmoil over the death of his mother as a weakness. Old Judd, after all, was as much a predator as any that existed in this world or any other.

Judd knocked back the rest of his tea and set the empty glass back down on the railing before stepping off the porch and looking back at Ray. "I know this ain't the best time to bring this up, and I know it's not somethin' you want to be talkin' about right now. But have you thought about what's goin' to happen to the home place here? Now that your mom has passed."

There it was, out in the open, all the cards on the table. Ray could see the hunger in Judd's eyes, the hunger of a predator stalking its prey, and knew this would be the worst possible moment to show signs of weakness because if he did, the old man would be on top of him like a rabid jackal. He expected Ray to sell him this land, the land that had been in Ray's family since 1846, the year George Sanders, Ray's great-grandfather, had bought it with all his savings. There wasn't a chance in hell of that happening.

"I haven't given it a whole lot of thought. Figured I might hold onto it, though. Too many memories in this place to let her go."

"You a young man, Ray. Might want to consider sellin' the place, don't let it tie you down. You sure don't want to be tied down in a town like Maple Grove, ain't nothin' ever come out of this place and I don't suspect anything ever will. But, like I say, you still young, yet. You'll figure it out."

Judd went and stood by his old gray Ford, half in and half out of it, the driver's side door open in front of him like a blast shield. "Appreciate the tea, boy. It hit the spot mighty fine. Now, you go on inside and get some rest. Next couple of days goin' to be a might rough on you. We'll have plenty of time to discuss business matters after you've done right by your mom."

Ray told him he was welcome for the tea and thanked Judd for stopping by. He watched the old man climb into the cab of the ancient Ford and slam the door, not out of anger, mind you, out of the fact the door wouldn't catch if you didn't slam it. Judd waved as he backed out, and Ray waved back and watched until at last the tailgate disappeared around the curve in the driveway and was lost beyond the pines and the oaks. The brief encounter with Judd Atkins proved to be as noxious as a backed-up sewer line, and Ray was relieved that it was over.

What would it take?

"Shut up!" Ray told himself and went inside.

The house was an old, white Victorian home Ray's great-grandfather had built shortly after the purchase of this land. There were four bedrooms, a study, and two baths upstairs; a living room, a den, a half bath, a kitchen, and a dining room downstairs. The house had both an attic and a basement. The attic was a dull place, full of stored away items and was hot as sin in the summer and cold as a well digger's balls in the winter. The basement was cold and dank; home to Earnest Sanders' workshop and Elizabeth Sanders' home-canned goods as well as her small sewing room. It was also the source of Ray's trepidation as a child. The floors were hard wooden floors, (no carpet for the Sanders family), and polished to a shine. Ray stood in the living room, staring at the walls and the four curio cabinets that stood against the walls. Dolphins, in all directions, even the glass-topped coffee table, littered with dolphins. His mother had always been fond of dolphins, but not until after his father had died, had she started to collect them so vigorously, and now, it seemed, she had been quite busy after Ray had moved out of the house. Extremely busy. The curio cabinets were full of glass, porcelain, and crystal dolphins, snow globes with dolphins inside; dolphin banks; a couple of dolphin-shaped ashtrays on the coffee table. Velvet dolphins hung from the walls along with oil paintings and photographs of *real* dolphins. Even the top of the big-screen television in front of the large picture window was overcrowded with a set of little dolphin statuettes and a couple of shot glasses with dolphins on the front of them.

Ray sat down on the couch and leaned back with a sigh. Was her obsession with the dolphins natural? Had she been mentally slipping? Then, on the other hand, could it have been that with her son and husband gone she had needed something to do to keep herself busy?

He noticed something else; something that bothered him far worse than the army of dolphins that had set up camp in the living room. All the family photos were gone; gone from the walls, from atop the television, and coffee table. She had taken all the family pictures down and replaced them with those damned dolphins. *I should have come home sooner, while she was still alive. How deep was her loneliness? I should have been a good son and came home a few years ago.*

There was no way to know if that was true or not, and Ray knew it. He was grieving and often people in the throes of grief believed that it was somehow their fault when a loved one died. That if they had done this or that differently, then the person they were grieving would still be in the world of the living. There was no cure for the pain of losing someone, no magical spell, or no pharmaceutical miracle drug, only time and time alone. He could sit here and blame himself until the world collapsed, and it would still be as meaningless as it was now. Ray kicked off his shoes, lay back across the full length of the couch, and cried himself to sleep. He slept dreamlessly and was fully awake by midnight. A noise had woken him; a sound like glass twinkling in the wind. Ray got up and went to the front porch, flipping on the outside light in passing, and walked outside. There, on the far side of the porch, above the porch swing, was a wrought iron dolphin wind chime.

CHAPTER TWO

There was a viewing, the day before the funeral, at the Whispering Light Funeral Home. Most of Ray's family was there: aunts, uncles, and cousins. A good number of his mother's friends showed up along with a handful of Ray's friends to pay their respects. As in most viewings of those departed from this Earth, or at least the ones Ray had attended in his lifetime, the mood was merry with somber undertones. If not for the corpse of his mother, dressed in her favorite blue Sunday dress, that lay in her coffin underneath the large stained-glass window, one may have thought this a family gathering; a reunion amongst family and old friends. Yet with the sadness of grief in the wake of passing, the gathering was quite pleasant. Even when his Aunt Martha, a big, burly woman with breasts as big as watermelons (and frighteningly shaped the same) came over to him with a snot-and-tear-drenched hanky in one hand and a tattered leather purse in the other, and enveloped him in a hug not unlike that of a big grizzly mauling some poor, unsuspecting hunter; he still felt it a pleasant experience. Ray became aware that he needed these people, at that moment more than ever. Even though a few of the faces in the crowd were still strangers, he needed them all the same.

Although there was a fair share of laughs, giggles, and friendly and warm pats on the back, tears were shed—a great many, in fact. It warmed Ray to be around his family but saddened him that it always seemed to take either a wedding or more commonly, a death to bring them all together. Partly, Ray understood with some certainty, it was because most of his family either lived out of state or so far on the other side of the state that traveling, especially with today's gas prices, was damn near unthinkable. In truth, Ray was quite touched that they had come down for the funeral, and risked the expense, to see Elizabeth Sanders into the afterlife. It said quite a deal about their character and quite a deal more about their devotion to the family. Ray loved them for that.

There was a small kitchenette in the back of Whispering Light: complete with a soda machine, a snack machine, a sink, a microwave oven, and a coffee pot. It was here he saw her, the first time in seven years, and she was as beautiful as ever. Beth stood next to the microwave with a coffee cup in her hand and chatted nonchalantly with Billy Danvers, Maple Grove's star quarterback back in 2006. She seemed to float like a vision or a mirage in the desert. Her hair was fiery red, hung to her shoulders, and seemed to Ray to catch the overhead lighting in much the same way the light of the sky did as the sun disappeared over the horizon. Her complexion was a light tan and her skin appeared to be as smooth, as soft to the touch, as he had remembered it to be, and Ray imagined how nice it would be to take her in his arms and hold her against him; to feel her skin pressed against his own. He still loved her, more than he thought possible after all these years, and immediately wished that he hadn't been such a fool to have let her slip away. She looked in his direction once, those eyes like brilliant emeralds set in the eyes of the statue of a Greek Goddess then went back to Billy, nodded and laughed at some joke he'd told, presumably, without giving Ray a second thought.

Ray had glanced down at the floor then, dull, scarred white tile, which had all the warmth of an undertaker's slab and shoved his hands into the pockets of his dress pants. He had considered going over, trying to talk to her, and ultimately was afraid of stumbling, bumbling, and blowing the encounter by saying something stupid. Instead, he stepped back into the hall, narrowly missing another encounter with Judd Atkins, now dressed in a light blue suit, an artifact from some 70's time capsule. He was talking burly Aunt Martha's ear off, trying to get her to talk sense into her stubborn nephew, no doubt, bidding for Ray's land even here at Elizabeth Sanders viewing. Ray ignored him and headed to the lobby.

The afternoon sun was warm and comforting on his face and the air, inhaled in deep, staggering breaths, was ambrosia. Tears streaked over his cheeks; tears for his mother, a woman of immaculate stature in the world of Ray Sanders; tears for Beth, the only woman he had ever had the courage to say, "I love you" to and mean it from the bottomless pit of his soul. What was going on? Why had his head felt like his stomach did after a ride on a roller coaster?

What would it take? Was she murdered? Does Beth still love me?

None of those questions was of the same nature, and yet Ray felt that oddly the answers were all the same or would at least come from the same direction. "Some things in this life don't have no answer, son," his father had told him once, but Ray could not remember when or what had prompted that conversation; a conversation lost in the unfathomable depths of his memory. "We have to accept it and live as good a life as we can and pray that the good Lord allows us through those Pearly Gates." It was sound advice, down-home country folk advice, but sound and his father had never lied to him, or at least as far as Ray knew (small white lies about Santa, the Easter Bunny, and the Tooth Fairy excluded) he had not.

Ray reached into his pocket and pulled out a pack of L&Ms, Marlboro's redheaded stepchild, and stared at the pack for a moment. He had quit smoking two years ago and did not understand what had possessed him to buy a pack of cigarettes on his way to the viewing. He remembered thinking that two years was an awfully long time to pass just to backslide into the old habit. So, he smoked a cigarette, with a few short, hacking coughs, relished it, and went back into the funeral home to visit with everyone and thank them for coming. As the afternoon faded into twilight and then into full nightfall, he sat with his mother; sat with the woman who had raised him; who had always had a comforting word when he had scraped his knees or gotten a cold. No words came to him in that time; the silence, after everyone had left them alone, was as cavernous and as empty as an undisturbed Egyptian tomb. He wept into the palms of his hands; the reality of it all sinking in hard and fast, and he wished that he had been a good son and had come home when his mother had asked him to.

Can we say feeling guilty, kids? I think we can.

Then, there was the funeral.

The sky, overcast and dreary, threatened rain and everyone in attendance had feared a monsoon would hit before the service was over. The rain had held out, however, but just barely. Reverend Blackstone, misty-eyed and solemn, had spoken and had read from the New Testament before praising the good deeds of Elizabeth Sanders and explaining to all in attendance that she was in the Lord's Heaven and that she would walk for eternity in the light of the angels.

The funeral, in its entirety, had held far less levity than the viewing and there had been a volley of sniffles following the reverend's words. Ray had sat there, under the black oval topped tent, flanked by his Aunt Martha and Uncle Richard on the left and his cousin Roy and Uncle James on the right. The white wooden folding chair had felt cold, intrusive and his mother's coffin, perched no more than two feet in front of him; waiting to be lowered into the earth, had seemed warped and surreal, not there at all. Aunt Martha had squeezed his hand and looked at him, fat cheeks wet with tears shed for her older sister and Ray had leaned over and kissed her on the cheek and had told her it would be all right, that his mother was in a far better place; that she was finally at peace. There was a wreath of dogwood blossoms and red roses atop her casket and Ray had managed a partial grin. Dogwoods had always been her favorite and he had felt slightly regretful that her little spot of ground, where she would spend eternity, was underneath an oak rather than a dogwood tree. Somehow, that felt wrong—a jip as his friends used to call it.

Ellie Sanders and Eliza Harrison, the youngest of

Ray's cousins; Ellie fourteen; Eliza fifteen, had stood next to his mother's headstone and played *Amazing Grace* and *What a Friend We Have in Jesus* on their trumpets, rousing another outburst of sobs, then laid single rose on the casket and wiped fresh tears from their cheeks. Mary Johnson and Dianne Townsend, two of the waitresses from the Kountry Kitchen, even Mom herself, Beatrice Alexander, the Kitchen's proprietor, had stood up and delivered sincere eulogies reflecting the times they had spent with Elizabeth Sanders, and how deeply they were going to miss her. As Ray had sat there and listened, listened to all the words spoken with such reverence for a woman who never again would enjoy bingo games on Saturday nights or bonfires by the river rehashing old times with friends and family; he recognized what it was that scared him. What chilled him worse than an endless parade of vindictive nightmares was the finality of death.

After the service, after the caretakers covered his mother's casket in a mound of fresh dirt, after the dinner at the Maple Grove V.F.W., Ray had gone home to begin the chore of sorting out his mother's belongings. Sorrow, life's mistress, grew nauseated by the task that lay before him and again, Ray had to rely on that unknown inner strength to cast a protective eye over his sanity, as he believed too much more of this; grief and disparity, would drive him insane.

"You know, Rayford, you don't have to do this right now," Roy Sanders said, using the childhood nickname he had coined for Ray eons ago, a nickname Ray had never really been fond of. But seeing that Roy was more like a brother than a cousin, Ray had never disputed it. "With the funeral just this afternoon and all, you should really put this off for a few days."

"Roy my boy," Ray's feeble attempt at a comeback. He had called him Royford once and had realized with a hint of embarrassment *after* he had said it, how pitifully stupid it had sounded. Of course, years later, sometime after high school, Ray had contemplated that "Rayford" sounded just as stupid, and he had laughed until his chest started to hurt. Dana Collins, Ray's girlfriend at the time, had come running from the bedroom of the little apartment they had shared; sure, that Ray had blown a fuse in his head, and had nearly slid right into the wall. He looked at Roy now, his truest friend, and continued. "I'd rather get it done and over with, while I still have the nerve."

"I know it's tough, Ray. And you know I'm here for you, dude—just like always."

Ray was sitting on the couch gazing out the big picture window, the one with the big-screen television set in front of it, watching it rain. A big cardboard box occupied the space next to him and scattered about around his feet were a few smaller boxes. The rain had held out all during the funeral and then, just as Ray had slipped his key into the front door, the bottom fell out, to quote his father whenever the rain fell hard and unyielding.

"I know you will," Ray responded thoughtfully. "We've been through a lot of shit together."

"Some of it I don't even want to remember. Some really *crazy* shit. Damn, if our dads had found out about just a third of it, I can say I don't think we'd be sitting flat on our asses. Not now or ever."

"Isn't that the truth. Think my dad would have shoved his foot so far up my ass I would have been able to taste his fucking shoe polish."

"Ray," Roy said, plopping down in Earnest Sanders old La-Z-Boy. "You going to be okay? I mean, this isn't going to have you climbing water towers with high powered rifles, is it?"

"*No.* But if I ever do decide to take that route, wear something bright, maybe something with a big red target on it."

Roy grinned and replied, "Sure thing. Because it doesn't matter what kind of scope you'd have on the thing, you still couldn't hit the broadside of a barn."

"I'm glad you have such great faith in my marksman-ship." Ray had a grin of his own. "But what makes you so sure I haven't gotten better over the years?"

"What's the name of the chair I'm sitting in again?"

"The La-z…hey, wait a second."

"Precisely."

"You're a dick," Ray said in a good-natured tone.

This was just a small fraction of the ribbings they had passed back and forth over the years and it felt good, the way a well-heated house felt when you came inside on a cold winter's day. It felt good to be reassured that not everything in this world was as melancholy as it so often seemed and that not every corner held a beast lurking in its shadows hunched and ready to pounce and rip you to bloody little chunks. It felt good to be alive, and for the first time since he had received word of his mother's death, Ray felt completely aware of the world around him.

"Beth was there, at the funeral. And the viewing, too."

"Was she? I didn't see her." *Damn it, Roy. Why did you have to go and bring her up? I was starting to feel all right again.*

"Bullshit you didn't see her. She was there with the steroid freak. Dude, you kept looking over at her every five minutes, you can't fool me. I see all and know all, remember?"

"She's water under the bridge, Roy my boy. And I don't intend to lose any sleep over her. I'm just glad she was able to put aside whatever bad feelings she has towards me and paid her respects to mom."

"Look, Ray, I need to get home before all that rain out there turns your driveway into Lake Placid and I have to borrow Uncle Earnest's old Bass boat to get out of here. But you really need to accept that you are in denial."

"Thank you, Dr. Phil. I'll try and keep that in mind."

"Hey! What's family for, anyway, if not to keep the stubborn ones in line?"

"Why don't you stay here tonight, Roy? You can crash in one of the guest rooms. No need to go out into *that*," Ray nodded towards the window to the monsoon just beyond its panes. "Besides, it's gotten pretty damn dark out and as hard as she's coming down out there, you'd be lucky to see past your hood."

Roy sat for a minute, seeming to consider such a generous offer as if he were an ancient scholar pondering the mysteries of the Heavens, or maybe the virtue of kings. "Alright. You talked me into it. You got anything I can sleep in, though? This suit would be a bit on the uncomfortable side."

Ray scrounged up an old *Grateful Dead* T-shirt and an old pair of gym shorts for Roy to change into, and Roy went off to the guest bedroom, returning shortly with a smirk on his face, almost hidden by his long black hair that hung around his face like an obsidian curtain. "What's up with all the dolphins? You got a Flipper fetish or something?"

For the next few hours Ray and Roy, cousins, brothers, best of friends, sat up and talked about old times. Ray told him about his mom's love for the dolphins and hence their infestation of the house. They talked about the trouble they used to get into as kids and about the times that they had gotten away with a few of their youthful pranks. Roy told Ray that he should consider moving back home and forget the bikini-clad women and margaritas on the beach, that in the end, it would all just wear him down. "You would feel much better living back here at the old home place," Roy said with a gleam of hope.

"I'll think about it. I do sort of miss this place. I had reasons for leaving, you know. I didn't—"

"Don't have to explain it to me. Just next time, don't let some two-timing bitch get you so worked up."

Ray nodded and took a sip of his coke. *Maybe you should move home, Ray. The past is the past, right?* Maybe he would do just that. He would have to find a job, but he didn't think that would be much of a problem. Until then, he could live off the thirty thousand left to him by his mother, money her and his dad had squirreled away over the years and settle back into the house. Admittedly, it wouldn't be as easy as that, least not until he sorted out a few personal issues, but it still sounded like a nice idea. A few more days here, sleeping in his old room and visiting with old friends, would decide all of that.

"You know, Roy, if I do move back home, I'll need some help on the bills."

"Shit! I'll do the roommate thing, so long as you don't try and sneak in my room at night to fondle my ass, you sick bastard."

"I'd be more worried about someone catching you in the act of fondling your own ass rather than someone sneaking anywhere near that nasty cakehole."

"My cakehole may be nasty, but nasty is as nasty does."

"What?" Ray asked, on the verge of some serious gut-wrenching laughter. "That makes no sense. At all. Nadda."

"Just think about it for a minute," said Roy with a yawn.

"Don't want to think about it." Ray stood up and did a little stretch walk before turning towards the hall. "Think I'm going to crash."

It was a quarter past midnight when they both headed off to bed, Roy in the first guest room at the top of the stairs and to the right, snoring as if he had swallowed a glass pack muffler, Ray in his old room and staring at the ceiling listlessly. His mind was being stubborn and refused to shut down to allow him a decent night's sleep. All he could think about was his mom, this house, and how lonely and abandoned she must have felt. *She must have hated you in her last moments, hated you for being so stubborn and selfish.*

"But I couldn't come home," he whispered into the dark. "I couldn't handle..."

Couldn't handle what? Beth dumping you for some brain dead jock? Or was there something else you were afraid of?

Ray rolled over on his side, twisted the blanket around him like a sleeping bag and covered his head with a pillow. *Just don't think about it. Any of it. Clear your head and get some sleep.*

However, no matter how hard he tried to sleep, it just wasn't going to happen. At some point, Ray got out of bed and walked over to his bedroom window. Ray's room looked out over the front yard and directly in line with his bedroom window was a floodlight. Ray stared at it for a moment. The light was barely visible, hazy, and illusory through the heavy rain, and again Ray had that feeling of being in a trancelike state. A little twinkling noise rose from somewhere out in the night and Ray immediately knew what it was; he just didn't understand how he could be hearing it. Surely the rain, as fiercely as it was pouring down, would drown out the little wind chime; surely, it would drown it out. But it didn't. Instead, the sound of the wind chime whipping in the wind only grew louder, persistently louder.

Were those brake lights? Ray's eyes caught the dim amber flashes as they blinked out and disappeared. His first thought was that Roy had decided to go home anyway, but his roaring, chainsaw snore was still present, drifting out of the guest room in a cacophony of snorts and whistles. Had someone come into the driveway to turn around? No. The house was too far off the main road for that, and he couldn't remember anyone ever doing that before. *Eyes must be playing tricks on me.*

Ray moved away from the window, planning to wake Roy, then thought better of it. *Wake him for what? Because you* thought, *you saw someone stop in the driveway.* That would be pointless, and besides that, Roy was an annoying prick when he first woke up. *It probably was just my eyes playing tricks. I'm tired and it's been a long day.* Regardless of any self-comforting, however, Ray was still awake and staring out of his bedroom window when the rain finally did stop, and the first rays of daylight seeped through the clouds.

CHAPTER THREE

Ray finally dozed off around six in the morning on the day following his mother's funeral only to wake up at noon with a crick in his neck and a headache. He had slept in the recliner in the front room, curled up into a ball and cuddling up with an old throw pillow he had snatched from the couch. Ray got out of the recliner with all the agility of a gazelle with a broken hip and went to the guest bathroom in the hallway to relieve himself. All the miseries of the previous day were still rolling around in the back of his mind, but it seemed like, despite his sore neck and pounding temples, he would be able to focus his attention on things a little more positively. "If ya shake it more than twice you're a playin' with it," his dad used to say, so Ray finished up, flushed the toilet, washed, and dried his hands. Now, it was time to hunt up some grub. *That* had also been one of his dad's favorite lines. *Damn if it don't feel weird as hell being here without them.*

There was a torn piece of notepaper on the kitchen counter and Ray picked it up and read it. It was from Roy, stating he had woken up and had helped himself to a ham sandwich and a glass of tea, and that he had to go meet his dad for breakfast.

Was going to wake you:

The note said.

But you looked like you were sleepin' pretty good, so I left you alone. Give me a call later and we'll hang out. Later. Roy.

Ray balled the note up and tossed it in the trashcan next to the counter. A ham sandwich didn't sound half-bad, though he wasn't sure that he wanted to wash it down with a glass of tea, at least not after just waking up. A tall, cool glass of milk or even a glass of orange juice was what he wanted. Ray nosed through the fridge for a moment, finally pulling out a pack of thick-sliced deli ham, bacon, cheese, and mayonnaise. He put it all on the counter next to the stove, and then returned to the fridge for further exploration. There was no milk or OJ, only sodas and tea, and that would just not do; he'd have to make a trip into town to pick some up. *Just have to tuck all this back in the fridge until I get back.*

As he was placing all his plundered items back into place, his eyes spied a carton of eggs and a pack of bagels. *I wonder,* Ray thought and shut the refrigerator door and opened the freezer on top of it. There was chicken, pork chops, more packs of frozen deli ham, sausage, and…*Eureka! A huge, thick Porter House steak! Why eat ham when I can have steak?* Ray took the steak and shut the freezer, then went over to the sink, put the stopper in the drain, and ran the hot water. When the water had filled the sink enough to submerge the steak, Ray shut off the faucet and put the packaged steak into the water, using a cast-iron skillet from the dish drainer as a weight to keep it from floating to the top. Once thawed and marinated, it would make for a fine steak and egg bagel breakfast. The only thing missing was the milk, and maybe a bottle of chocolate syrup to mix with it. *No problem there.*

Half an hour later, Ray pulled into a spot in front of the Maple Grove Piggly Wiggly and stepped out of the Tahoe, patting his front and back pockets to make sure he had both his keys and his wallet before shutting and locking the door. He looked around the parking lot, at the scant few vehicles scattered around it, and was somewhat amazed at how some things about a place, no matter how long you are away, never change. Out front, on either side of the entrance and exits, were a couple of soda machines with a handful of teenagers on either side hanging out next to them. Ray smiled; he remembered when he and Roy had used to do the same thing, usually right before they went down to Atkins Park for some baseball or down to the river for an afternoon of fishing. Of course, Roy was never what you would call an angler, especially once he had discovered heavy metal music and video games, but up until then, when they were still around eleven or twelve, they had fished quite a bit. That was when not being harassed by Bo Atkins, a local bully and future candidate for incarceration. Bo had been one bad attitude on legs, always picking on the younger kids, a typical town bully. Lord knows he gave Ray and Roy their share of grief; he was a real bastard and from what Ray could tell; Bo's baby brother Donnie was exactly the same. At least he didn't have to worry about contending with both this time around. Last Ray had heard old Bo was doing time somewhere in Georgia for armed robbery and assault, which meant he wouldn't be in Ray's hair or anyone else's for a long time.

That's all in the past now, Ray. You are a grown man.

Bully or no, pretty damn fair bet that you could kick the shit out of either one of those Atkins boys if they gave you a problem.

This was true, but sometimes it was so hard *not* to fall back into your old role of victim when surrounded by all the sites and memories of home. It felt like he was twelve and Roy was eleven and Bo Atkins was standing over them with the tip end of Roy's broken rod and reel and popping them across their bare legs with it, laughing harder with each pop against flesh. Ray remembered that day and remembered it well. He and Roy had worn jeans for the rest of that summer to hide the red marks.

"Well, ain't you a sight!"

Ray looked up to see an old man, hunched over at the back, ambling towards him on an old wooden cane, mouth opened wide in a smile, white false teeth (*falsies* his dad would call them) glistening in the sunlight. Ray met him near the entrance of the Piggly Wiggly and got a closer look. The man was dressed in a stained white tee and faded brown slacks and a pair of ratty old loafers. He was all but bald, with a few strands of spider-web-thin, white hair poking out from beneath a worn brown fedora and his liver-spotted skin had that leather look sometimes associated with the elderly. But one look into those deep-set brown eyes and Ray knew who the man was. Mr. Mills, former town caretaker and co-owner slash operator of the Drunken Horse Bar. In his prime, Jimmy Mills had been a lightweight boxer and local tough guy. His fists were not all people remembered Mills for, however, as most knew him as having the biggest heart in the county: donating blood to all the blood drives, giving money and toys to the Toys for Tots, and he had been seen on more than one occasion volunteering at the homeless shelters on Thanksgiving and Christmas. Of all the people in town,

Ray was happy to see that the old man was still alive and kicking.

"How's it going, Mr. Mills? Long time no see."

"Well," Mills said, in a wispy, old man's voice. "It's a goin'. Has been a while, though. Where you been hidin' yerself, boy."

"Florida. I moved down there a few years back. I've been home for a few days, thinking about staying this time."

"Well, hope that you do. You a good boy, no matter what they say about you." The old man smiled again. "Just joshing ya, boy. Glad to see you home. I'm sorry to hear about your mother. Was a good woman. Her and your dad. About the finest people in the Grove. But when it's your time to go, there's no arguing with the Man upstairs, that's all His decision."

It was basically the same thing Judd Atkins had said yesterday, only with Jimmy Mills, Ray knew the sentiment was true and not some load of crap aimed at prying a land deed out of him. "Thank you, Mr. Mills. It means a lot." *I've been saying that way too much lately. Please don't let me bump into anyone...*

"I understand old Judd done been by your place. Tryin' to push you into sellin' your land, I suppose. You listen up, ya hear, don't you go sellin' that property to him or anyone else. Your great-granddaddy worked his self to the bone for that land, him, and your great-grandma both. They was proud of that place, they was. I'd sure hate to see some jackass pop a damn burger joint or one of them strip malls up on that piece of ground."

"Pardon me!"

Ray turned to see a rather chunky woman in a bright pink wind suit pushing a buggy load of groceries emerge from the store with an even chunkier toddler riding on the front of the buggy. He couldn't be sure, but he thought it was Mrs. Barnes, his old music teacher from elementary school, although a lot heavier then he remembered.

"Pardon me," the woman repeated.

"Yea!" the butterball in front of the buggy chimed in. "Pardun us."

"Oh! Excuse me," Ray said and stepped aside. "Sorry about that, ma'am. I didn't realize I was blocking you up."

"You just need to keep an eye out for where you are standing, that's all," the woman said. "People have to get through here."

"Yes, ma'am."

The woman pushed on by and Jimmy Mills stood aside and gave her a slight nod as she trundled by. When he was good and sure that she was out of earshot, he turned to Ray and said, "Out of all the money that woman spends on food and out of all the food she stuffs down that kid's throat, she can't ever seem to find her purse when it comes time to help those in real need."

Ray nodded in agreement; although he really wasn't sure he even knew who the woman was, even if she did sort of remind him of Mrs. Barnes. And the Mrs. Barnes he had known had always been kind and giving. Ray didn't believe the woman to have ever had an unkind bone in her body. Not that he could recollect, anyway.

"I ain't goin' to hold ya up too much more," Mills said.

"Oh, no, sir. It's cool. You aren't bothering me. It was nice to see you again after all these years."

"Maybe not botherin' you, but botherin' myself plenty. Gettin' up in years these days and if I don't have at least one nap a day, I ain't worth a damn the next day. All I wanted to tell ya was to be wary of Judd Atkins. The man is crooked and a backstabber. You watch out for him, now. No tellin' what he'd do if he bought yer place. No tellin' what he'd do to get his hands *on* your place."

"I don't intend to sell anytime soon. It's like I told Judd, too many memories of my parents there. Don't think my conscience would let me get rid of the place."

"Yup. I imagine you have some sentimental attachment, at that, but that don't mean he's a-goin' to give up. Sentimental value means jack squat to a man like him and I wouldn't put it past him to try and… Well, don't want to go makin' accusations, but wouldn't put it past him. Just be careful, boy." There was a knowing glint in Mill's eyes, eyes that were just as sharp now as they had been when he had been young and going round-for-round in the ring.

"I will. Thank you. And it was good to see you again."

"You're plenty welcome. Just mind me and be careful."

Jimmy Mills headed across the parking lot, stopped briefly to raise and point his cane at the woman Ray had thought was Mrs. Barnes, said something the woman apparently disapproved of, then disappeared amongst a small cluster of pickup trucks at the end of the parking lot. Ray waited a moment longer, then went inside and bought what he came for and went home.

A few hours later, Ray stretched out across the living room sofa, full and satisfied, having finally gotten to eat, and was now ready for a well-deserved nap. Okay, maybe not *well deserved,* but deserved as his stomach was packed and all he wanted to do was pass out here on the couch; his encounter with Jimmy Mills at the Piggly Wiggly temporarily forgotten, all but that sharp, knowing look in the man's eyes. And what the old man had said about Judd was true and worth spending a minute or two to think about …Crooked…. backstabber… Ray agreed with both of those definitions of Judd, as both definitions fit that man as snug as an overweight person squeezed into a pair of too-small jeans. But what could he do? Judd couldn't make him sell his land and there was no way he would hand it over to him willingly. Ray meant to give more thought to the whole mess but was asleep before he even realized he had dozed off.

Don't wake momma, Ray thinks as he strolls down the old red rock road towards the little cabin on the river. She'd be pissed if you woke her up for no good reason. Let her sleep; let her rest. Why was everything so dismal tonight? Where was momma? Why was she sleeping?

WHY DID SHE LEAVE ME ALONE! His mind screamed. I DON'T WANT TO BE ALONE! I WANT MY MOMMA! MOMMA COME BACK! I'LL BE GOOD, MOMMA! I'LL COME HOME! PLEASE COME BACK, MOMMA! PLEASE!

Ray fell to his knees and clawed at the ground, the pleas of his little boy mind echoing in his head. "Come back momma, please come back," he whimpered into his soil-stained hands, then stared up into the silver face of the moon; the evil, twisted face of a demon; a monstrosity that seemed ready to fall from the sky and devour him; consume his soul. And it was laughing... a hateful, hysterical laugh, like some demented, depraved jester bent on the torment of human minds. Laughing at him, toying with him, stabbing that jagged blade of torment deep into his heart.

Ray slowly stood up on unsteady legs, quivering like a junkie trying to dispose of the elusive monkey that had taken residence upon his back. The ground felt moist underneath his bare feet, not like the plush carpet of grass that had covered the small clearing for nearly a century, but more like a grotesque, slimy bog. Not that he could see the ground at his feet, as a dense fog had blanketed the clearing and rose just an inch or so above his knees. The cabin, which had been his father's most cherished spot in the world (other than the Drunken Horse Bar in town, that is), was a dark and foreboding silhouette against the backdrop of the pale moonlight. A loud cracking sounded as somewhere in the woods around him a branch broke, shortly followed by the sound of something crashing into the underbrush. The hairs on the nape of Ray's neck stood on end for a few seconds as he listened, listened for whatever beast that had broken the branch to come for him. To come rushing through the clearing; big, razor-sharp claws chewing up the earth and spitting out chunks of dirt, like blood clots, into the air; big, powerful jaws like a brake press and filled with needle-sharp teeth.

But nothing came except an onrush of bitter silence.

Silence akin to that of a mausoleum.

Then, a sound as loud as a thunderclap roared from somewhere inside the small wooden cabin and the windows, previously hidden in the murky darkness of shadow, glowed a bright crimson hue and something that looked like lava began to run from the corners of them in thick streams. The cabin shook and shimmied, floorboards and rafters rattled in a hell-born symphony that made his headache and his heart stutter. There was an explosion of glass, wood, and fire as the front door was blown off its hinges and flung out into the clearing, immediately swallowed by the fog. Long, twisted arms of fire erupted from the doorway and reached into the sky and seemed to be reaching for that eerie demon moon. Paralyzed by terror and unable to issue a scream, as Ray turned to run his terror grew tenfold. In every direction, he looked, stood a cabin, each one belching fire from the open doorways and spewing that gooey lava substance from every crack and crevice.

There was a low, throaty growl behind him, just over his right shoulder and a warm, putrid breath rolled past his ear, staggering him with the stench of decay. Something cold, wet, and hairy brushed against his arm and Ray tried yet again to scream and found yet again that he was unable to do so. Am I going to die? *He thought.* Is this how I am going to go? Mauled down by some unknown beast and then probably eaten? Oh, dear God, please don't let this be how I die! Please don't let me die alone in this hell! Don't let me die with that son-of-bitch dining on my guts!

Crackle-pop-crackle-pop.

The cabins were completely ablaze now, the ones that Ray could see anyway; he was far too scared to turn around and come face-to-face with whatever stood behind him, but he knew, felt, that the cabin behind him was burning as well. All the cabins burned like massive, unattended bonfires feeding the night sky with yellow-orange light and smoky entrails that drifted aimlessly into the darkness before dissipating into thin air.

"They can't hurt you unless you let them in."

It was the voice of a stranger and no stranger a voice had Ray ever heard. It wasn't male or female but a combination of the two; an alien voice synthesized in some science fiction studio, perhaps, or maybe just born of madness.

"You are not crazy, Ray," the he/she voice said and the growling behind him stopped, that rank breath disappeared and the thing behind him whined. It was the whine of a puppy that had been whacked across the snout with a newspaper for chewing up its master's slipper or for

pissing on the carpet. "However, you will go crazy if you let them rape your mind. Only if you let them. You have to be strong, Ray. Just as strong as all of the men of your family before you."

"Who... What are you?" Ray managed the question weakly, speaking as a person speaks when in desperate need of water and on the verge of dehydration. "What are you talking about?"

"You have seen the movies, Ray, read the books. You know I cannot go much further...not yet. Not until you have seen all the truths of my existence."

"This isn't a movie, damn it!" Ray shouted and a chorus of schoolgirl giggles met him in response.

Off to his left, a fish jumped, a rather big fish, Ray thought, as the splash was much larger than any of the fish that lived in those waters was capable of producing. Ray walked over to the riverbank, as moist sediment and what Ray prayed was mud, seeped through his toes. What he saw next frightened him, puzzled him and fascinated him all at the same time. In the middle of the river was the dark silhouette of a man, walking on the surface of the water as if it were solid ground. There were other outlines around the man, surrounding him like a pack of wild dogs, four-legged beasts that seemed to taunt the man with snips and snarls. They were not like a pack of wild dogs; Ray became aware of dourly; they appeared to be a pack of wild dogs. Even though Ray could not see the man's face, he knew what was on it, confusion, and fear. The beasts closed their circle around him, growling in deep, menacing growls that seemed to rumble the way the Earth did along an angry fault that had become bored with dormancy and had decided to stir up trouble. Ray suddenly found himself fearful for the man who, as far as Ray knew, did not exist; a phantom that lingered over a river that was unnaturally still and under a moon that seethed evil.

Crackle-snap-pop-pop-snap-crackle.

Ray turned back towards the burning cabins; only now, it was a single cabin again and barely on fire at all. Within a few moments, the flames ceased, and it was just another shadow amongst shadows. A single, ear-piercing howl reverberated in the air and Ray's blood turned as cold as a corpse. He snapped his head back towards the river, half-expecting to see the shadow-man torn apart by those vicious shadow-dogs that had cornered him, but saw nothing but the river, shimmering as glass caught in the sun. What would it take? She was murdered, you know. They put her down the way a biting dog is put down after it has turned its teeth on people and has tasted human blood. Like a biting dog, she was a danger, a threat.

"SHUT UP," Ray wailed. "JUST SHUT THE FUCK UP!"

The fog began to clear—no let's be honest, the fog vanished, there one moment, gone the next—and Ray got his chance to see, for the first time since this nightmare began, just what it was he had been walking in. The ground was not the bog he had initially thought it to be but was a mass of bloated, disfigured human bodies that writhed in agony. Ray looked down and felt his stomach twisting and turning; he was ankle-deep in the naked, mutilated corpse of an elderly woman. The old woman's eyes suddenly flew open. She screamed in pain, and Ray became disgustedly aware that her intestines were slowly snaking their way up his legs. He started to scream, and then doubled over, wretched and...

...heaved and released his gorge all over his sheets and comforter. For a moment, he sat up in his bed, the acrid smell of vomit, *his* vomit, burning his nostrils, and then he threw the bedcovers to the floor and shakily got to his feet. He needed something to drink, something to get the bitter taste of regurgitated steak and eggs out of his mouth. Ray stumbled through the darkness and fumbled a hand around the wall near the bedroom door, found the wall switch, and flicked it on. The overhead light came on, a little brighter than it should be, and burned his eyes.

"What the hell kind of dream was that?" Ray asked the empty room, as he opened the door and headed for the stairs.

Ray, still shaking uncontrollably, got to the stairs and groped the railing like an old man in the grip of severe arthritis, and took the steps one at a time. He had never felt so rattled in his whole life; he had never had a dream like that in his whole life. It had seemed so real; all the sounds, sights, and smells had seemed so *real.* He had felt those slimy entrails...*Just a dream, Ray. Nothing but a dream. Probably something you ate didn't agree with you... The eggs, or possibly the steak was bad or not cooked enough. And dreams can't hurt you. Right? They are just byproducts of your mind shutting down when you go to sleep. Right?*

Actually, he did not know if that was right or not. He knew nothing of dreams or what caused them, and he didn't think that he would ever have such a dream that would cause him to wonder about its meaning. Surely, though, nothing substantial could come out of such a twisted vision, nothing that in any way could or would affect him or anyone else in his life. Dreams meant nothing, had no bearing on reality, he was sure of it, *had* to be sure of it, if not for the sake of arguing against things that sounded silly, but for the sake of rational, coherent thought. Nevertheless, it had scared the hell out of him.

Once in the kitchen, Ray hovered over the open refrigerator door indecisively; eyes roving from coke to milk to tea, then snatched the six-pack of canned coca-colas and set them on the kitchen table. Ray then took a glass from the cabinet above the sink, filled it half-full of ice, and set it next to the cokes. One more item, which he prayed that his mother had still kept there, as it was the only thing that would quench his thirst tonight, and he was desperate to find it. Ray went back to the sink, shuffled around underneath it, ruffling aside empty plastic grocery bags, cleaning agents, and utensils until… There it was. His hands happened upon what he was looking for and his eyes shone with triumph. *Hot Damn!* his mind shouted as he held the bottle to the light. *Bring on your bad dreams, now, you bastards.*

Ray set the bottle of Jack Daniels on the table as he sat down and began the task of mixing his first drink. Jack and coke embraced and savored by the late Elizabeth Sanders, and now to be indulged by her alive, if somewhat distraught, son. Ray had always been a beer man and had never even once sipped a mixed drink, let alone actually mix one. Now, as he knocked back his first swallow, he wondered why he had never tried it before. It was a bit strong and burned slightly as it went down, but it was not all bad, so after the first drink was gone, Ray mixed another. By midnight, completely shit-faced and laughing at jokes only he could hear; Ray was in utopia. It was a good feeling, to be drunk, to be able to forget the nightmare that had stolen him from sleep's warm embrace.

When the bottle of Tennessee sour mash was empty, and but one can of coke remained, Ray stood up, almost falling right back down in the process, and staggered towards the hallway. He stared in want at the stairs for a few seconds, yearning for the comfort of one of the upstairs beds, and then decided against it. In his present condition, he was afraid he would end up tumbling back down and breaking his neck. Instead, he moved past the stairs and into the living room and found the couch, as if it had been mysteriously lost and, just as mysteriously, returned. There were no more thoughts as he passed out and, for better more than for worse, no more dreams, either.

As Ray Sanders shut his eyes and drifted away to that purgatory only known to and reserved for those cast out in drunken sleep, the world around him stirred awake. Underneath the little cabin by the river, his father's last known achievement in the world of the living, the dank, hard-packed soil began to stir.

On the other side of town, on a small patch of land even more secluded than the Sanders land, sat a house. A ramshackle old house not much bigger than the little cabin Ray's father had built by the river. It was white once, a testament to that fact was the few specks of white paint that held on to the wood the way a dying man might hold onto to a life preserver. Mildewed cardboard wrapped in thick plastic covered a few of the broken windows. The yard around it was a mixture of gravel and mud and a handful of scraggly hedge bushes that struggled for survival around the outside of the house. Empty beer cans and cigarette packs littered the yard, and here and there rested the rusted hulls of riding lawnmowers, a few of them entombed in weeds. Behind the house, parked next to the porch steps, was Judd Atkins' old Ford pickup.

On the porch, shaded from the moonlit sky, Judd Atkins sat in his old rocker, taking long drags from a cigarette as he stared past his little lean-to shed and into the woods. He could smell them now. They were close, but not quite enough. Preparations would have to be made for their arrival. They would be hungry, oh yes, as hungry as one of those people he saw on the television, the ones that girl from *All in the Family* used to always mouth about. Judd would make sure *they* fed; he would make damn sure of that.

Judd thumped the ashes from the end of his cigarette and swallowed the last bit of beer in the can. He crushed the can in his palm and tossed it over the rickety porch railing, reached down into the old blue igloo cooler beside the rocker, and fished out another beer, popping the tab.

Yup, things are turning out just fine.

CHAPTER FOUR

While Ray Sanders lay passed out on his mother's couch, a puddle of drool forming under his chin, Donnie Atkins, nephew of Judd, that patron saint of Maple Grove, made his way north along Highway 78. He couldn't believe the bitch had had the nerve to put him out, *him* of all people. She was damn lucky Donnie had taken to her so, cause everyone in town called her a skank or a Satan baby—all but Donnie, of course. He was infatuated with the black lipstick and her smooth pale skin; the way her breasts heaved beneath the black corsets she wore and the way her legs seemed to grow from beneath her black miniskirts. He had wanted her, wanted to discover the secret beneath those skirts ever since he first saw her down at the parking lot of the Piggly Wiggly. Even though his friends had made jokes and lewd remarks, he had wanted her just the same. And since that day, he *had* had her, several times, in fact. Julie Fontaine was a regular slut, or at least had been his slut, and now she had the nerve to kick him out of that raggedy-ass little Stanza of hers and make him walk. Who did she think she was? Did she not know what kind of trouble he could cause her? *Stupid bitch!*

In some way, the fault laid at his feet for agreeing to go with her to that club over on the Southside of Birmingham. The Raven was a club for others like Julie, those who seemed to relish the night. Yet, he had agreed and there was no need worrying over spilled milk, as his mom would say. What is done is done and all that. However, it did not change the fact that he was pissed, did not change it at all. The bitch could have at least dropped him off in town where the walk would not have been as bad. What the fuck was her problem, anyway? Just because Donnie had changed his mind about that Club Med for freaks, decided that it was not his scene, that gave her the right to be pissed at him? He didn't think so. She didn't have the right to be pissed at anyone but herself for being a stupid, little cunt.

"Fuckin' bitch," Donnie mumbled to no one but the few passing cars along the highway.

The more he walked, the madder he became, and his head filled up with vengeful thoughts. Each step brought cruel and demeaning ways to get back at her, to make her wish she had never messed with Donnie Atkins; things he would do to her that would make her learn what respect was. Yeah, she would learn *really* fast.

"What's wrong with you?" she had asked, as they stood in the parking lot outside the club while others of her kind stood gawking at them. "You said you would at least give it a chance! You promised me you would! So, what's wrong with you? Tell me, what the fuck did I do?"

"Nothing," he had replied uneasily. A small group of freaks had circled around them and seemed to be thriving on their words as if this were some gothic soap opera open for their amusement. "I think we should just go."

"Why?" she had pleaded, her eyes wide with questions, some of those questions he knew deep down she had been afraid to ask. On some level, he knew she was scared of him; he could smell her fear, the way a beast in the wild smelled the fear of its prey.

"'Cause I don't want to be here… There ain't no other whys about it. Let's go, Julie, let's get the hell out of this shithole."

He had seen defiance in her eyes then, had seen her anger and knew she wanted to argue, but again her timid self, which she fought tooth-and-nail to hide, surfaced as undaunted as a submarine parting the surface of the ocean. She had given in, as she always did, and had given Donnie his way, just as she had given into him in the cab of his Chevy two nights after he had seen her at the Piggly Wiggly. But there had been something new in her eyes tonight, hadn't there? Yes, there had been something with more power than defiance and it had a sharp row of teeth. It had wanted to bite, yearned to bite, and Donnie had felt pain when it sank its teeth into his ego inside the cramped little Nissan.

She had sat in silence as she drove them from the Raven, her anger brewing and ready to boil over, and Donnie had not even noticed. He'd thought she had forgotten how mad she was and that in another few minutes she would be riding his manhood out at Cedar Point; the little argument completely lost as they both came and fell to the soft grass pressed together, panting and dripping with sweat. That, however, had not been the case. About three miles out of Adamsville, she had slammed on the brakes, dead in the middle of the highway. Donnie remembered thinking that if anyone had been behind them, one of the big rigs more than likely at this time of night, it would have plowed right over the top of the little Stanza and crushed it, and crushed them right along with it.

"Get out, Donnie. Get out of my car and don't ever call me again. I don't want to see you anymore." Her voice had been calm, but anger had taken shelter underneath her words.

"What the… Are you fucking crazy? You could have gotten us killed!"

She had looked at him with those dark brown eyes; an ebony ribbon of hair curly cued over her forehead and said, "I'm not crazy. I know what I am doing. You used me, Donnie, used me for a fuck! That's all I was to you and you know it! I was stupid…so, so, stupid. Now get out of my DAMN CAR!"

She had started to tremble then, and rivulets of tears had streaked her eye make-up down her face, reminding Donnie of a movie they had both watched about a week before, *The Crow*. Not the same but close enough to win the race. What had disturbed him, more than the eerie comparison of his girlfriend to Brandon Lee in white face paint, was the way the amber light of the streetlamps had crept into the car and cast her in a ghastly, supernatural glow. For a few seconds Donnie had just sat there in the passenger seat of the Stanza, frozen, mouth open, eyes wide; a screaming wax figure in a museum of horrors. Then he had composed himself, afraid and a tad embarrassed to let Julie see that she had frightened him.

"Damn, baby! Why you raggin'? You *know* I love you. C'mon, let's just go." Donnie leaned over and had tried to cup one of her breasts, wanted to give it a good tease. The way the slut in her liked it. But she had pushed him away.

"I said *get out*, Donnie. Save your 'I love you's' for the next gullible little thing in a skirt that falls for your shit. Now get out!"

"You fuckin' whore! Fuck you then!" he yelled at her as he climbed out. "You'll come crawlin' ba…"

She had reached over and slammed the door, then shifted the little Nissan into drive and had sped away. He had stood on the side of the highway for few hopeless minutes after she had left him there, thinking that she would realize how stupid she was acting and would come back to pick him up, but she never did, and so Donnie had started his long walk home.

An old, white Mustang full of teenagers peeled out of the Kountry Kitchen parking lot and onto the highway as he was stepping onto Pine Lane, whooping and hollering obscenities at him that he couldn't make out, not that he would give a damn one way or the other about what was said, even if he could have. Just a bunch of high school kids having fun; he could relate, as he was one of their kind a few years back. There were no streetlights on Pine Lane and it didn't take long for the light from Highway 78 to fade out behind him, no time at all before he was in complete darkness as the trees along the road formed a sort of canopy over the two-lane stretch of blacktop, and little to no moonlight shone through. But that did not bother Donnie; he had spent most of his time in the woods at night 'coon hunting with his uncle Judd when he was little. He knew what lived just beyond the trees; he knew there was nothing that could do him much harm. It was pretty damn refreshing walking along in the dark; it helped him to think. It helped him to think of ways to repay that damned little whore for putting him out on the side of the road in the middle of the night.

The bitch had some nerve. Treating him as if he was

some dumb, old country bumpkin was not a very wise thing to do, and if she thought for a minute that he was done with her–she was dead wrong. *He* was the one who would decide when and if it was over and if she refused to give him what he wanted; he would take it, just the way his uncle Judd was going to take what *he* wanted from that Sanders prick. Sometimes people got a little big for their britches, a saying his uncle Judd was fond of saying when someone was running off at the mouth. And it was *so* true. Julie had definitely grown a little big for her britches tonight, and shortly she would find out how big a mistake that was. By the time the sun rose up in the morning, she would be begging Donnie to forgive her; begging for another chance.

Up ahead, the treetop canopy opened up to allow in the prying radiance of moonbeams, and soft, silvery light poured through to bathe Pine Lane in the morose ambiance of a grave burrowed from the bottom up. The steadfast regiments of trees along the road were gray ghosts amidst an army of shadows and the old, worn asphalt road a fading scar on the face of Mother Earth. The rhythmic drone of the crickets and toads tapered off into a black hole of nonexistence and Donnie Atkins became acutely aware that he was scared. Even more scared than that time his brother Bo had let him stay up late with him to watch the *Omen* on late-night cable. A sickly vision of that little possessed boy, Damien, and his psychotic and obsessed nanny stalking around out there somewhere in that maze of pines and oaks, homicidal smirks on their faces and hands clenching the hilts of blood-stained daggers, permeated his horror-stricken mind.

Easy, boy. What would the guys say if they saw you standing here about to piss yourself? If they saw you were scared of the dark like some punk-ass little kid? I'll tell you what they would *do. They would laugh their asses off, that's what they would do. You would be a big joke. Get a hold of yourself, for Christ's sake. Before you do piss yourself.*

Onward ho, brave soldier, Donnie thought and laughed; the old joke buried so deep in his childhood memories that he forgot what had made it so funny, to begin with, and then he proceeded forward. Acting like a snot-nosed, little brat afraid of his own shadow was getting him nowhere and he had an important appointment to keep with a certain disrespectful little tramp. That caused a stirring down below and Donnie smiled a razor-thin and misshapen smile; it looked like an incision made by some mad doctor suffering through a bout of hysterics. He could almost feel the bitch squirming around while he ravaged her, and that grisly smile widened considerably, as did the bulge in his pants. Punishment *had* to be served; there were no ifs, ands, or buts about it. She would beg, oh how she would beg, but Donnie would have none of that. *Well, if she was begging on her knees...*

A long, deep howl infiltrated the night and shattered his perverse visions as the snot-nosed brat in his mind returned for an encore and his erection deflated to a smaller and more insignificant state.

"That sounded like a coyote," he murmured through trembling lips. "There haven't been coyotes around here in—"

The howl came again, louder.

"—five or ten years."

Probably just a loner. That made sense to him, or eased his mind, anyway. There had been an occasional stray coyote through here from time to time, those that were for some reason or the other rejected from their packs. As for an actual pack of coyotes, he could not remember ever actually seeing one. It was possible, no two ways about that. There had been a time, before his time, that is when coyotes were not that uncommon in Maple Grove and its surrounding areas. Nowadays, though, they were scarce and many of the folks around these parts had a tendency to shoot them on sight.

It could be a stray dog or someone's mutt. Did you consider that?

Of course, he had considered that but had dismissed it as soon as it had popped into his head. No dog he knew of had a howl like that and there was no mistaking that high, quavering cry, the trademark of the American coyote. Why was he worried about it? Coyotes did not attack people. They were generally more afraid of you than you were of them. But had he not heard somewhere that they were getting more aggressive? Would not a starving coyote be apt to attack opposed to sitting idly by?

The streetlights at the edge of town were visible now, only about two and a half miles and he would be crossing the short, wooden bridge crossing Sanders Creek, and onto Main Street which ran between Dale's Bakery and the Ace Hardware run by Tim Haney. And from there, Julie Fontaine's meager apartment was only a short walk. For some reason, he did not feel as eager as he did earlier to administer the punishment, he felt she so rightly deserved. He just wanted this business over with so he could get some sleep. In this case, sleep meant leaving his bedroom light on and pulling the covers up to his chin. The snot-nosed little brat didn't want to be in the dark.

Forget it. Go home. Close the door, lock it, and barricade the shit out of it. Just go straight home.

That was not a bad idea. Yeah. He would go home and

then tomorrow, after he got his head straight, he would give Julie a visit. Then everything would be as it should be, and he could shut this night behind him, lock the door, and throw away the key.

And he would have done just that if not for the lone coyote that trotted out of the darkness into the pallid moonlight. Donnie froze where he was, heart, beating in a rapid crescendo, and stared in frightened disbelief at the four-legged scavenger before him. *Won't hurt me,* he thought, without much conviction. *He's more afraid of me than I am of him.* He took a hesitant step forward and the coyote took a step towards him and started to growl, the hair on its neck and back bunching up around its shoulders.

"Easy, boy," Donnie said pleadingly and held out his hands, palms forward in an I-mean-you-no-harm gesture. "Just trying to get home. You're okay. Just going to ease on by now." Donnie tried to take a step around the coyote, but it cut him off. Its growl deepened and its lips pulled back over its gums, exposing its small, yet efficient, canines.

Reluctant to do so, but afraid to do anything else, Donnie stood where he was and watched carefully as the coyote stopped growling and sat on its haunches. They stayed that way for a few moments, man, and beast, eyes locked on one another in the world's most bizarre staring contest, until the coyote threw its head back and howled. Donnie backed up a few steps with that wild baying ricocheting in his head like a bullet fired into a room with steel walls, debating if he should make a break for it before the wild dog tore out his throat.

Then things got weird.

Too weird, even for an aspiring sex offender like Donnie Atkins.

A scant dozen coyotes staggered from the woods on both sides of the road and a few more crept up behind him. But not just coyotes, Donnie noticed, there was a mixture of stray dogs (some were not strays at all; a few were the pets of people he knew in town) and cats. *Cats and dogs were supposed to be enemies, right? And coyotes were known cat eaters. What was wrong with this picture?*

Donnie whipped his head from side-to-side, near panic and on the verge of tears. This kind of shit was not supposed to happen. Not to him. Not to anyone in real life. All around him, his unlikely entourage of felines and canines began to bark, and meow and Donnie broke out in a panicky sweat. This was not natural. No way in hell this was natural.

He snapped his head back towards the team leader, the lone coyote that had initiated this unusual encounter and his jaw dropped. Randy Sloan's old collie was sitting next to it and nuzzling it with some deep animal affection that Donnie could not comprehend. Then, it let out a string of hoarse coughs that almost sounded like…

Is that son-of-a-bitch laughing at me? Is that even possible?

But, before he could give it anymore thought, his world was bathed in white, for a brief moment as darkness soon closed around him in a pall. So intent was his focus on that strange, mocking animal laugh, that Donnie never even saw or heard Sonny McLain's big Mack truck as it roared down Maple Lane. And Sonny had not seen Donnie until he was right on top of him, literally. It was not until Sonny had brought his rig to a stop and climbed out that he realized that it was not his tired mind playing a cruel joke on him but something far more serious.

Sonny knew nothing of laughing coyotes or the joining

of cats and dogs getting along in a bewildering harmony; all he knew was he had just run someone down. In evidence of that, there was a large smear of gore from where Donnie first was drug and then chewed up and spat out into a twisted, bloody parody of a human body. Sonny McLain, a man strong of stomach, if not strong of mind, went back to the cab of his truck and snatched his cell phone from the console. He started to dial 911 when some inner urge forced him to look up. In the middle of the road sat a lone coyote staring at him in an oddly quizzical fashion. It barked a short, yipping bark and darted off into the woods. Years later, Sonny McLain would take his own life in a drunken fit of depression and the last thought to flash through his mind before pressing the barrel of his .357 to his temple and squeezing the trigger would be of that lone coyote and whether or not it had been smiling at him.

Ray nearly rolled off his couch; he woke with such a start. Outside the house, howls rose and fell. Still light-headed and a little drunk, he managed to sit up. *Probably be a good idea to check things*, he thought and used the arm of the couch to help himself stand, which he immediately regretted. The living room was dark, with only a hint of light falling into it from the kitchen at the other end of the hall, and his head was spinning. It reminded him of when he was a kid, and someone would dare him to spin around in a circle until he got dizzy and then try to walk around afterward, only about ten times worse. "Getting drunk" is what they called it and Ray figured that was pretty much what it was, only without the alcohol.

Confident that he could make it to his front door without taking a fall, Ray steadied his footing, released his hold on the couch and stagger-swayed around the coffee table, careful not to bump against it and knock any break-ables off onto the floor. When he got to the door, he pulled back the curtain and spied out the window.

The glare from the porch light left him blind to anything beyond the porch railing, so he reached over and flicked it off. There was nothing out there, not that he could see, and he was ready to forget it and go back to bed when a single howl forced him to stop in mid-turn. The hairs on the nape of his neck prickled and suddenly, he had a strong urge to drain the main vein. *Grow some balls, Sanders. It's just a wild dog.*

He walked back towards the couch, heavy-eyed and heavy-footed, nothing else on his mind other than passing out, when that shrill, forbidding cry repeated, followed by the thunderous report of a shotgun. *Yup. Just some poor wild dog going after somebody's chickens. Wonder if the guy hit the poor mutt.* It was hard to miss with a shotgun, unless whoever used it was firing from a fair distance away, but coyotes were quick and generally people shy.

It doesn't matter. You don't own any chickens. So why worry about wild dogs? You don't have anything for them to come after.

If that was true, then why worry about it?

Because it's what you were used to worrying about as a kid and it's what your dad was always concerned about. You're falling back into your old role again, Ray.

Why worry about any of it at all? Especially in his current condition, this was nowhere near sober, not in the least. However, inebriated though he was, his mind, no, his memories rather, would not shut off. It was like having a defective DVD player stuck on repeat and you could not find the remote to shut it off. *This is getting me nowhere,* Ray thought. Trudging back to the couch he lay across it face down, nuzzling his face into one of the throw pillows. Finally managing to push his thoughts aside and drifting into unconsciousness, the wind chimes on the front porch, rattling out a frantic tune, and a long, strangled howl, woke Ray once more and put a chill in his blood.

CHAPTER FIVE

"Maybe you should try sleeping pills," Roy said as he speared a piece of link sausage from his plate and stuffed it in his mouth. "My dad has a prescription of Ambien. I could grab you a couple of those. See if they do you any good, or you could try Lunesta. Friend of mine says they do him wonders."

"Don't think that's the problem." Ray was drowning his pancakes in maple syrup and debating whether he should have a second helping of bacon. It had been two weeks since he had had any form of decent sleep and he had yet to find anything that would ease the issue. Perhaps it was that dream, which kept recurring like a crazy person with a vendetta, or maybe it was this town, which should seem warm and inviting but instead felt like some dark, brooding entity from the reaches of some abysmal land-scape. Whatever it was, it was not doing him any good. When he did manage sleep, the rare and dreamless kind, he would wake tired, aching, and wanting to do nothing more than sleep the entire day, doing nothing.

"No. It wouldn't be the problem; it'd be the solution."

Roy waved over to Dianne Townsend, who was refreshing a cup of coffee for a skinny, middle-aged man in a grey sweatsuit and dirt-yellowed Nikes and looking very annoyed. The man was sagging against the counter and bird-pecking at a plate of scrambled eggs. Dianne held up one finger and lipped, "Just a moment."

"You know what I mean. I don't think any sleep aid is going to do much good unless you know of one that'll put this whole town to sleep."

"Huh?"

"Nothing."

From behind the counter came the pop and crackle of hot grease and the aroma of cooking pork; a nostalgic scent that took Ray back to a billion mornings before school (or before chores on weekends and summer days) with his mom standing over their old gas stove preparing breakfast for him and his father. A sudden, sharp longing for the immortality of youth struck him with the force of a shotgun blast to the chest. *Everything was so much easier then. Back before the reality of the real-world complicated things.*

"Could be worse, you know. A lot worse things than not sleeping well. Take poor old Sonny McLain, for instance. That poor bastard is *really* going through some head- numbing shit."

"I imagine so," Ray said and shoved a forkful of pancake into his mouth. Sonny, who was under persecution by damn near everyone in Maple Grove and was under the investigative eyes of both the Richards Trucking Company and the state police, was slowly slipping away from the shores of sanity like a raft drifting aimlessly out to sea. The rumor was the tragedy out on Pine Lane had turned him into a slobbering drunk, and he'd been holed up in that firetrap house of his out behind the Maple Grove High School. "From what I heard they were picking pieces of Donnie up about a half-mile from where Sonny stopped his rig. That's not the kind of thing a person can just put out of their mind."

"No doubt on that one, Rayford. I just feel bad for the guy, you know."

"I know what you mean, and I feel about the same, but some things can't be helped. I was always taught that everything happens for a reason and maybe this, well maybe this was supposed to happen."

"Supposed to or not, it still sucks the bone for old Sonny. This shit always seems to happen to the good ones."

Dianne Townsend stepped over to their booth, pulled an order book and pen from the pocket of her apron, and gave Roy a disapproving look. She did not like his wardrobe: The black ICP shirt with The Great Milenko on the front, the faded blue Levi's jeans with more holes than a colander and the scuffed, worn combat style boots. Dianne had been the second wife of James Sanders and she had always given Roy hell about the way he chose to dress, even after being divorced from Roy's dad for almost six years. In some ways Ray guessed she still thought of herself as his cousin's mother, and being she was the only real mother Roy had ever known, he supposed that was only natural.

"Don't tell me you want to order something else," she said to Roy.

"Just another chocolate milk." Roy patted his stomach and gave Dianne a pleasant smile. "I'm too stuffed to eat another bite. I swear."

Dianne shook her head and looked over at Ray. "What about you, hon? Can I get you anythin' else?"

Ray looked back at her, a forty-ish something woman

with honey blonde hair, the body of a showgirl, and a heart of gold, and he wondered just why his uncle had let her slip away. "No, ma'am. I think I'm pretty stuffed."

"Well I don't know about all that 'ma'am' crap, but I'm happy to see you got a good meal down your throat, you been lookin' a bit scrawny last couple of weeks."

"Haven't had much of an appetite, I guess."

She offered him a warm smile and gave his left hand a light squeeze. "You just make sure you start takin' better care of yourself before you make yourself sick. And you–" her gaze shifted to Roy. "—need to buy you some new pants. Those things you got on look about to fall apart. You got the money to spend on video games, DVDs, and God knows what else and you can't pick up a decent pair of pants?"

She gave Roy a pat on the shoulder and another disapproving headshake and walked off. A huge smirk spread across Ray's face.

"Laugh now," Roy said. "Laugh all you want. Ha-ha. Dick."

"Sorry, my man. That shit's just funny as hell."

"Yea, it's fucking hilarious, huh? Ha-ha."

Something gave way then and Ray barked warm laughter, and Roy mocked as if he was going to hit him with the ketchup bottle causing Ray to laugh even harder. Dianne returned and set a glass and a pint container of chocolate milk on the table, eyed the two of them earnestly, shook her head, and walked off.

"Sorry, man." Ray let his eyes wander out the window into the light of the morning sun, watching as it glided over the fresh blacktop and dance across the few cars parked out front in tiny hypnotic sparkles. He embraced its warmth, felt its comfort, but it was a charade; the hideous, pock-scarred face of a witch masked by the succulent glow of beauty. There was darkness in Maple Grove. Darkness like a thousand shadows on a moonless night and Ray believed it would turn him into a drooling fool if he did not find someone to confide with his fears. And that someone was Roy.

"Have you ever seen anything strange in Maple Grove?" Ray asked suddenly.

"Depends on what you consider strange."

Well, Roy my boy, I consider this whole damn town strange. I know I've only been back for about two months…but let me tell you this place is reallllllly *strange. Strange is what I need you to see, so I don't think I am losing my goddamn mind. Strange is what happened in my basement…*

…Two days after Donnie Atkins's funeral. It was a Saturday. The July sun was a red-hot ember against a curtain of baby blue; rabbit-tail tufts of clouds drifted along with a cool breeze. Birds were singing and a fat rattlesnake disappeared underneath the lean-to shed out back of the house as Ray stumbled across the back yard with a big cardboard box marked "memories of mom" in black permanent marker. He had spent most of the day packing away his mother's cherished dolphin collection. Starting with that eerie wind-chime that he snatched from its little hook with a rapturous grin and ending with what seemed like three or four hundred snow globes. Now, as he set the last box on a dusty wooden table in the back of the shed, he armed away the sweat on his brow and let out a sigh of relief. The next task was to find those missing family photos, the ones his mother had whisked away in order to make room for the inevitable coming of a certain irritating sea mammal.

Half an hour later, Ray sat at the kitchen table nursing a Miller Lite, bare all but his sweatpants, and staring holes into the wall. He had stripped off his sweat-drenched tee shirt and tossed it on the counter next to the sink. It wasn't hot in the house, but it wasn't on the verge of becoming the next Ice Age, either. Eventually, the air conditioning would go out all together and Ray knew he would have to replace it—replace it or burn up for the rest of the summer.

He tossed the empty bottle into the wastebasket next to the sink and went to the refrigerator for another. His fingers had just enclosed around a cold, refreshing bottle of brew (Less filling! Tastes great!) when he heard a low, scratching sound off to his left and became mannequin-still. He was poised that way for a few seconds, minutes, bent over, cold beer in his hand and cool refrigerated air blowing in his face, waiting for that scratching sound to repeat. When it didn't, he straightened up, shut the refrigerator door, and went back to the table with his beer. *It's just a mouse or a rat behind the walls or under the floorboards somewhere. I have to go to town and get some traps and poison.*

Then he heard it again, louder and with a frantic, hurried urgency that caused Ray to stop in mid-gulp and set his beer down. He swallowed hard and it hurt his throat to do so. But he would not notice this until later, nor would he remember until later the family pictures he had wanted with such desperation. His focus, for now, was the door about three feet to the left of the refrigerator, the one that led down into the basement, and the fevered scratching behind it. Mesmerized, Ray sat and stared at the basement door for a period of time that escaped him and listened as the scratching grew steadily in volume and intensity.

Suddenly, near the bottom of the door, the wood began to splinter and crack. A hole opened up; small at first, then as Ray watched with frightened fascination, the hole widened; white splintered wood and sawdust drifted down to the shiny green linoleum in slow motion. A furry head poked through, nose twitching, and eyes as dark as coal. Then the body squeezed through, as big as a house cat, and it tumbled to the floor, convulsing and bloody and trailing a tendril of blue-gray smoke. Ray had a moment to think his next course of action through but ignored it. He went over to the dying rodent, not sure exactly why, but believed it had to do with curiosity. *Curiosity killed the cat. You remember that old saying, don't you?* He knelt next to it and studied it as a lab student may study a frog he or she is about to dissect.

The rat was much bigger than any he had ever seen and from the tip of its nose to the tip of its tail it was soaked in blood; its little paws no more than nubs and its sharp little beaver teeth chipped and jutting from a crimson mass that had been its gums. As he watched, the rat's eyes went from black to white, more of that blue-gray smoke spewed out, and smell like rotting meat burned his nose.

This is impossible, Ray thought as he staggered to his feet. *There is no way in hell that what I'm seeing is possible.*

That was when the basement door flew open.

"You all right?"

Ray looked up and saw the worried expression on Roy's face and in his eyes. "Huh?"

"You went all pale and shit. You all right?"

Dianne Townsend was now taking an order for an elderly couple seated in the corner booth adjacent to Ray and Roy and had him fixed with a grave, concerned stare.

"I'm good. A little bit of heartburn, that's all."

"You sure?"

"Yeah."

"All right. Just checking. Can't have my fav cuz go and collapse on me before he picks up the check." Roy was smiling, but it was a false smile. *You are not okay, and you are feeding me a line of horse shit*, that smile said. It was hard work to hide something from someone who knew you as much as you knew yourself.

"I'll pick up your breakfast tab on one condition, Roy my boy."

"Yeah. And what's that?"

"You come over to the house tonight and have a couple of beers with me. We could watch a movie or two or play some video games. My old Super NES is still there, I think Mom may have packed it away in the basement." Just saying the word basement and Ray could feel goosebumps rise on his skin. Roy apparently did not notice.

"Super NES. Now, that is old school."

"I got a PS3 and PS4, but they're in Florida. I'll have to bring them up when I go down there to get my stuff."

"So, you are moving back. Hell yeah!"

"I called my boss and gave him the bad news. He was cool about it and told me he understood. Said he hated to see me go and that if I ever got back down that way, I could have my job back. But I doubt I'll be moving back to sunny Florida in the near future."

"Going to be just like old times. I really miss those days, Ray. We used to have some hellacious good times, remember?"

Ray pushed his plate out of the way and killed the remainder of his orange juice. "Yeah, we had some good times, no doubt there. And I think we're going to have some good times, yet." *That is if I'm not locked up in a padded cell upstate somewhere.*

As Ray pulled onto Pine Lane and headed for town, his thoughts drifted back to that Saturday almost two weeks ago. He thought about that smoldering rat carcass and of what he had seen in the basement. How it had made him feel so small and afraid, and how for a few moments he had thought…

What would it take?

… About driving nails into his eyes so he would see no more. But that was crazy, and Ray liked to believe that he was still sane enough to know better than to commit suicide. But what he had seen… What was it exactly?

Then those dreams, those nightmares, that haunted his sleep and tortured his mind. What were those? A slip in reality? A message in the proverbial bottle? What?

The basement door flew open… And what? What was it that was so monstrous…? So awful that it felt like his mind was going to collapse like a card house in the wind. And the smell; a smell like burning wood and fermented apples that had assaulted his nostrils as soon as the door had flung open.

It didn't happen, Ray. It was a dream, just like the

*burning cabins down by the river. You went to the base-
ment the next day and it was just a basement*

But that hole was still there in the door, the one that mammoth rat had made. That was still there, so how could it have all been a dream? And the rat, he had scooped it up into a garbage bag and buried it out behind the shed; that had not been a dream. He remembered that clearly. The deadweight of it as he carried the bag out back and that awful decayed flesh stench, and the way it had slid around inside the bag had been all too real.

What am I getting Roy mixed up in? He thought as he pulled to a stop in front of his house some fifteen minutes later, jolted by a pang of guilt. Then aloud, he said, "Sorry, Roy my boy, but I need to know if all this shit is really happening. And you're the only one I can trust."

CHAPTER SIX

She stood like a soldier on the edge of some foreign battlefield, a can of Raid Ant and Roach Spray in her hand, frenzied determination in her eyes. "Take this, you little fucks!" She depressed the valve on the aerosol can and began her assault. She sprayed her trashcan, behind it, under it, and inside of it. She sprayed the floor, where the trails of ants led from the trash to the sink. She sprayed the sink and behind the faucet. "How you little pricks like that?" She grabbed the red plastic cap off the sink and popped it back into place on the can, then set the can on the glass-topped dining table behind her.

If Julie Fontaine hated, *loathed,* anything; it was ants. The only other member of the insect kingdom that came anywhere close to second on her "Most Hated" bug list was the cockroach. They were nasty little things, and although Miss Haney, Julie's seventh-grade science teacher, had told her once that cockroaches were actually very clean, Julie had doubted it was true. Still did, in fact. How could anything that fed off everything from package glue to shit be clean? She even read somewhere that they had a bad effect on people with asthma. So, again, how did that make the cockroach worthy of defense? Well, that did not matter; they were nasty and icky, case closed.

After taking a quick death toll on the invading ant army, Julie snatched the drawstrings of the hefty bag, hefted it from the trashcan with a wet, sucking plop, drew it shut and tied it off. Then, holding it by the yellow draw-string and keeping it an arm's length away, wary of any stray ants that had survived insect D-Day, and revolted by that sickening garbage smell, Julie took the bloated hefty bag out to the dumpster provided by River View Apart-ments. *River View? What view?* The only thing to view was the Maple Grove Elementary across the street and an old corrugated building housing Danny Johnson's wood cabinet and craft shop outback. *Some view, huh?*

Julie slung the hefty bag into the dumpster. There was a clinking of glass as her bag landed amongst the refuse of the other tenants, and an even deeper gassy garbage smell wafted out. She wrinkled her nose, backed up a few steps, and fanned a hand in front of her face. Why hadn't some brainy nerd created a huge, dumpster-sized air freshener? That would be *so* much easier on the old snout. Of course, maybe someone had invented one and the River View management was just too cheap to buy one. Who knew? She didn't, that was for sure. It would be nice though, instead of ruined milk and spoiled meat, if you would get a whiff of strawberry or jasmine. *Dream on. That's something you won't see in your lifetime. Just mark it up with winning a big check from Publisher's Clearing House and finding your soul mate.*

She was halfway back to her apartment when she caught a glance of old Mr. Reed leaning against the railing of the second-floor breezeway and looking down at her, no doubt with a rock-hard boner (that is if he could still get the old trouser snake up) and greedy lust in his sunken dull eyes. Julie suddenly felt self-conscious, not because she thought she looked bad, but because despite her efforts to be unappealing: baggy jogging pants, huge oversized T-shirt and unkempt hair, that old pervert still gawked at her every time she walked out the front door. *The old bastard really creeps my shit,* she thought as she pushed open the door of apartment A-2 and stepped inside. And to think the old geezer was probably picturing her while he was flogging the bishop was just too…

That is a thought better left in the dark, girl.

And dark was just how she liked it. Despite the burning gaze of the sun outside, and because of the black homemade wool curtains covering her windows, every room in her apartment was as dark as the bottom of a well, except for the overhead light in the kitchen that spilled out into the living room with a surreal, foreboding glow and the *Family Guy* lamps on her end tables that burned dim circles from underneath their shades. The central air was pumping out fresh, cool air that was cold against her sweat-drenched skin, cold and intoxicating, a welcome embrace from the blast furnace-like heat that consumed the world outside.

She lay back on the couch, shut her eyes, and exhaled softly. And before she even realized it was happening, she was sound asleep, unaware of the fat, black rat atop her coffee table that stood watch over her, little soulless eyes locked onto her sleeping form, its tiny wet nose twitching.

At quarter until seven, Roy knocked on the door. The world outside was easing into twilight in a cricket serenade while the rest of the woodland nightlife began to stir. Ray opened the door, half-asleep and groggy from an unplanned afternoon nap in his dad's old recliner. Roy held up a six-pack of Budweiser in one hand and a fifth of Jack Daniels in the other. The smile on his face was big enough to shame the Cheshire cat.

"Wake up, sunshine. Time to get tore up."

Ray grinned, or what passed for a grin from anyone waking from a deep, exhausted sleep, and waved him in. They went into the kitchen and Roy put the beer in the refrigerator and the whiskey on the table, and then took a seat. Ray stared at the basement door for a few seconds, then pulled a chair out from the table, glanced over at Roy as he sat down, and let out a monstrous yawn.

"Watch it. That shit's contagious," Roy said as he unscrewed the cap to the Jack Daniels and took a quick shot, wincing as the whiskey burned its way down his throat. "How long you been asleep?"

Ray took the bottle from his cousin, knocked it back, and set it on the table with a sour look on his face. "About six hours, give or take. Damn! Need some coke to mix with that. It's good, though, hit the spot."

"Mixed drinks are for pussies. Drink it straight, puts hair on your balls. Guaranteed."

"Maybe so, but who wants to walk around with a 'fro between their legs? Besides, I like the taste of it. Tried it the other night and I have to admit that it's not too bad."

Roy leaned back in his chair and shook his head. "I knew Florida was a bad idea. You done went and turned all girly and shit."

"Girly? I can still kick your ass."

"You wish."

Ray reached for the bottle of Jack, thought about it, and pulled his hand back. "While the beer's getting cold, you want a soda or anything?"

Roy said he would take coke and Ray fetched two cold Coca-Colas from the refrigerator, handed one to Roy, and kept one for himself. Ray showed his cousin the hole in the basement door and told him about the rat and its unnatural entrance into the kitchen, saving for later what he saw during his frightful exploration into the basement. He had to be good and sure Roy believed him about the rat first. Because, if he did not believe Ray about that, no way in hell would he believe what Ray had to tell him about the basement. He then went on to tell Roy about the weird dream following his mother's funeral and about the eerie dolphin wind-chime and that he believed he could hear it every now and again, even though Ray had packed it away at the very bottom of his mother's things out back in the shed. Roy took all this in, nodded in between pauses, sipped his coke, and nodded some more.

By the time Ray finished his story, Roy had a look on his face that Ray was unable to decipher. He knew his cousin would have either some smart remark or maybe even a concerned response, but from the look on his face, Ray did not know what to expect. He could not tell if it was a good sign or a bad sign, or maybe a sign that indicated a visit from the men in white coats. Whatever it was, he hoped he would get some kind of response soon because uncomfortable silences weren't his forte.

"Well…" Roy trailed off. He took another shot of Jack Daniels. "Well…"

"Come on. Spit it out."

"Well, it's one hell of a story. That's for sure."

"It's true."

"Your mom's…" Roy hesitated, searching for the proper word. "…death. You took it pretty hard. Maybe you just—"

"I saw what I fucking saw! Dude look at my basement door! What the fuck you think did that? I even buried the damn thing out back."

"C'mon, Ray. You know it's a lot to swallow. Either you're poking fun here, or you're cracking up and I'd sure as hell like to believe that you're just screwing with my head. Be a lot easier to take than my fav cuz going bonkers, you know. So, which is it?"

"Come on," Ray said, as he stood up and headed for the back door. "I'll show you the rat."

Roy followed Ray onto the back porch, fighting the urge to protest further. He decided to humor his cousin rather than upset him any more than necessary. The shovel Ray had used to dig the makeshift grave was in the flowerbed next to the steps, leaning against the banister, and he snatched it as he cleared the last step.

"You'll see. You'll see exactly how strange all this really is when you see the rat."

They stopped at the shed for a few minutes while Ray went in and retrieved two flashlights and a small hunting knife, the latter of which he was tucking into his waistband as he emerged from the shed.

"What you going to do with that?" Roy asked as he took one of the flashlights and flicked it on.

"In case it isn't dead."

"Well, okay, you buried it two weeks ago. I think it's pretty much dead unless you just imagined it."

"No, I didn't imagine it. You'll see."

As they approached the grave, a mound of dirt two weeks fresh, Ray noticed that there were young blades of grass growing already. The rat must have been some good fertilizer. He shivered, reluctant to start digging. Seeing that monstrosity once in his lifetime was more than enough, but to have to see it twice was an invitation to insanity. He could feel Roy's eyes on him, waiting, curious to see what had made his cousin talk about things only a lunatic would dare speak of in front of others. *Come on, come on, come on. Don't make me a liar. Roy has to see this… He has to know I'm not crazy. I have to know I'm not crazy.*

For the next ten minutes, Ray dug, Roy watching in silence and taking the occasional swig of Jack Daniels. He finished the fifth of whiskey around the same time Ray struck the bag with the end of his shovel. "Now, you'll see." Ray dropped the shovel and hopped into the freshly dug hole, grabbing his flashlight in the process, and sprawled his legs over either side of the bag. Twin beams of light landed on the soiled black plastic and Ray took a deep breath, wishing instantly that he had not. The smell irritated his nose and watered his eyes. *It's been two weeks. How can it still smell so bad?*

"Damn, dude. I don't know what you got buried here, but damn, smells like ass mixed with sour milk. Damn, that's nasty."

"Well, hold your breath. It's going to be even worse when I open the bag."

"Is that a good idea…I mean…? Hey, I take your word for it."

"No," Ray looked at Roy as he felt for the knot at the top of the bag. "You have to see this. I'm not ready for a padded cell yet. Just keep your light on the bag and try not to get too big a whiff."

Ray took the knife from his waistband and cut the top off the garbage bag. The smell that rolled out of it was horrendous. Behind him, Roy lost control and sent his lunch to meet his shoes. Ray couldn't blame him, he felt like throwing up too, but he held it in, trying to ignore the ungodly stench that hung around him in a haze; he had to finish this and prove he wasn't losing his mind. Ray reached into the bag.

He almost lost his war against nausea as his fingertips brushed against fur and decaying flesh, hard chips of dried blood pricking at his skin as he closed his hands around the carcass of the dead rat. Something was not right. It didn't feel right somehow. It felt *different.* No matter, it was probably just his mind playing tricks on him. Without further hesitation, he removed the corpse from the bag and held it up towards Roy. "See! I told you! Believe me now?"

"Sweet Jesus!" Roy's eyes filled with disgust and he appeared on the verge of vomiting a second time. "Ray, what the hell did you do? Good Lord!"

"What do you mean, 'what the hell did I do?' Look at the rat."

"Dude, that's not a rat."

Stunned, Ray brought the thing in his hands down to where he could get a good look at it, not quite grasping what he was seeing in his hands. It was the severed head of a German Sheppard, minus the eyes and ears. Then, as if it were a molten piece of metal, Ray dropped it and scrambled out of the hole, leaving both his flashlight and knife behind. "Jesus!"

"Was that Lady?" Roy asked frantically. "Mrs. Johnson's dog, Lady. That was her! Oh please, dude, tell me you didn't—"

"I didn't kill Mrs. Johnson's dog. Two weeks ago, that was a rat! A big fucking rat! I swear on my mother's grave! I swear it! I don't know how the fuck that... *That* got in there. I promise."

Roy began to pace around the hole, his flashlight beam bobbing up and down, then he stopped and looked at Ray. "That dog's been missing for a couple of weeks. Mrs. Johnson, she came by the apartment and asked if I'd seen Lady and I told her, that if I did, I'd let her know. What am I supposed to tell her? 'Hey, Mrs. Johnson, I found your dog. Well, part of her. My cousin has her head buried in his back yard.' Jesus, Ray! What am I supposed to tell sweet old Mrs. Johnson about her dog? Jesus!"

"First, you just calm down. Second, I didn't kill Mrs. Johnson's dog. And third, we don't know for sure that..." Ray paused, trying to gain some form of composure. "... For sure that head belongs to Lady."

"Are you blind? How many other people in the Grove own a German Sheppard? Mrs. Johnson is the only one I know that does. And it's buried in *your* yard! Dude, this is crazy. I don't know how to take this, it's just too messed up."

"You believe me. Right?"

"I don't know, Ray? It's hard *not* to believe that you hacked off Lady's head. After seeing this, anyway."

Ray started to plead more in his defense when he heard the growl, low and muffled, but definitely a growl, like that of a dog, coming from the small grave and he wanted to run as far away from it as possible. Roy heard it too and both men froze, slowly turning their heads toward the hole, as the growl grew louder, meaner, as if the severed head that lay at the bottom of the grave was going to climb out and bite into them with its rotting teeth.

"I'm not hearing this," Roy said as if trying to convince his inner self.

"Me either," Ray said.

"Think maybe we should check to see if the beer is cold yet."

"Yeah, I think maybe we should."

———••+•••——

Julie Fontaine bolted from her couch and dashed down the hall to the bathroom. She slapped a clumsy hand at the light switch a few times before finally hitting it and hurried to the sink. She turned on the cold water, cupped her hands under it, and flushed her face for several minutes before shutting the water off and looking into the bathroom mirror.

That dream.

It had been so real. Already it was beginning to fade, but his face, pale and lifeless; stitched together. Donnie? The funeral had been closed casket. How in the hell was she seeing this? And he had spoken to her, spoken to her through lips that were not lips but bloodless sacks of meat. What had he said? Something about a sacrifice. No, that couldn't be right. Could it?

"It was just a dream, girl. So don't you go freaking out."

But it had been so real.

Donnie had been here, in her apartment, standing in front of her television, watching her sleep, a big, fat, black rat perched on his right shoulder. The rat was nibbling on his ear. However, it was not the Donnie she remembered. This Donnie was the Donnie that rested in a grave no more than ten miles away, his body so mangled that his casket had remained closed during the viewing. Julie had not personally seen Donnie's body, that what remained of him was a poor, sloppy stitch job, but she was positive that the specter that had visited her in her dream was exactly how his corpse had looked beneath that closed lid.

Donnie had been motionless for several minutes, that fat rat on his shoulder squeaking at such a high pitch Julie had feared all the glass in the apartment would shatter. Then he had spoken, a voice as gelid and empty as open space had issued forth and Julie had shrunk as far back against the couch as she could manage, pulling her blanket with her.

"*They* fear him," Donnie had said. "But you, you fill *them* with pure terror. There are others, their roles are insignificant, and distractions to what you and he must do to rid Maple Grove of *them* forever."

"Donnie?" Julie had thought her own voice distant, fuzzy. "Are..."

"Do not speak," he had said, cutting her off. "Only listen."

Julie had nodded, too afraid to speak; lest she upset the ghoul speaking through Donnie's ruined lips.

"The orb must be silenced, the sacrifice must be made, and Maple Grove must be cleansed of *them* and of those that collaborate with *them.*"

"I don't understand..." Julie had started, and Donnie had silenced her with a look so disturbing that it was beyond her ability to put into words.

"Find him," he had said. "Find him and destroy the nest, silence the orb, and end *their* time in this realm."

Another squeak had issued from the rat and much to Julie's disgust, it had burrowed into Donnie's shoulder, the bulk of its body plainly visible as it moved around beneath his skin and popped few stitches as it worked its way down his throat and into his chest. At this point, her eyes had opened, and she had realized she had been dreaming.

Looking into the bathroom mirror, rivulets of water running down her face and dripping from her chin, Julie had yet to feel any true fear. The dream was short, and her ex-boyfriend had been horrifying, in both looks and the way his voice had been hollow and cold, but it hadn't scared her so much as it had confused her.

For a dream, this one had seemed almost tangible, as if not a dream at all, but some weird supernatural encounter. An encounter that held such a sense of urgency that Julie could not even begin to fathom the depths of its meaning. And what was this shit about a sacrifice? And who were *they?* Or for that matter, who was the *him* Donnie had mentioned? Nests, orbs, realms, a mysterious man that was supposed to help her save the world. Julie giggled.

Girl, you have been watching way too many scare flicks. That shit has your dreams twisted.

Julie flipped the bathroom light off and started back towards the living room when a flash of Donnie's decomposing face popped into her head along with an image of a large black rat burrowing through his rotting flesh, and Julie turned on her heels and beelined it to her bedroom. Jumping into her bed and pulling her comforter up over her head, she began to pray. She hadn't prayed since she was fourteen, but Julie felt for the first time in years, that she needed protection by a higher power.

CHAPTER SEVEN

The drive home from the Kountry Kitchen was its usual depressing trek along with a mangled combination of paved and dirt roads. The same trip she had made to and from work, day in and day out, for the last eighteen years. From navigating around the potholes of Pine Lane (ever wary of the trees and weeds that bordered this dismal strip of road, making it seem isolated and forgotten) to driving through the humdrum scenery of Main Street through to her double-wide mobile home on the northern outskirts of Maple Grove. Then, back again. The monotony of it was awful, sour, bitter, like lemon slices sprinkled with vinegar.

As a girl, Dianne Townsend had had many daydreams and fantasies of leaving Maple Grove, going out west to California, where she could write poetry by the sea and have tea with celebrities. *How naive was I? Who actually had tea parties in Hollywood?* For an eleven-year-old girl with bony knees and a retainer, it had been a formidable dream. Along with meeting one Andy Griffith, the lovable sheriff and best friend to Barney Fife from the *Andy Grif-*

fith Show, and her secret celebrity crush. While most girls her age and older were idolizing rock stars and big-name movie actors she had fallen in love with a comedian that starred in a sitcom about a small-town country sheriff and his bumbling deputy. That was why she kept it a secret. Her friends and peers would have laughed, teased, and ridiculed her to no end. Dianne believed there was no such person on the face of the earth with a tongue as venomous as that of an adolescent schoolgirl.

It was around her nineteenth birthday when all her dreams of leaving Maple Grove had drowned beneath the tides of romance. That was the year she had met James Sanders at a dance down at the VFW and fell in love with his smile, among other things, and that slight wild streak that shone in his eyes. It didn't hurt that he had some slick dance moves, either.

James was ten years older than Dianne and raising a nine-year-old son whose mother who had decided to pick up and run off. She had left James and baby Roy behind without a word. A year later and they were married, and her parents had thrown one hell of a tantrum over that decision. "You've got no business being that man's whore," her father had spat as she stormed out of the house. "He's just using you to raise that little bastard son of his and to get in your drawers when he's done with the other whores!" Her father had shouted this last part as she walked away from him, teary-eyed and hurt by her parents' rejection of her good news.

Dianne eased her Datsun to a stop at the intersection of Main and Maple and checked to see if all was clear along Maple, then continued forward. The little car lurched and backfired as she pressed the accelerator, a sound like a gunshot along these empty streets. That was another thing about Maple Grove: after eight o'clock, everyone seemed to go home to roost, as her mother used to say 'they 'as gone to bed with the chickens'. On the weekends, you might catch some of the younger high school kids out, but mostly they hung out in Birmingham, Hoover, or some of the other larger, more populated cities. A scant few prowled the parking lot of the Piggly Wiggly or the Laundromat over by the elementary school.

She made a left onto Oak Avenue at the next intersection and her thoughts drifted back to her ex-husband and stepson. She loved them both, always would, and she missed them so much she didn't know if her heart could survive such a vicious ache. Twelve years as a mother and wife, some feelings were eternal. *Can't change the past. Can't make things the way they were. You know that. So why even bother thinking about it?*

Fifteen minutes later found Dianne in her meager kitchen, staring out the window over the sink as she washed the few dishes left over from breakfast and the bowl of Sweet Sue chicken and dumplings she indulged in when she got home. A floodlight out back lit her yard up in a dim yellow glow, giving it the appearance of a night-time scene in some old classic black-and-white horror film. It was *way* too eerie for her comfort. The closest neighbor was about a mile up a stretch of dirt road and all the years she had lived here, she hated nights, partly because James used to work nights, partly because she hated that James hadn't chosen to set their mobile home up closer to the main road. The only consolation was that she could see the lights of her neighbors' houses from her front porch, thanks to open fields along either side of her driveway. James always wanted to farm…

Leave it alone.

She could not help but wonder just how her ex-husband and stepson were getting along in their little apartment. Roy came by the diner on a regular basis, but she hadn't spoken to James in about six months. And that was just because they had bumped into each other over at Barry Smith's service station at the end of town.

Leave it alone!

Dianne looked back through the window, across the unfinished deck that hung from the back of her trailer like some discarded relic to the rusted swing set skulking at the edge of the tree line. Her heart ached with sorrow at the memories excreted from that old swing set. James pushing Roy on the swing on clear warm afternoons, or that time Roy and his cousin Ray had the brilliant idea to coat the slide in baby oil and slide down on their bellies. They couldn't have been more than ten at the time, and both of them came to her crying five minutes later; Roy holding his bleeding elbow and gushing tears like a broken sprinkler head and Ray clapping hold of his forehead with both hands and wailing. Neither of them had been hurt badly, but the way they were carrying on, you would think they were about to drop dead. She had cleaned their cuts, bandaged their boo-boos, and assured them they were going to live. Then, that time…

Leave it alone. For Christ's sake, don't think about those things.

With the dishes done and air drying in the drainer, Dianne dried her hands on the dishtowel hung on the oven door and went into the living room, switching the lights off on her way out. Maybe a little TV would help clear her head. *Divorced six years and you still can't let them go. You're just lonely. Time to go out and find you a good man, don't let the past drag you down.*

The problem was she had dated or tried to, anyway. Disaster after disaster was what that had turned out to be. Ben Walker, who had been so nice when she met him, turned out to be a sex-crazed pervert. The one time they had gone out, they had ridden up to Jasper to see a movie. Everything was going well until she had gone to use the ladies' room. When she came back, Ben was sitting there with his fly open and his thing hanging out. "It's dark… Ain't nobody gonna know," Ben had begged. The bastard even had the nerve to try to put her hand on it. There were other dates after that, none as disturbing as the one with Ben Walker, but none of them was worth mentioning, either.

"Do you have a job? Do you have three hundred dollars? If so, we can put you in a new car today." The car salesman pitched as Dianne curled up on the sofa and clicked the power button on the remote. *"Bad credit, no credit, no problem! We…"*

All these channels and nothing on, she thought as she began to surf. Waste is what that was. It was a waste of money on cable. After a few minutes, she found an *Andy Griffith Show* marathon and dropped the remote on the couch beside her. *They don't make shows like this anymore. Nowadays, it's all sex and violence.*

Somewhat relaxed and content, Dianne Townsend lit a cigarette, shifted into a more comfortable position, one that didn't cause too much strain on her back, and three hours later she was still there, covered in a thin sheet and in a deep sleep.

It watched as she got up, grabbed a sheet from the hallway closet, and then crumpled back down on her battered old couch. It watched her laying there in the glow of her television. It was ravenous, but it would not let its hunger impregnate its conscious mind. In time, it would feed, and it would feed well. For now, all it could do was watch and wait, wait for the sign, wait for its instructions. Which one would it take first? Old slut, young slut, who would it be? It began to salivate.

The boy was a problem.

The boy Sanders would get in the way of everything.

It went to flick its cigarette to the ground but realized in time where it was. Instead, it crushed the cigarette out in the calloused, greasy palm of its hand. The pain was searing and intense and it had to grit its teeth to endure the pain. *Better safe than sorry,* it thought and pulled its mouth into a grin; yellow, rotting teeth exposed from swollen, diseased gums. Smoking had been its host body's vice, and the awful habit had become its habit, but not for much longer.

It was knee-deep in the underbrush, dry, brittle, and flammable. It hadn't rained in a few weeks and had been terribly hot. If it had tossed its cigarette, it might as well have thrown down a match and some gas. Burned up corpses were no good. No good at all.

The boy. It had to do something about the boy. Maybe it would burn the boy; after all, it had no interest in feeding on the boy. Maybe it would do that. First, it had to watch, though. It had to wait.

Whispering Willows was home to Maple Grove's most prestigious residents as well as anyone who enjoyed a higher tax bracket than the rest of the town. It was a quiet community located off Wood Street with a scenic cul-de-sac along the bank of the Locust Fork River. Among those that lived there were Judge Addison, Jefferson County Deputy Miles Reed, John Hicks, and Randal Davis; two attorneys from Birmingham, and Dale and Maria Atkins; parents to the recently deceased Donnie Atkins. Since their youngest son's death, their happy home had become morose and apathetic.

Maria Atkins, formally Maria Jackson and Maple Grove High School's 1995 prom queen, was now a creature of isolation and degradation. No more were her happy smiles or her cheerful representation at the local bake sale. No more was a woman so full of life it burst from her in a glow so bright you needed sunglasses to look at her. Now she lived in a cheerless, lifeless void plagued by nightmares of her dead son and his entourage of demons; vile creatures with charcoal gray skin and large mouths full of teeth. Teeth like daggers and eyes like dead souls. If not for the morphine, Dale Atkins feared his wife would take her own life. Couldn't have that, now could he?

She had begun having the dreams two days after Donnie's death and had told him all about it and had asked Dale if he thought she was going crazy.

"These dreams!" she cried, her eyes swollen with tears. "They're so real! I can't take it, Dale. I'm scared. I'm so scared. I want my little boy back."

He had held her hand and comforted her as best he could, but she was slipping away from him. Therefore, two days later he went across the road to Doc Holden's house and persuaded the old man to bring him some morphine. Well, persuasion *is* a kinder word than blackmail. All it took were a few well-backed threats to disclose certain information to the hospital board, information that would end the old coot's career, not to mention his marriage and all the respect of the town.

Now he sat beside their bed in a leather wingback chair, a gift from her parents, and watched the rise and fall of her chest as she slept—not that being hopped up on morphine was real sleep. It would be so much easier to just let her slip away completely… An overdose, perhaps.

"I had no idea she was on that stuff, officer. It's been so hard on us since our son died. If only I had paid more attention to her." Nah, that sounded bogus. Maybe he would just stop giving it to her, let her off herself.

He ran a hand through her midnight black hair and then gently touched a hand to her olive skin, soft and warm to the touch. She was beautiful, so beautiful. His hand had left her face now, tracked along the dip of her neck and glided over the silk surface of her nightgown, around her breasts, her stomach, her thighs.

"Yes," he whispered to his nearly comatose wife. "Maybe that would be best."

CHAPTER EIGHT

Judd caught the phone on the second ring, almost dropping the receiver in the process, and lifted it to his ear. "This better be damn important," he growled.

There was a pause on the other end of the line, then a deep, shaky male voice. "Judd, I need to talk to you."

"You are talkin' to me. Who in the shit is this at–" Judd glanced over at the wall clock above his kitchen sink. "—four in the goddamn morning?"

"It's Dale. I need to talk to you face-to-face. It's about Maria."

Judd picked the old rotary phone up and walked with it to his kitchen table, the dirty, mildewed telephone wire trailing behind him. It snagged once on the exposed head of a nail sticking up from the floor, but Judd gave it a hard tug and it came away with no further incident. A clutter of plates and dirty glasses were scattered about the tabletop helter-skelter, and the smell of gone over food and spoiled milk hung in the air so thick you could almost taste it. Judd made space on the table for the base of the phone by shoving a maggot-infested plate and a glass of curdled milk off into the floor with one meaty hand. The plate hit the floor with a loud crash as it shattered, sending moldering food and maggots in all directions. The glass didn't break but spilled its ruined contents to run along the cracks in the floor in tiny streams.

"What about Maria?" Judd asked, pulling a chair out from the table and sitting down. "What's so damn important you couldn't call me at a decent hour?"

"She's having the dreams, Judd." Dale sounded frantic, in a panic. "I've been giving her morphine… But I don't know how long it's going to work. *The dreams, Judd! She's having those Christ forsaken dreams! Fuck!*"

"Are you sure? You had better be goddamn sure of that, Dale. Or so help me—"

"She sees Donnie… And she sees *them.*"

"Donnie's dead," Judd said, deadpan. "As for *them*, you ought not worry too much about it. I know what *they* want."

"But if Maria realizes what the dreams are if she figures them out—"

"—Then you do what has to be done, boy. I ain't got time to worry about some dumb cunt."

"She's still my wife, Judd. I thought…I thought I…" The panic in Dale's voice was thicker and Judd, disgusted by his brother's weakness, hocked up and spat a large wad of phlegm into the floor.

"Tell you what. Being you done gone all chicken shit on me, I'll meet you tonight at Earnest's old cabin. You remember it, don't you?"

"I remember it." Dale sounded a little calmer, but he was still trembling as he spoke.

"Come up the river. You'll see my boat, so just tie off beside it. Be there around ten."

Judd cradled the receiver.

White-hot pain shot through his already throbbing head as he sat up, and somewhere, distant or near; he could not tell for sure which, came the sound of breaking glass. Ray eased back into a prone position, rolled over on his side and blinked a few times; much like a television with poor resolution, the objects in the room swam around him in a blur of color and incomprehensible shapes. The left side of his face pressed against something cool and smooth, and a draft was blowing through the room and up his bare legs.

Bare legs? Where are my pants?

His skin was alive with goosebumps and out of habit, he reached behind him for a blanket, one that was not there, and he became even more distressed. He blinked his eyes with a little more gusto now and the white and brown blur before his eyes transformed into the bottom half of a General Electric stove and a row of cabinet doors with fancy little brass handles. The cool, smooth surface, he was now aware, was the green linoleum of his kitchen floor and the draft issued from the direction of the kitchen door, which stood cracked open about a foot, allowing a cool morning breeze to squeeze through. In front of him, dead even with his line of sight, was a broken juice glass, explaining the noise he had heard upon waking. He lay there for a few minutes, fascinated by the plight of a small black beetle struggling to right itself. He watched as it squirmed around amidst jagged shards of broken glass and liquor. But that fascination was short-lived, as he knew he could not lie here on the floor forever.

What did I whack my head on?

Looking up at the pine underbelly of his kitchen table, he answered his own question. *Way to tie one on, Ray. Go ahead and get drunk again… Still, plenty of rooms left in this big old house you haven't passed out in.*

What if I had passed out in the basement?

That last thought was more than uncomfortable, and Ray shoved it out of his mind as he slid from underneath the table. There was a brief struggle as his legs tangled up in the chair, he had knocked over during his unexplainable drunken urge to sleep on the floor, and then he cast it to the side. Once on his feet, he leaned forward on the table and closed his eyes. He was still woozy and light-headed and realized there was still plenty of alcohol circulating through his system.

Ray opened his eyes slowly, knowing he was going to be sick and unable to prevent the inevitable. Everything was spinning around him, as if the earth's rotation on its axis had suddenly accelerated, like an enormous planet-sized basketball spinning on the finger of the universe. He stumbled to the back door on unsure feet, flung it open, and staggered to the porch railing. Finally, he could hold it in no more. The muscles in his stomach began to spasm and kick, and he leaned over the railing and let it flow.

As he came back inside the house, he grabbed a dish-towel from the back of one of the kitchen chairs and wiped his mouth, then made the vow that so many, from the beginning drinker to the seasoned alcoholic, had made before him: "I'm never drinking again."

Tottering down the hall, bracing himself against the wall a couple of times to keep from falling flat on his face,

Ray made it to the bottom of the stairs and gave the banister a firm, determined grip. He had managed two steps and had a foot poised to take a third when the stairway illuminated in retina-searing light.

"I was wondering where you had run off to." Her voice was soft, angelic, a seductive melody drifting along a field of roses. "You know how much I hate to wake up alone." The last sentence was a playful pout.

With eyes half shut against the light, Ray lifted his gaze to the top of the stairs. Beth was standing there, hands behind her back and wearing one of his button-up shirts. A funny thing, memory, how it could abandon you, leaving you utterly clueless, then pop back up as quickly as a released spring and slam into you like a bullet. It all came back to him in a head-numbing rush.

After the incident in the backyard, Roy had claimed to need more alcohol and had made a trip to the county line, bringing back two more fifths of Jack Daniels and a case of Budweiser. He wanted to get drunk and forget what he had heard and seen, and Ray couldn't blame him. Who wouldn't, after hearing a severed dog's head growl at them? Sometime after that, Ray had called Beth and asked her over. Surprising enough, she had said yes and within the hour was knocking on Ray's door with her friend Amy, a petite brunette with a cute face and a friendly disposition; friendly enough to bring a *big* smile to Roy's face. Everything beyond that point was still lost in the fog, but Ray didn't think it would be too difficult to fill in the blanks.

"You coming back to bed?" Beth asked, then turned and hiked up the tail of the button up, exposing a perfectly tanned teardrop fanny, and teasing him with a little shake.

"On my way, sweet cheeks," Ray said and felt a

familiar stiffness between his legs. As he slipped in bed beside her, she grabbed his hand and guided it between her legs. Ray pressed against her and found her lips with his.

Leeann Willis, Lee, or Lil Ann to her friends, of which she had many, had just scored the best homegrown bud she had ever smoked. "Primo Bud," as her best friend Susan Burkett would say. It was definitely prime grade-A weed, that was for sure. One hit and you were sailing. Best high she had ever experienced and even though she was only sixteen, Leeann didn't think there was anyone, at least not in Maple Grove that knew more about bud than she did. She was an expert on subject and material. In fact, her knowledge of marijuana was so well trusted that Paul Baker, Maple High's star athlete and all-around hunk, had asked her personally if she would score *him* some of that "Primo Bud." To which her response was, "Hell yeah!"

No one said no to Paul Baker. He was like a god at Maple Grove High, the guy all the girls wanted to be with, blonde hair, blue eyes and a body like an Olympian statue. Another one of her friends, Paula Elliot, told her that she had seen Paul naked one time when she was over at his house hanging out with Dina, Paul's little sister. Said she had accidentally walked in on him in the bathroom while he was changing clothes and it had made her so hot, she had to go home. When Leeann asked Paula about his thing, she said, "Oh, my God, Lee, he's hung like a fuckin' horse." She swore it was about as big as a twenty-oz. soda bottle, only much longer.

Leann doubted it was that big, but she still wanted to see it, and if she could score him some of that good weed, she may get to do more than see it—a lot more.

Out of the three joints she had rolled last night, two of which she had smoked with Susan and Paula in Paula's basement, there was one left. As she crossed Main Street onto Atkins Park Road, and once she was out of sight of nosey passersby, she reached into the inside pocket of her blue jean jacket, took the joint out and fired it up. She exhaled the thick smoke in a hacking cough, her eyes tearing up, making the world around her appear as if she were looking at it from underwater. Stopping next to a young pine, Leanne leaned back against it and took another drag. Only two hits and she felt free, weightless, and sailing amongst the clouds.

Damn, this is some good shit!

Overhead the sky was a collage of color as fresh morning light cut through the gossamer fabric of retreating darkness. Far off to the east thunder rolled, the low rumble of waking giants, and dim flashes of lightning scarred the heavens, briefly tinting it the color of fresh blood. Leeann frowned. She hated storms. Not that she was scared of bad weather, but it was a buzz kill when you had plans—sunny weather plans, like going to the lake to hang out with your friends or chilling in the park getting stoned.

She carefully put out the joint by moisturizing the tip with saliva, and then tucked it away in her jacket pocket. She had to save as much as possible since she wouldn't have any more money until next weekend and without cash Doug Feldman, the guy she bought her dope from, would only give her the weed if she fucked him. And that wasn't happening. The guy smelled like ass, and not just every once in a while, but all the time. Besides, if she ran out before next weekend, she could always get high with Susan or one of her other friends, it wasn't as good as Doug's weed most of the time, but it was better than nothing.

Better get moving before the rain hits.

Doug Feldman lived at the end of Atkins Park Road. In fact, he was the *only* person that lived on Atkins Park road, and it was about a two-mile hike from where she was now. If she wanted to beat the rain, she had to haul ass. Days like this, she wished her parents would buy her a car and stop being so cheap. What good was having a driver's license if you didn't own a car?

Leeann stepped into the road and began walking along the side of it. She had only made a few steps when she caught a glimpse of movement out the corner of her eye. She stopped and looked to see what it was that had caught her attention—probably an animal, or maybe she was just high, but she wanted to be careful, she didn't want to end up like that Collins girl they found in the river last year.

Jenna Collins was a sophomore at Maple High who had gone missing last year after walking home from the homecoming game. It was big talk for a while; everyone loves a mystery in a small town. They found her two months later out by Ben Walker's Salvage yard. Her body had gotten wedged in the moorings of Ed Watson's pier and he had found her, quite by accident, he had said when he was checking his trotlines. The story was that the guy had raped and beaten her to death, then dumped her in the river. Someone even said they had found bite marks on her body, but after two months in the river, with fish and turtles going at her, Leeann figured that was just someone's idea of an urban legend. No one knew who killed Jenna, which was a frightening thought. One she had never really thought about until today.

Across from where she stood, she saw the gazebos; the covered benches and the restrooms and concession stand (*Closed for repair,* proclaimed a big sign out front of it). Beyond it was the ball field where the high school and little league teams practiced, as well as the girls' softball team. She could see the aluminum bleachers and the dugouts, all empty. Pine trees provided the shade for the park, their needles like a prickly carpet layered the ground, and they swayed in the wind like silent ghostly sentries watching in quiet discord over the raping of their land. Even with daylight slowly filling the day, there was a peculiar feeling in the air—an almost spooky feel.

Fuck the weed! Get the hell out of here.

She was coming down from her cloud, her high brutally murdered by paranoia and fear. Leeann turned and headed back towards Main Street in long, hurried strides. She fought the panic that swelled in her chest. She was just passing the tree where she had stopped to take a couple of tokes when she heard something rattling the underbrush next to it. Her heart was performing summersaults in her chest and she stopped, frozen, as still as a headstone.

Probably just a snake or a rat, she thought, as if that were any better. *It's not some loony rapist that's going to kill me and drop me in the river itsnotitsnotitsnot...*

Something brushed against her ankle and she let out a high-pitched, broken squeal that was too weak to be a scream. After a moment, she looked down, terrified and curious as to why nothing had attacked her. Much to her relief, it was only a stray cat. It was an emaciated Siamese with dirty, matted fur. It rubbed up against her leg lovingly, purring loudly, and meowed. "Well, ain't that a bitch cracker," she fumed. "Fuckin' grade A fuckin' weed got me paranoid of a fuckin' cat."

Leeann leaned down and stroked the top of its head, and the cat closed its eyes and purred even louder. It sure was friendly, so it wasn't wild. Someone must have set the poor thing out. She picked it up and walked to the pine tree she had leaned on earlier and sat down next to it. The cat had no tags so whoever set it out didn't want it back, which was normally the case. Why else would you abandon an animal on the side of the road?

"You scared the shit out of me, you know," she said to the cat as she held it up. "Thought you were some crazy psycho rapist."

When it happened, it happened fast—faster than Leeann could react. The cat's teeth sank into her right hand and she was too terrified to notice that its neck had elongated to accomplish this feat. "You little bastard!" she screamed. "You fucki…" Cutting her off was another sharp set of teeth clamped over her mouth. Her eyes widened and bulged in horror when she realized the mouth attached to her face was a part of some grotesque, wormlike appendage snaking from the cat's back.

There was so much pain, but not much blood… The creature was suckling it, feeding off it. She reached out for the beast latched to her face in an attempt to save herself and another of those wormlike appendages shot out from what remained of the cat's side and bit into her wrist. She tried to stand but her legs were numb and unresponsive. Leeann knew she was going to die, and she started to cry.

From the cat's eyes, two, segmented limbs erupted and hovered in front of her face for a second before boring into her eyes. Her struggling ended after a while and her body went limp, falling to the ground with barely a sound, and the creature continued to suckle.

A pair of dirty, calloused hands reached down and removed the creature from Leeann's corpse. The creature made a catlike whine and then fell silent. Moments later, just as Doug Feldman passed by in his car, stereo blasting the screaming lyrics of BloodFist, a local metal band he enjoyed, Leann's feet disappeared into the brush.

CHAPTER NINE

Thunderous roars ripped open the midmorning sky as streaks of lightning cast deadly judgmental fingers towards the earth. The wind raged as if it scorned mankind's very existence, kicking, biting, or whipping anyone or anything in its path. The rain came in torrents, saturating the soil with its cleansing tears, and lending its strength to rivers and streams. Spring was the last time a thunderstorm such as this had hit Maple Grove, and it seemed that Mother Nature was making up for lost time.

At the Kountry Kitchen, Dianne Townsend watched nervously from behind the big glass windows of the diner at the darkening skies, crossing her fingers and praying that she would not see a funnel amongst those clouds. A thunderstorm was one thing, but a tornado was a completely different beast altogether.

She turned to Connie Alexander, Beatrice Alexander's granddaughter, who was leaning across the counter on her elbows gaping at the dark skies and pouring rain as if she was bearing witness to the apocalypse. "You know," said Dianne, "if it gets much worse, we'll have to shut her down and hunker ourselves down in the back."

But Dianne knew that if a tornado did birth from this storm, and if it was big enough, the diner would fare worse than the straw house that the big bad wolf blew over in the *Three Little Pigs.* Counting her, Connie and Johnny Barlow, the short-order cook, there were fifteen heads in the Kitchen this morning. Fifteen lives. *Lord, let it be your will to let this storm pass us by.*

A loud thunderclap and a flash of lightning as bright and as white as new fluorescents, accompanied by an ear-splitting crack of thunder made Connie jump and take a few steps away from the counter. A few heads turned towards the window and a few of the customers murmured uneasily amongst themselves.

"God, I hate storms," Dianne said and pulled her notepad and pen from her apron pocket.

Across town in an old white Victorian, deeply secluded from the town by a mote of pines, oaks, and cedars, Ray Sanders woke to a fusillade of rain beating against his bedroom window. Beside him Beth was still sleeping soundly, curled up next to him, one hand on his chest, her head resting in the little nook his shoulder made as his arm wrapped around her. Between blasts of thunder, he could clearly hear Roy snoring in the room adjacent to his own and wondered just how in the hell poor Amy could sleep next to such a racket.

If it got too bad they would all have to make a beeline for the basement, but after what had happened down there, he wondered if it would be better to take his chances with the storm. All of those faces and all those voices… And the screams, the screams had been the worst.

Today, he had to face it today. After the storm was over and once the girls were on their way home, he would take Roy down there and… What? What if nothing happened?

Then he *was* crazy.

An explosion of thunder rattled the house and Beth snuggled in closer. Ray leaned over, kissed her lightly on the forehead, and closed his eyes.

In the filthy kitchen of his decrepit old house, Judd Atkins finished the last of his coffee. He tossed the plastic mug at the sink and missed; it ricocheted off the pile of dirty dishes already occupying the sink and hit the floor with a hollow thud. Ignoring this, Judd got up, stepped onto his back porch, and sat down in his old rocker. He loved storms, loved the violence behind them, and it had been so long since one had blown through. However, he could not find solace, even when the wind picked up a rickety old rabbit cage next to his shed and dropped it on its side, could not find the comfort and relaxation that nature's fury usually afforded him.

Something was wrong, and not just with his brother's dumb cunt wife. It was one of *them*, something not right about one of *them*. What was it? Why couldn't he *feel* what was wrong? Judd reached into his shirt pocket, removed a crumpled pack of cigarettes, took the last one out, and lit it. He threw the empty pack to the floor of the porch to join other discarded trash.

For the last couple of hours, the power had threatened to go out, blinking on and off in random spurts. Julie was digging through her bedroom closet: clothes, shoe boxes, a couple of issues of *Vogue*, remnants of her little sister's last visit, were strewn across the floor and her bed in untidy little piles where she had haplessly tossed them. With a frown, she leaned back on her knees and pulled the hair away from her face. *Where did I put them? Know I had them somewhere.* But where? Then her face lit up with recollection. She got up, hurried to the hall closet, and yanked it open. Dropping to her knees, she rummaged through the blankets and quilts, flinging them out into the hall, regardless of the mess she was creating.

"Not here either. Damn."

The world outside rumbled and the lights went out. Then the lights came back on, held for about thirty seconds, and went out again.

Shit!

Using the doorknob on the closet door, Julie pulled herself to her feet and felt along the wall into the living room. She made her way to the couch, or in the direction of the couch, anyway, feeling out in front of her with her hands. If possible, she wanted to avoid a collision with the corner of her coffee table—bruised knees were the last thing she needed. After stumbling through the darkness for a few awkward minutes, her fingers, at last, brushed against the arm of the couch. She leaned forward and brought a knee up and, despite her best efforts, banged her knee on the coffee table.

"Ow! Shit, shit, shit, shit," she cursed under her breath as she reached out for the curtain, snagging it between her fingers and tugging at it. It didn't budge. It had to be wedged between the couch and the wall. Not to be daunted by her drapery, Julie clenched the folds of the curtain in both hands and heaved. There was a small metallic pop as the curtain rod snapped free and dropped to the windowsill with a clang.

Dull grey light spilled through her window as she leaned back and rested her feet up on the coffee table. She was massaging her wounded knee with both hands when the power came back on.

"Oh, yeah. *Now* you come on after I bang my fucking knee." Bitter sarcasm.

Adding insult to injury, Julie saw the objects of her earlier search. Next to her flat-screen TV, on the entertainment center, sat two fat blue candles. She sat stewing over it for a moment or two, then got up, and brought the candles back to the couch. After setting the candles down on the table, she shoved her hand into a pocket of her sleep pants, pulled out a scratched yellow Bic lighter, and laid it between them. Now, she was ready for power failure.

"Can't believe those damn things were right in front of my eyes the whole time," Julie said, peeved at herself. "Stupid, stupid, stupid."

All but the rain drumming against the pavement and walls of the building and the occasional bouts of thunder, everything was quiet. She could hear the water pouring from the rain gutters and could imagine the little rivers it created as it ran downhill from her building to the street. There was a brilliant flash of lightning and a loud crack somewhere in the distance and the power was out again.

"Damn, I hate storms," she complained as she lit the candles.

Scratch, scratch, scratch, scratch.

Julie raised an eyebrow. *What was that?*

Scratch, scratch, scratch.

There it was again.

She picked up one of the candles and carried it with her towards the hall, the flame flickering with every step she took. She looked down the hallway towards her room and started towards it.

Scratch, scratch, scratch, scratch.

The door that opened up on the bathroom was a few feet ahead of her to the left, and that was where she would have sworn the scratching had come from. Easing up to the door, Julie took a deep breath.

If it's rats the landlord is going to get an earful, especially for what he charges me on pest control. An image of a large black rat burrowing into dead flesh popped into her head and Julie cringed. *It was just a dream,* Julie thought and took a deep breath.

She pushed open the door and let the waning light of the candle lead her as she stepped inside. In the dim light, she could see her toilet, the bathtub, with the *Snoopy* shower curtain and the single basin with her toothbrush and other personal hygiene products scattered on top of it. The only ominous thing she could see was the dripping faucet in her tub and she reached over and twisted both knobs until the drip stopped.

Then, something furry scuttled across her foot and she screamed and dropped the candle. There was a splash as it landed in the toilet bowl, and then darkness. Julie cursed under her breath some more while she fumbled in her pockets for the Bic. Then she felt cool plastic in her hand, brought the lighter out of her pocket, and struck a flame.

The face before her was pale and scarred with blood-red eyes set in deep sockets and a grin like death itself.

Soggy red hair clung to the side of his face and a putrid smell emanated from him—the smell of dead things, the dead animals she had smelled alongside the highway or in the woods. It was the smell of backed-up sewage and rotten fruit. His laugh was the laugh of tortured souls screaming in anguish, and it echoed inside her skull like an air raid siren. Julie dropped the lighter.

CHAPTER TEN

After the storm had ended there was uncanny tranquility settling throughout the house, a dreamlike calm as unsettling as a festering corpse slow cooking under a desert sun. The sky outside was cast in an unnatural, orange glow as fresh daylight filtered through the legions of bruise-colored clouds, lending a foreboding shadow throughout the house and splashing the walls and objects of the room in a strange amber-crimson hue. Floorboards creaked and shrieked as if in mortal agony, protesting against even the slightest of movement as if it only aggravated their suffering and in some deep shadowy corner of the house, a cricket played its lonely, brooding concerto.

Ray moved through the hallway and into the kitchen in a lumbering, zombie-like fashion, clenching an old red Eveready flashlight in his left hand and a mottled, and moth-eaten dolphin-shaped pillow in his right. A fine mist rose from the floor up to his waist, rolling throughout the house, restless, indifferent to the world in which it was lost wandering. Something wet and slimy writhed beneath the opaque fog that surrounded him, wrapped around his ankles, and then passed on. Ray didn't seem to notice and continued forward.

Before him now stood the basement door like the gate of some forbidden city; posted warnings leaped before his mind's eye: DO NOT ENTER, OFF LIMITS, TURN BACK NOW! Near the bottom of the door was a gaping hole, the hole the rat had made, jagged, splintered wood jutted from the hole's inner perimeter; it was like looking into the gaping maw of some giant, disfigured worm with rows of sharp crooked teeth. From behind the door came the sound of some rustic old tune, one that Ray was not familiar with and was sure he had never heard before. The instruments he recognized, the tune he did not. There was a banjo, and fiddle and an acoustic guitar, mingling their rhythmic and fast-paced country melody together with an edgy, demonic score.

"Got to do this. Now or never," his voice, distant, slurred, trembled from his lips and escalated his fear.

Like a character from one of the many suspense films archived in his memory, his hand hovered over the door-knob, trembling and uncertain. He was really going to do it. He was going to face his fear. But where was Roy? Roy was supposed to go down there with him—that been the plan, anyway.

"No! You, Ray! You and you alone." It was that alien he/she voice he had heard in all the nightmares that had plagued his sleep since returning to Maple Grove, nagging and persistent, an invisible force pushing him towards the edge. The edge of what, he did not know—his sanity, perhaps—a climactic duel between reason and delusion.

"To hell with you!" Ray shouted back. "To hell with you." This last dropped off from a shout into a whisper and, rather than feeling bolstered, Ray felt more unsure than he had previously.

The doorknob was cold, yet warm at the same time, and Ray shuddered at the thought that the simple turn of his wrist would hurtle him into the deepest, darkest realm of the aberration ravaging his mind. To walk again in the company of the dead, hear their screams and, worst yet, to see them, to see their mangled, twisted bodies were torn apart so brutality, was the cause for his trepidation.

"What would it take?" Ray asked himself with a sarcastic, contemptuous laugh. "It would take me being a man for once in my life; that's what it would take. I've got to do this. Got to grow some balls some time."

"NO!"

Ray whirled around. It wasn't the unisex entity he had heard just a few minutes before. This was a new voice, and definitely female.

"Don't do it, Ray. Don't be their sacrifice. Don't let them get to you."

Somewhere in the house or outside of the house, Ray was unable to determine which, came the sound of a wind chime, loud and vicious, as if it were caught up in a tropical wind. Then he saw her: pale white skin and raven black hair, dressed in a halter top and leather mini the same shade of black as her hair. She stood with her back pressed to the kitchen counter, clutching a worn, old, dolphin pillow in her hands, pressed to her breasts as if it were a shield. Ray looked down at his hands. The Eveready was still in his right hand, but the pillow had vanished. Only it hadn't vanished, had it? It had just changed hands, from his hands to hers. But how...and when?

"They want you to go down there, Ray. They need you to go down there," the woman said.

"Who are you?" he asked, but he knew before the words had left his mouth that he did know who she was. He couldn't place her face, but he knew her, recognized her from somewhere.

"Does that matter?" she asked impatiently. "No. What matters is that you listen." She leaned forward, squeezing the little dolphin pillow in her hands so tightly that Ray expected to see the stuffing burst out of it. There was urgency in her dark eyes, even with the murk and the crazy way the light was entering the room, he could see that. There was something else in her eyes too, panic, fear, all the above. She was scared. And for all of this, Ray still couldn't help but wonder where he had seen her before, why she was so damned familiar.

"YOU WILL NOT LISTEN TO HER, RAY! SHE'S JUST A LITTLE WHORE! SHE WANTS TO HURT YOU!"

Reeling from the intensity of anger in the he/she thing's words, as if struck in the chest by some invisible fist, Ray slammed into the basement door hard enough to rattle his teeth. Lucky for him, the door didn't swing inward or he would have spilled down the stairs and would have probably broken his neck in the process.

"I'm not trying to hurt you, Ray. I want to help—"

"SHUT UP!" the he/she thing screamed. SHUT UP, SHUT UP, SHUT UP! YOU LYING LITTLE BITCH!"

Whatever it was, it was pissed. What was going on here? Just what in the hell was happening? There were tears in the woman's eyes and she was trembling as if she were cold as if freezing. Ray stepped towards her…

***

… And woke suddenly, confused and afraid, afraid of

the strange nightmare, afraid of how real it had been. He was confused because it was different from his other dreams. Usually, when he dreamed, he was down by the river and his dad's old cabin. This time, however, he had been inside his house, in his kitchen. And there had been someone new, someone other than the strange entity that usually haunted him. A girl, or rather a woman, someone he knew but couldn't place, and she had been trying to warn him of something, even as terrified as she was, she was trying to warn him. Already her face was fuzzy in his mind but the familiarity of her nagged at him. As did her words, 'Don't be their sacrifice', and this was just as frightening, if not more so than the dream itself.

As he sat up in his bed, the thin white bed sheet covering him slipped down to his waist. There was a constant tap, tap, tap against his bedroom window as a steady downpour continued to fall outside and his bedroom, occupied by a battalion of shadows, was intruded upon by the slightest touch of smoke gray light that crept in through the window in thin slivers. Wish you were here, mom. You and dad both. I don't know if I have what it takes, not this time. I'm scared…terrified. I can't do this, not alone.

He slung his legs over the edge of the bed. The floor was cool under his feet, not cold, but cool enough to give him a case of the shivers. A constant, throbbing ache seemed to ricochet off every muscle in his body, a remnant of a night spent of heavy drinking and sexual escapades. There were always consequences, sometimes bad, sometimes terrible, but always consequences. His head had a mild ache but nothing too major; for him to have headaches during hangovers was rare, usually, he just had an all-over body ache like the one he had now. Maybe it was time to stop being so juvenile and leave the booze alone before he became one of those people, he saw on the street corners accosting passersby for spare change. Just maybe it was time for him to grow up and be a little more responsible for his actions.

Ray stood up, his bed sheet falling away completely, cool air sending chill bumps dancing along his skin, and glanced over at the alarm clock on his nightstand. It was steadily flashing 12:00 a.m. and he realized that at some point during his slumber, the power had either gone out or surged. Blatantly aware that he was naked, that his door was standing wide open, and the spot on his bed where Beth had lain was empty, fuck me, and leave me, he thought miserably, he walked over and shut his door. Modest he was not, but the last thing he wanted was for Roy to come sauntering down the hall and see him in the buff. Talk about uncomfortable situations—that would be the Mt. Everest of uncomfortable situations, and one Ray preferred to avoid.

While slipping on a fresh pair of boxers, his mind flashed back to, not just last night's dream, but to all of them since arriving back at the home place. Up until just recently, he couldn't ever remember having the same dream twice, and never any that seemed to connect as strongly as the cabin dream and the kitchen dream from last night. They seemed to be two parts to the same story, instead of random images that had no link whatsoever, the normal type of dream. What was the link between his dad's old cabin and the basement of this house? Ray was not a firm believer in the supernatural, well at least not until the smoking rat, the rat that had later mystically transformed into the growling severed head of a German Sheppard, after it had eaten its way through the basement door. Then, there were the dolphins.

Sometimes, like last night, dolphins made a cameo

appearance in his dreams, usually in the form of a pillow or a wind chime or some other knickknack from his mother's collection. But what was the significance in it all? How did a giant rat, a severed dog's head, and a bunch of keepsakes tie in together? Then, there was the basement. Had what he seen down there been another dream or something a little closer to reality? Of course, just lately his dreams did have a hint of reality to them, didn't they? Ray could still hear that grating unisex voice screaming for the lying bitch to shut up. And the girl, woman, whatever she was, insisting she was trying to help and not hurt him as the weird entity had proclaimed. He could still see her dark, pleading eyes, eyes that begged him to believe her, eyes that showed no signs of deception.

There is another option, here, Ray. You could just be crazier than Stalin or Pol Pot.

Roy had witnessed some of it—well, just the severed dog's head—and he had heard it growl; he may be trying to ignore it or block it out of his memory, but he had witnessed that much of it, at least. Ray was damn sure of that if he was sure of nothing else.

***

Listening to the rain pattering against the glass calmed him to a point that if Maria hadn't screamed out in her sleep, Dale would have eased into a sleep of his own. Jumping up from the wing-backed chair, which he had brought over to her bed and away from the window, he administered Maria her scheduled dose of morphine, gently wiping away the sweat on her forehead with a damp dishtowel as he did so. Her body was adjusting to the drug or the dosage of it, and she was no longer susceptible to long periods of sedation. He was no medical expert and could only go by the instructions Holden had given him, but he could up her dosage, no problems, no worries, but as sure as he was yesterday that he could let her die, she was still his wife.

Your wife, yes, but you are turning her into a junkie. Don't you know that? With tolerance comes addiction… Didn't that sink in from your own mother's ride on the coke train? What kind of wife will Maria be if she is always droned out? What other drugs will she shove into her veins, up her nose or whatever orifice she decides on? Wouldn't it be better just to let her die?

"She's still my wife, damnit! I can get her help."

She's having the dreams, Dale. She's seeing things, things she should not see. You should listen to Judd; big brothers always know what to do. Just like with your mother and father. Judd took care of that problem, didn't he? No more booze or nose candy for either of them, not where they are. No more beatings either and no more drunken father doing dirty no-no's to you and your brothers. All thanks to big brother Judd. Don't you think you owe him?

"No. I can't."

You will.

Dale reached over and took one of Maria's hands in his and squeezed, not too tight, but as tender as he could manage, and his eyes swelled with fresh tears for the first time in years. Not even when officer Clardy had come to his door to announce the death of his youngest son did he cry. When Donnie's coffin, and what remained of his son, lowered into the ground, Dale's eyes were as dry as a Nevada heat. Now, as he sat next to his wife and clutched her hand in his, well aware of her fate as well as his own, Dale Atkins wept.

CHAPTER ELEVEN

As Doug Feldman pulled his rusted old Toyota Corolla up in front of the Maple Grove Post Office, the car belching and coughing out blue-gray smoke from its tailpipe like a crop duster caught afire and spiraling earthward, the heavy rain that had been drenching the town since early that morning came to a halt. The Post Office, like most of Maple Grove's buildings along Main Street, was old and constructed primarily of red brick. A bright new American Flag hung in a wet clump over the entrance and just below it, in fading blue and white paints, was the head and crest outline of the American Bald Eagle. Doug popped the Toyota into park and let the car idle while he took a crumpled pack of cigarettes from the dash, took one out, and tossed the pack back onto the dash. Lighting his cigarette and staring indifferently at the cluster of Xeroxed announcements taped to the inside of the Post Office door, he rolled down his window and leaned his head against the headrest, exhaling a puff of smoke that eerily resembled what was spewing from his car's exhaust.

"C'mon damn it," he whispered under his breath. "I ain't got all fuckin' night."

There was a gold Zippo lighter dropped down in the console, not the one he used to light his smoke, as he didn't have any fluid for it, and he reached down and grabbed it, flipped open the top with his thumb, then slammed it shut with the palm of his hand. He had a right to be nervous, especially with four lbs of weed tucked under the spare tire in his trunk. Normally, in a town like Maple Grove, you could deal smoke all day long and not worry about getting busted: one, because it was a small country town and two because Maple Grove had no active police department. But these days the Grove was hot, not only because of Leon Phillips and his fucking little Meth lab, but because of that incident with Sonny McLain running down Donnie Atkins, and now that little skank Leeann Willis and her disappearing act. It was not official, not yet, anyway, but her parents, in a fit over her not coming home and on the edge of panic, gave rise to Doug's fear's that even more cops would descend on the town over the next few weeks.

"Fuckin' pigs," Doug mumbled in an edgy, contemptuous voice. "Always fuckin' with my shit."

The breeze blowing through his open window was mild and cool and on the tail end of it was the sharp yet dull scent of wet grass and pine. Around him, the night was quiet, all but the dragging squeak of his windshield wipers wiping a windshield that was now dry, and he reached over and shut them off. Listless amber light spilled from the old-fashioned dome-shaped streetlamps along Main Street and formed dismal circles on the shiny wet asphalt. The water-soaked sidewalk in front of the Post Office was dark gray, giving it the look of freshly poured cement. Doug felt a hazy sluggishness overcome him, as if he was high off some really good shit and remembered the feeling as what they used to call in school as a "Natural High". It felt good, it felt right, but somehow it felt as if there was nothing natural about it.

Don't freak. Don't you do it. Be calm, wait for Alan, then you both can haul ass over to the park and get the hell out of here. Get out of sight of nosey eyes and ears.

"Hurry up, Alan," he whispered between two quick drags of his cigarette. "Just hurry the fuck up."

Alan was Alan Donaldson, local stoner and all-around slacker, and for much else, he was useless. Alan Donaldson was Doug's gofer, (gofer this, gofer that), and would never be held for questioning in the case of being too smart, nor would he ever win any contests for good looks, but he was loyal. Loyal to a fault and Doug sometimes felt bad about taking the idiot's money for weed, especially since said money just came from Doug's pocket. Alan didn't spend his entire pay on weed, he sometimes clung on to twenty or thirty bucks, but he might as well have spent it all. Doug *could* just pay Alan in weed—that thought had occurred to him on more than one occasion—but Alan was the type of person that puts two and two together and always comes up with five instead of four and would somehow believe that he was being cheated.

A series of short yipping barks shattered his thoughts and Doug jumped, dropping his half-smoked cigarette into a muddy puddle of water next to his car where it made a slight sizzling sound before it was drowned out.

"Shit!" he spat in agitation and stared down at the ruined butt floating next to the front tire. "Shit! What the hell else is going to go…?" His words died off as his eyes met with those of an old stray dog sitting a few feet away. It was a mangy old mongrel dog; a 'Heinz 57', as his dad would call it, with dirt-spattered red fur and a swarm of gnats as thick as a thunderhead buzzing around its sore-infested muzzle. A dopey looking mutt with a slack face and eyes set up high on its head…but those eyes. They almost looked intelligent, as if this dumb-looking dog was capable of rational thought.

That's fucking stupid. It's just another dumbass mutt.

Yet, there was that glimmer, that all-knowing glimmer that screamed sentience.

"Go on! Go on, you stupid flea-toting bitch!" Doug flinched at the way his voice carried along the rain-soaked streets, and somewhere another dog barked and then another.

"See what you got started, you son-of-a-bitch. Now, just look at what you went and got started."

The dog did nothing, not even bark in response to its canine comrades, and stared at him with those deep, somewhat intelligent, eyes.

Suddenly it just cocked its head to the side, let out a low whine, and took off across the street. Doug watched after it for a moment, as it disappeared between the Paradise tanning salon and the corrugated steel shed where David Sullivan stored supplies, then started his hand out for another cigarette.

"You ready to roll?"

For the second time tonight, Doug was startled; he dropped the crumpled pack of Marlboros to the floorboard and looked up. Alan was leaning up against his car, arms folded on the roof, fingers tapping restlessly, head lowered to look in. A brief instant of anger passed, an instant where Doug visualized knocking the stupid little stoner's teeth out, and then he reached down to pick up his smokes.

"The fuck took you so long?" Doug asked as he

straightened in his seat. "And why the hell you standin' there like that? Get in the car before someone makes something of it."

Alan said nothing; he just leaned back, gave Doug the thumbs-up gesture with his right hand, and bolted around the front of the car, giving the hood a little pat in passing, then slid into the passenger side. The door shut with a slam Doug could have done without, and he said so.

"What you so damn jumpy for, man?" Alan asked as he was rifling through the pockets of his tattered camouflage jacket—searching for his own pack of smokes was Doug's guess. "Ain't a soul out there, man. Fuckin' ghost town."

Doug offered his pack of cigarettes to Alan and Alan grabbed one, lit it, and took a drag then exhaled slowly. "Cops don't need to be seen to be there. Christ, Alan, don't you ever think? Or are you just too much of a burnout to care?"

"Hey, man. I'm not brain dead. I was lookin'. Damn!" There was a hurt look on Alan's face.

"To hell with it," Doug said and reversed the Corolla out onto Main Street. "Let's get this shit over with."

As he put the car in drive and eased forward, he caught a glimpse of movement on the other side of the street. *It's the police and I'm busted,* he thought. Frantic and rocking along the line of panic, Doug snapped his head towards Paradise Tan, anticipating the worst. In his mind's eye he saw an army of county cops coming towards him, some with batons and blast shields, others with rifles targeted at his head. He nearly lost control of his senses then, freaking out as Alan would call it, but he regained control. What he actually saw was a mangy red dog with glowing red eyes and a foaming mouth. It was growling, a deep, vicious sound that sent thoughts of gnashing teeth and sharp, hooked claws, claws sharp enough to slice open his flesh as easily as a *Ginsu* would slice through an aluminum can. The dog barked once and then launched forward in a trail of smoke.

Pinning the pedal to the floor and turning the Toyota's stereo as loud as it would go, Doug Feldman shot down Main Street with the smell of hot rubber burning his nose, and cold, hard-edged fear impaling his heart.

***

Atkins Park, and the gravel parking area out in front of it was a blur as they passed it at better than sixty mph. Alan Donaldson was holding on to the little leather padded bar, commonly known to him and all his friends as the "OH SHIT!" handle, just above the passenger side door. BloodFist's lead singer was screaming about anally raping some politician or a goat, Alan couldn't make out the words well enough to be sure which, not with the shitty factory speakers in the Corolla that carried so much distortion and static that it sounded like the band was giving a concert at the bottom of the ocean. A lock of greasy dirty blond hair fell over his panic-stitched face and Alan brushed it away. Taking a nervous breath, he reached for the stereo's volume controls.

Doug slapped Alan's hand away and shot him an uneasy grin. "Don't fuck with my radio, man. Don't ever do that again."

"Slow down!" Alan roared over the music blaring from the speakers. "Slow down before you wipe out and kill us, man! Shit!"

But Doug couldn't do that; he wouldn't do that, not with that weird-ass dog following them. *Must be some new type of drug dog or something.* This was a thought born of his long association with paranoia. *Fucking pigs training 'em to hunt us down.* "Fuckin'pigs!"

Alan felt discontent at the sudden outburst, but not at the outburst itself, not entirely, it was that lost, doped-out, crazy gleam in Doug's eyes as he said it. A weird thought struck Alan, probably the first and last halfway intelligent thought that would ever cross his hollow mind. *If he's so damn worried about being noticed by the cops, then why's he drivin' like this?*

It was right behind them. Doug could see it in the review mirror, but it was no longer some stray mutt. It was bigger now, almost as big as a horse, its dingy red fur replaced by flames and smoke. Its eyes were the color of burning brush and its teeth looked as big as railroad spikes. Moreover, it was coming for him, a breath away from the rear bumper. A growl as threatening as that of a monstrous wolf protecting its pack rumbled from somewhere deep within the beast's belly.

"Slow down! Slow down! Jesus Christ, Doug, Slow Down!"

Alan was running off at the mouth about something. Although Doug couldn't hear him since his focus was on outrunning the monster on his heels, a monster that Alan seemed too oblivious to even notice. He pressed the accelerator to the floor and the Corolla's tired, poorly maintained V-6 engine whined and sputtered but accepted the command to go faster.

He should have known something was wrong when he first saw the dog, but it hadn't registered in his mind then, not in the slightest. It wasn't until he had pulled away from the Post Office that he noticed it was following them, *chasing* them. It wasn't until he had turned onto Atkins Park Road that he had noticed just how big and fast the damn mutt was. *Clever, clever, you fuckin' pigs…* Stopping in mid-thought, Doug wondered if the police were even capable of creating something like that. *Of course, they are. Fuckin' pigs!*

Asphalt gave way to gravel and the Toyota tried to fishtail, but Doug brought the car back under control. That, however, wouldn't last long and he knew it. High speeds and gravel roads didn't tend to go hand and hand. *Almost home, though. Just a couple of miles. I can actually see my porch light. I'm gonna make it.*

The car was going too fast. Much too fast and Maria knew that if the driver didn't slow down the outcome would be fatal, but she was helpless, forced to watch and unable to call out and warn them. It was like watching a movie that you knew was going to frighten you and you could not cover your eyes to avert from seeing every horrid detail. Dear God, why must I watch this? Pleasepleaseplease make it stop. Pleasssse. But the image remained, as clear and vivid as if it were happening right in front of her and she felt warm wetness streak across her face.

Up ahead of them was a dingy doublewide trailer under a grove of pines and bordered by a rusty chain-link fence. A weathered, lopsided porch clung to the front of it, soggy, wet tee-shirts and several pairs of men's underwear hung over the railing. There was a dry yellow light emanating from a single 75-watt bulb that swayed back and forth from a wire disappearing into the porch ceiling.

Now she was a passenger in the speeding car, watching as the double-wide, the fence, and the trees, as all of it came rushing up before them. Gripping the back of the passenger side seat in her hands, she looked over at the passenger, who was screaming and yelling at the driver to stop. The boy couldn't be any more than eighteen or nineteen with a head full of nasty dark brown hair and an army jacket, camouflage is what they called it, which was faded and torn. His face was a deep, terror-filled grimace and his eyes shone with the awareness of oncoming death.

Oh God, Oh God. I'm going to be right here next to them when it happens. Oh please, God, no. Don't let me see this.

"Fuckin' A! Almost home! Whew!"

This was the driver and Maria turned to look at him. He was a little older than his passenger but no more than a couple of years. He was sweating and a thick, musty stench seemed to exude from every pore on his body and he had a grimace of his own, but not one of fear. His grimace was one of fierce determination and loathing. His fists were blood-red knots on the steering wheel, and he was shouting so loud that the cords in his neck stuck out.

That one's crazy. He's going to kill them both and he doesn't even realize it. Dear God.

There was a sudden jolt as the car struck against something hard and then she was spinning, driver and passenger screaming, one in terror, one in a mad exaltation. A loud metallic screech and shattering glass, and then she drifted away.

Her eyes flew open. No crazy-eyed kid shouting in disillusioned defiance, no terrified kid screaming in terror, only her bedroom ceiling. Maria sat up and began to cry.

What was happening to her? Why was she seeing these things? And where was Dale?

Dropping back on her bed, she pulled the covers over her face and prayed between each hitching, sobbing breath that this was all a dream; that her Donnie wasn't dead and that this was some terrible nightmare. However, deep down, she knew that the terror was real. Donnie was dead, and hell was just a hop, skip and a jump away.

record for domestic violence and his not- too-reputable presence around town, Judd's claim of self-defense had held all the ground it was meant to hold, and he had continued on with his life. He had cold-bloodedly murdered their father and came off the victim.

Dale was looking around, searching the fog through squinted eyes when Judd reached out, took a handful of his shirt, and spun him around. Dale let out a gasp, which sounded more like a weak hiccup, and braced for impact, but there was no impact, no striking fists, nothing. Judd steadied him so he wouldn't fall, then drew his hand away and made a half-hearted attempt at straightening out the wrinkles in Dale's shirt.

"C'mon," Judd said, cocking a thumb towards the cabin. "We'll tend to business in there."

The first thing to hit him as he stepped through the door was a dank, musty smell; it reminded Dale of the vacant dwellings of those that had passed on, either in death or to wander and had remained uninhabited. The second thing was how typically male-oriented it was, like the clubs they had as kids with postings like "Guys only" or "No girls allowed", only with more adult themes. There were posters on every wall of scantily dressed women with big breasts and big smiles, blondes, brunettes, redheads, all promoting various numbers of alcoholic beverages. On the far wall was a dusty old couch, missing two feet in the front and resting on what looked to be chunks of concrete blocks, with a cedar end table on one end and a derelict T.V. stand on the other. Stacks of grimy porno magazines and automotive repair manuals occupied the lower half of the T.V. stand and atop it rested a couple of ashtrays and what the kids of the 80's used to refer to as a "boom box". In the center of the room stood a pool table that was, layers of dust aside, in better condition than any other piece of furniture in the room and on the wall next to it was a homemade rack used to store the pool sticks. In the middle of the pool table set three Coleman Lanterns. Their waxing, waning light gave the interior of the cabin a haunted house feel. Dale almost expected Judd to start telling a bunch of ghost stories. He knew different, though; he knew that whatever Judd was about to say was far from some harmless yarn about ghouls and goblins.

Judd went over to the couch, looked as if he might sit down, and then turned to face Dale instead. "You know why we're here? Well?"

"Maria. You want me to kill Maria."

"Don't look at it like that, boy. No, not *kill*… Not at all. What you're goin' to have to do is give her to *them*." Judd hocked up and spat out a large wad of phlegm onto the floor. "Sorry about that. Been congested as all hell lately. Think it might be all this crazy weather… Cool, hot, cool, hot… Keeps me a might on the sickly side."

"She's my wife…I don't know…"

"Don't give me that shit again! You didn't have a problem puttin' Donnie's head on the choppin' block. And he was your *boy,* for Christ's sake!"

"Sonny McLain…"

"You let it happen, Dale." Judd's voice dropped to a low, husky, malevolent tone and there was intelligence in that voice, intelligence beyond his limited six-grade education, and a long since extinct sentience longing for rebirth. "You *knew* what *we* wanted. You *knew* that in order for the rejuvenation to begin that an *Atkins* had to be given over to us. Just as a Sanders will be needed to secure the pact. This partnership cannot be disrupted, if we are to survive."

"She doesn't even know what the dreams are. For all

anybody knows, she's just having a tough time dealing with Donnie's death. No one's going to believe…"

"There are those few who believe that the second coming of Jesus Christ will be aboard a massive space-craft," Judd interrupted. He was alarmingly placid, and his eyes were obsidian marbles set deep on his haggard, unshaven face. "Dreaming of that day when they will travel with their Lord and Savior throughout the cosmos to a Heaven of eternal bliss."

The pool table creaked under Judd's weight as he leaned forward against it. "And there are those that believe Elvis, Kennedy, and Monroe are alive and well, living the good life on a sunny little island in the South Pacific. People, you ignorant bastard, the human popu-lace, will believe anything—given the right circum-stances."

"I'll go to prison for murder," Dale said. He couldn't help it; he was scared and trembling. He grabbed hold of the pool table and leaned forward, eerily similar to his brother, and afraid that if he let go his legs would buckle and fall out from under him.

"That depends on how much actin' you can pull off, boy. The cunt's already on the juice, there's as good a start as any on a story." This was Judd's voice. Judd was back, or at least for the time being. "That shit can be a might addictin'. You know that, don't you?"

"Ye…yes." Dale stuttered. "I…I've never killed anyone before. I don't know if I can."

"It'll be a lot more pleasant if you do it, boy. A hell of a lot more pleasant than if I do it."

"I don't want her to die."

"*You goddamn thick-headed son-of-a-bitch!*" Judd roared. Dale flinched and took a couple of staggering steps back. "*How you think Maria is goin' to react when she comes to an understandin' about what happened to Donnie?"* Judd, rounding the corner of the pool table faster than a man his size should have been able to, strode its length in just a few long and heavy strides. Dale was trying to back away when Judd reached out for him, but it was useless. Judd was a big man, but not a slow man and one huge calloused hand clamped around the side of Dale's head while another secured the opposite shoulder. "Why you got to be foolin' with me like this, boy? Big brother Judd is just out to keep an eye on you."

In a shaking, scared voice: "I'm afraid, Judd. I…I'm…"

"Shhh." Judd shushed him and the hand on Dale's shoulder tightened, and then Judd became the other one, the voice of them, and the one that had stalked Dale's nightmares for as long as he could remember. "Do *not* take us for granted. We will survive. We will see our struggle end, no matter how many of *you* we have to decimate. Your Maria will die, to that there is no argument."

Like some master chef kneading dough, Judd's sausage-like fingers massaged the back of Dale's neck, rough and painful, and he used the thumb of that hand to apply pressure to Dale's cheek. "We're allowing you the chance to see that she has some form of dignity in death. However, our generosity is limited."

"So, what you say, boy?" That was Judd again, and the pressure on the back of Dale's neck and cheek ceased. "You goin' to take care of business?"

"I'll do it. I'll do it… Just don't hurt her."

"Don't hurt her?" Judd let go of Dale with a hearty laugh and slapped him on the back. "Boy, that's purty damn funny. What you're about to do is a hell of a lot worse than death. Don't hurt her, damn, boy." Judd was shaking his head and laughing even harder. That laugh turned Dale's blood as cold as the water beneath a frozen lake.

A few minutes later, and after a couple of rough hacking coughs that sent more wads of blackish phlegm to the floor, Judd straightened up, took a cigarette from the pack in his front pocket and lit it. "Brother or not," he said between wisps of exhaled smoke. "I'll open you up. Let them sons-of-bitches have a buffet. Now, go on ahead and handle your business and I'll check up on everythin' later."

"But what do I do, Judd? After… Well, after I'm finished with my business."

"You don't worry none too much about that. I'll make sure *they* get a hold of the news. Everythin' will turn out just dandy if you do what *they* want. Now, go on now and do what you been told to do."

Dale said no more and turned towards the door. He was expecting Judd to call after him, as they do in movies, or books, with some last-minute threat or ultimatum, but none came. Judd stood statue-still in a plume of cigarette smoke and watched him go.

Julie Fontaine was resting on her couch with a washcloth wrapping up a few cubes of ice pressed on her forehead when she heard the first of the sirens outside of her apartment. She sat up and put the impromptu ice pack on the coffee table, then turned and knelt on the couch, peeling the curtain back just a tad. She couldn't see any flashing lights, but it sounded like they were moving in the direction of Atkins Park road. By the sound of it, they were hauling ass, too. Which meant either a car wreck or a fire, and she didn't hear any of the big fire engines, just an ambulance, and the police, so it must have been a car wreck. *Wonder what in the hell happened out there. I hope no one was hurt too bad.*

Twisting around so that she could sit on the couch in the way it was intended to be sat on, Julie wondered if what was happening with the paramedics and police was related in any way to the dream she had had earlier. *That was no dream, girl, and you know it. That shit was way too real. If not a dream, then what was it?* A vision? Some fraction of clairvoyance she was unaware she had? No, it was something different. Julie had never had a dream where she woke up wearing a completely different set of clothes than what she had been wearing when she went to sleep, and she had never gone to sleep on the bathroom floor. There had been a few parties when she was younger where she had passed out on the floor, among various other locations, but never had she done so while she was sober. Was it possible she was sleepwalking?

That was a laugh, too. Her parents had never mentioned her sleepwalking, neither had any of her old roommates or ex-boyfriends. But what had happened? There was a storm, she remembered that, and the power had knocked out the power. Julie wasn't sure if everything following the lights going out really happened or was a part of one big nightmare. *When you woke up, you saw the candle floating in the toilet. If you had dreamed that part, the candle would not have been there. And what about your clothes? When, exactly, did you change clothes?*

When had she changed clothes? She had no recollection of that at all. Could it have been before or after the dream with Donnie Atkins' mutilated face staring at her? She did know that in the dream, she was wearing one of her Goth outfits, the one she wore most times when she went out—the one she was wearing the night Donnie died. But how did she go from silk sleep pants and T-shirt to a black halter-top and a leather mini? And what about the dream itself? Why was she having a dream where she was warning Ray Sanders to stay out of his basement? Shit, she hardly even knew who Ray Sanders was. She knew him from high school, but Ray had been three years ahead of her and they never hung out in the same circles (even in high school, Julie hung with the punk and Goth crowd) or went to the same parties.

There was something else. Do you remember what it was?

She did remember. Not long before she woke, there was mention of a woman in town who would be in contact with her. This woman would be able to explain everything. *It was a dream. How can you believe something is going to happen based on a dream? Do you really think some lady here in town is going to call up out of the blue and guide you to unlimited truth? Some old, wrinkled-up female version of Yoda is going to appear and scream, "Use the Force, Julie! Use the Force!" Do you really think something like that will happen? Get real, girl, this is the real world. That kind of stuff only happens in some Hollywood screenwriter's head.*

Still, she couldn't help but wonder who this mysterious woman was or how the woman even knew who she was. Even more headache-inducing was the fact that she was even thinking about any of this when it was all some subconscious signal left over from some low-rate horror flick she had watched as a kid. The rent and utilities are what she *should* focus on since bill-time was only a few weeks away, and she still hadn't found a job. *Those are real-life issues and you know dad isn't going to bail you out this time. And if he does, he sure won't do it next month.*

Getting up from her couch, grabbing her makeshift icepack from the coffee table— the ice all but melted, and creating little puddles (which in turn created little streams that ran over the edge and onto her carpet)—Julie was thinking of bill money and how to obtain some quick cash rather than the mysteries of her dreamscape. She was so deep into her thoughts in fact, that the heavy footfalls on the landing outside of her apartment gave her a start. It was a quarter past midnight, a *little* unusual for someone to be out at this time on a weekday, at least in Maple Grove, and she was curious as to who was out there. There was an old saying/cliché about curiosity killing the cat. Well, if Julie was a cat and the person on the other side of her wall was an ax-wielding maniac, she figured she deserved that swinging ax for being so nosey since she ordinarily didn't care one way or the other what happened outside of her private sanctum.

Julie was on her couch and peering out her window before she realized that she had pulled open the curtain a little too far. She let it drop down again, peeling it back just enough to look through with one eye. *And what before my wondering eyes should appear? Roy Sanders?* How odd and coincidental at the same time. Odd because Roy Sanders was usually home as early as most of the town, not like those his own age or the younger crowds. It was coincidental because she had just been thinking of his cousin Ray. But wait; he wasn't coming home at all but going out. Yet another oddity for old Roy. And what was with the gym bag and plastic shopping bags? They were full of something and he kept looking around in nervous little jerks as if he was afraid someone might see him. *Yes. And someone has seen him, haven't they?* Julie felt somewhat guilty about that, at what her dad used to call a "Peeping Tom" or a "Nosey Nelly," and she was praying that Roy hadn't spotted her staring at him. She quickly let the curtain fall shut and eased around on the couch.

Wonder what that's all about? Nothing you should be worrying about, Julie. Now go to bed.

Yet, as Julie lay across her bed and as her head and pillow reunited with one another in a hoped-for union of sleep, all thoughts of bills and money to pay them faded away, while thoughts of mysterious women and basements ripe with danger tormented her.

"Wake up, Dianne. Snoozers are losers, remember, and I need one last favor from you. One last favor for an old friend."

"Who…dere…?" A groggy Diane Townsend asked. Her eyes opened in the darkness.

"One last favor…"

"Who's there?" she repeated with more coherence.

No answer.

Only the sound of a light wind brushing against the aluminum siding of her doublewide and the constant tick, tock, tick, tock of the old-fashioned wind-up clock on her nightstand.

"You're hearing things, girl. And talkin' to yourself to boot."

Dianne shut her eyes, content that the voices talking belonged to the world of dreams and weren't serious enough to demand her attention. Then, something cold grabbed onto her shoulder and shook her until her eyes popped back open in surprise and fear. She was fully awake now and too scared to do anything other than lie still, her heart pounding like a high school band bassline and her nerves jittering on the brink of panic. Someone had shaken her, had reached out, took hold of her shoulder and shook her, and since that she lived alone, it meant someone had broken into her home and crept up on her while she slept. Was that person staring at her with some horrible, crazed grin on their face? Were they waiting to see how she reacted before they did whatever harm it was, they meant to do to her? She didn't know. Fear was a powerful force and it had locked onto her with all of its might.

"Don't go getting all catatonic on me, Dianne. Now, why don't you get up and make us a fresh pot of coffee?"

She knew that voice. But it couldn't be; there was no possible way; crazed burglars didn't sound like dead friends. Dianne sat up and threw the blankets aside; afraid she was about to come face-to-face with some horny, deranged transient, but found herself as she was when she came to bed..., alone, just her and that damned ticking clock. Alone with the clock and her paranoia, that was. She looked around at the objects in her room, from the dresser to wardrobe to T.V. stand, all of it was fore-boding in the dark like shifting, slithering unknown beasts waiting to pounce. I'm not leaving this room, *she thought and reached out and grabbed hold of the comforter.* I'm just going to wrap back up and go to sleep. *But was it actually going to be as easy as that, to just drop off into sleep after such a weird awakening? Easy or not, she had every intention of closing her eyes and going to sleep, in spite of what she may have heard or may have felt. Besides, she was too old to be afraid of the dark, way too old for that sort of nonsense.*

"Dianne? Are you getting up to make us that coffee, or do I have to drag you out of bed by your ankles?"

Dianne was in the process of pulling the comforter

around her and nestling back down into a more comfortable position when the voice returned and she froze that way, eyes scanning left and right trying to pick out its source. Again, she was hit by the notion that she knew the owner of that voice, knew her quite well, actually, but it wasn't possible, not unless Dianne had become some kind of receiver of paranormal signals, which she doubted. It was actually funny, ironically funny, and she would've laughed if she hadn't been so scared. She could see the headlines now: "Woman from Jefferson county talks to the dead." It would be perfect to print in some sleazy tabloid, and as a bonus, Dianne lived in the country in a doublewide trailer. The tabloid freaks would eat it up. On the front cover would be a picture of her trailer, with a picture of her standing beside it crying into some kind newsman's hanky, and then off to the side would be a piss poor artist's rendering of the malevolent spirit that spent its nights causing Dianne all her woe. The truly depressing part of it all was that out there somewhere, some cooped-up busy body would read the whole thing and go "Oh! That poor dear! What a terrible and tragic plight." Well, maybe not that dramatic, but you get the picture.

"You going to sit there in la-la land or are you getting up? We haven't got a whole heap of time on our hands, girl."

"Lizzy? Elizabeth?" Dianne shook free of her tabloid fantasy at the repeating of her deceased friend's voice.

"I'm in the kitchen, dear. Now get that skinny behind of yours in here and put us on a fresh pot of coffee. I don't have all night, and neither does that stepson of yours."

"Roy? What's wrong with Roy?" And why am I talking to myself? She wondered. The idea that Elizabeth Sanders was having a conversation with her, and from all *the way in the kitchen, at that, was absurd, being that Eliz-abeth has been dead going on two months now.*

I will not go in there. I will not, no way, no how. I will not…

Then she was up, tossing the comforter to the floor and tottering out of her room and down the hall. The walls swayed and rippled like the current of a river post-rainfall and the pictures hanging on them became the faces of the dead. The cold, pale, and withered faces looked down upon her with vicious, contemptuous sneers. Dianne felt nauseous and disoriented and she tried to lean against one of the walls for support, but one touch of its surface gave her the chills as the wall was ice cold and slicked over with grime. Recoiling from her contact with the wall, as if inflicted by sudden, stabbing pain, Dianne continued up the hallway, which had now seemed impossibly long, appearing to have no end. The kitchen light burning at the other end was about as inviting as a lighthouse engulfed in a dense bank of fog. Gelid, knotted fingers grabbed at her arms, seeking purchase, but Dianne quickly moved from their reach, turning to look back the way she'd come, curious as well as frightened. Madly flailing arms, decom-posed and laden with scars, formed from the surface of the walls and extended outward, searching, desperate and blind, for some hapless soul to claim in their grasp.

What…

"Don't go worryin' about any of that, Dianne. The reapers only take the ones carrying a punched ticket. It ain't your time, girl, or they would have taken hold of you. Now get on in here."

"Liz…" Dianne started, choked, and then tried again. *"Liz, is it…I mean, are you…"*

"Hurry."

"I'm hurry…" Then she was in her kitchen, sitting at her

quaint cedar wood dinette table. *"…ing."* The first sound to further rattle her already rattled mind was the sound of running water. She looked up. Over next to the sink was a short, petite woman of about fifty with long gray hair. The woman was dressed in a light pink jogging suit and was filling Dianne's coffee pot with water from the faucet. Dianne watched as the woman reached over to shut off the water. The woman's hands, wrinkled by age, were not pallid or frail, but tanned and strong. She knew those hands, just as she knew the voice that had called out to her. Though both were strong indications that the woman standing at her kitchen sink was her long-time friend and ex-sister-in-law, Elizabeth Sanders, who had died of a heart attack two months ago, Dianne hoped and prayed that the woman would not turn to face her, old friend or not. What would one look like, even after buried only a short while? Diane didn't want to know. And the thought of seeing her dearest friend in such a condition would tear her heart out.

The woman turned and Dianne sucked in air, preparing to scream.

But no scream came. Elizabeth was exactly as she had been when Dianne last saw her: sky blue eyes, deep and thoughtful, high, well-sculptured cheekbones, pearly white teeth, luminescent smile brighter than all the suns in the universe. It was the face of a kind, hardworking Southern woman in her prime, the face of kindness and Southern charm. It was a face Dianne missed dearly.

Elizabeth carried the pot of water over to the coffee maker on the counter next to the refrigerator and started it to brew. No words passed between them and the only noises in the room was the ticking of an old grandfather clock in the corner by the door, the steady hiss and pop of the water as it percolated and the occasional sizzling *when a stray drop of water landed on the coffee maker's hot metal eye. After the brewing stopped, Elizabeth took two coffee mugs from the cabinet above the stove, filled them to the brim, as they say, and mixed sugar and creamer into both cups. Hadn't the two of them started many of their mornings at the diner in this exact same way right before their shifts began? Elizabeth brought the cups over and set them on the table, then pulled out a chair and sat across from her, sipping at her coffee as if it was no hotter than a glass of chilled milk.*

"Go ahead, hon," Elizabeth said. "Don't let it get cold. I know how much you can't stand drinkin' that stuff cold."

Dianne slid a finger through the mug's handle, lifted it to her lips, and stared at its contents with unsure eyes.

"It ain't nothing that's goin' to kill ya, girl. I ain't that desperate for company."

Dianne took a hesitant sip, winced as the hot brew scalded her tongue, and put the mug down in front of her.

"Now see, that didn't have ya foamin' at the mouth, now did it?" Elizabeth asked, taking a sip from her mug. "Now we must get down to the grit of why I'm here, hon."

Curiosity etched across Dianne's face, as well as frightened awe. This was either a nightmare or dream—which of the two it was, she had not the slightest idea. Dianne knew or wanted to believe, rather, that there was no way in Heaven or on Earth, that she was sitting here in her kitchen having a conversation with her dead friend over a cup of coffee. Earlier, she had jokingly thought about this experience as being something she would probably read in the tabloids. Though all the levity had departed from her situation, she still thought that this experience was identical to one of the ridiculous articles found in one of those rags. The very idea that this encounter could be anything more than a figment of her imagination was beyond Dianne's reach; to contemplate it being anything other than that was laughable.

"Well, shit, I should have put out three cups." Elizabeth shook her head as if to say dumb ole me. "Forgot all about poor ole Donnie. You don't drink coffee do ya, hon?"

There was movement to Dianne's left, accompanied by a wet, tearing sound. She turned towards it, slow and frightful, heart pounding, eyes wide with confusion and fear. At first glance, the young man sitting in the chair next to her was just an ordinary twenty-something man with firebrick red hair, garbed in the normal rustic wear of the average good ole country boy. Other than the fact that his skin was a bit pale and he seemed to be sweating from every pore on his body, he appeared as normal as all the other young men in the Grove. Then she got a closer look. Her stomach cramped and her bowls threatened to give way. From his forehead down to the collar of his shirt, was a tangled network of stitches and some portions of his face were uneven with one another, one eye lower than the other, and so on. His eyes weren't eyes at all, but discolored clumps of gel resembling spat up mucus. Dianne dropped her gaze to his hands, the only other parts of his body not covered with clothing. As it was with his face, so it was with his hands; the stitching appeared to be hurried and unprofessional with the fingers on each hand splayed apart unnaturally and hooked at crooked angles.

"I know Donnie here ain't looking his best, but he's learned a thing or two about humility since his incident and he's been tryin' to help, bless him. But we can only do so much, bein' disembodied spirits and all of that nonsense."

"Disembodied...what? Liz, I..."

"No worries about that, girl. You just listen up. Ray and Roy are depending on you."

"What about Ray..." Dianne gagged as the rancid smell of rotting flesh wafted under her nose. "...and Roy?"

"Ole Donnie is a bit ripe, sorry about that, hon. But it can't be helped."

"It's okay, I guess," Dianne said. "What about the boys?"

"I think you remember, or at least, you should, if you haven't switched over to selective memory."

"Liz. I don't understand you. Remember what?"

"Them. That help ya any, hon? You were there. It was you, Earnest, James, and me... Think it was '98 or '99... Somewhere in there."

Dianne suddenly wanted to wake up from this horrid vision. She did not want to go where Elizabeth was going. It was nice to stroll down memory lane, yes, but that was only if the memories were good memories. Why did you and James divorce? Was it not because of the incident under Earnest and Elizabeth's house all those years ago and the fact that James could not let it go? You held on as long as you could, almost twelve years, but it was hard, wasn't it? It was very hard.

"Dianne."

"Yes."

"There's a girl in town that has the ability to see, just like you are seeing now, through her dreams. We were wrong about how we handled things. It never was meant to be us, neither Sanders nor Atkins. The two families never were meant for anything special. They just needed us to help them get on their feet... Needed loyalty from willin' human hosts to help them get stronger. It was the only way they could ensure their survival, Dianne. We fell for it. Us and all of the ones before us. We can't let our

sons make the same mistake, and this girl, she is some-thing special. She can hurt them in a way we never could've dreamed of. Find her, protect her, and get her to the cabin. You have to start at the cabin."

"How? How am I…?"

"I'll leave you with a way to find her. Together, you will both go to Earnest's cabin and find the key."

"What do we do with this key?" Dianne asked, still in disbelief, convinced that this was only a dream and that it meant nothing. But Elizabeth had never lied to her… *"What do I do with the key?"*

"Nothing. The girl will know. She will see what to do."

"Liz. Is all of this real? It can't be."

"Afraid so, girl, and I hate to ask you to do this, but it's the only way," Elizabeth said, sorrowfully. *"Here, take this."* She slid a tarnished silver trinket across the table to Dianne. It was a dolphin. *"This is my talisman; I suppose that's the right word for it. You take it. There's a part of me in it somewhere, and it is as good a charm as any I imag-ine. It kept them from taking my soul, whatever good that's done. Make sure it gets to Ray. I've tried reaching him through his dreams, to warn him, but the boy hasn't picked up the clues. Let him know that his mother loves him, and that I never hated him for leaving."*

"Liz, I need…"

"Bye, Dianne. You just let Ray know his momma loves him, okay?"

"Liz."

"Let Ray know his momma loves him."

Dianne sat up in her bed, copious amounts of sweat exuding from every pore, soaking both her nightgown and bedsheets. She was crying and clenching an old tarnished dolphin pendant in her right hand. *Why me, Liz? Why does it have to be me?*

As Julie Fontaine battled in torment over a good night's sleep and Dianne Townsend spoke to dead friends, James Sanders stood at his living room window and watched his son tossing bags into the back of the cherry-red Chevy Nova SS he had had since high school. He had feigned sleep when Roy came in, trying not to make a sound that would wake his sleeping father. The sad thing was that Roy Sanders was about as good at being quiet as a thumbtack was at holding down a stack of paper in a windstorm. Whatever it was his son was up to, James didn't like the feel of it. He had a feeling that he *knew* what was going on but hoped in every way that he was wrong.

But everything's pointing to one answer. Sure, the hell is.

Donnie Atkins' death, the missing Willis girl, and a few minutes ago the sirens of paramedic vans and police cruisers wailing away towards Atkins Park Road, all of these had the same feel. Had Ray stumbled onto a secret that he was dragging his cousin Roy into? A secret that neither of them should be meddling with? "Every corner of every small town has a shadow," James's granddad had told him once. "And in those shadows, there are always secrets. Shadows and secrets, Jim, that's all small towns, are. Nothin' on the surface ever is what it is. Someone is always hidin' somethin'." *Got that right, granddad…and we have one doozy of a secret in our family, don't we?*

James went into the pantry on the backside of the kitchen, picked up his work boots, and then headed to his bedroom to change. Those boys didn't have a clue as to what was happening, and he had to get over to his late brother's house as fast as he could. If something were to happen to his son or nephew because neither he nor Earnest had felt it necessary to explain to their sons, the truth… *Then there is no way in hell I could ever forgive myself. But this was all supposed to have been over twenty years ago, Earnest and me saw to it. How…*

It didn't matter how. It only mattered that he did what he should have done years ago when Roy was old enough to understand things like a man. Of course, there was the offshoot chance that he was reading all of this wrong, that maybe the boys were just doing typical male bullshit and having fun. *You know better than that. You know what's happening. You felt it months ago before Lizzie died, and you ignored it.*

"I'm such a bastard," James said to his empty bedroom as he slipped on a chambray work shirt. He had just pulled on a pair of jeans and was putting on his work boots when he heard the scream.

He stood there for a minute (maybe two, maybe six, he lost track) next to his bed, the laces of his left boot hanging limply between his fingers. His chest tightened and it felt like he had a pair of slinkies for legs. Then, another scream issued, and James Sanders finished tying his shoes. Grabbing his shotgun from inside the closet and a handful of shells from his top dresser drawer and shoving them into his pockets, he hurried through his tiny two-bedroom apartment and out the front door. The scream had come from the apartment next door, to the right of his, he knew the young woman who lived there lived alone, and he feared the worst. A robbery, a rape, or God knew what was happening over there, and he didn't intend on letting that young woman get hurt.

James barely had the time to palm the doorknob to Julie Fontaine's apartment door and twist it when his world was swathed in light, followed by intense pain from head-to-toe as an unforeseen force propelled him backward. His back slammed against something cold and metal and he was swimming in a lake of shadows.

Minutes later—James wasn't sure how many, since he had lost track of time earlier—he opened his eyes to a distorted collection of jumbled images, and even more screaming assaulted his ringing ears. He was vaguely aware that a crowd had gathered, and his shotgun lay at his feet. *The hell hit me?*

The whirling world around him began to settle somewhat and James was aware that someone was pushing through the crowd and running into the girl's apartment. Then he heard her voice, a voice he would not forget no matter how many bumps he took to the head. It was the voice of the only woman James Sanders would ever allow into his heart. She shouldn't be here; she should be leaving this crap alone. This wasn't her fight.

What if she came over here to see me? After all this time, what if... And now, what if Dianne died because I'm too slow to save her? NO! Too many have died because of them. There was no longer any doubt in James Sanders' mind what he was dealing with this night. Pushing the charred apartment door off him, he slid off the hood of the old sedan he'd been pinned to, knelt to pick up the shotgun, and moved toward the apartment.

Entering the girl's apartment with a slight limp, James Sanders took in the scene and assessed the situation. The girl—Julie was her name, Julie Fontaine, he had gone to school with her father and her mother—lay collapsed near the little archway to her kitchen wearing only a white halter-top and gray sweatpants. At first, he thought her dead; a big crimson patch of blood soaking the front of her shirt, but then the steady rise and fall of her chest eased his mind.

To Julie's right, the grisly remains of a man had Dianne pinned against the wall with a grimy hand around her throat, a small welling of blood soaking through her blouse at the right shoulder. Snaking from the corpse's back was a slimy gray appendage. It hovered over her face, a small spear-like spur from its tip dripping some unknown, clear fluid. James lurched forward, crossing the short distance between them in mere seconds, heart beating sonic booms in his chest. Once within reach, James reached out with his left arm and took hold of the dead man's left shoulder, pulling the creature away from Dianne and spinning it around. Then, pressing the barrel of the shotgun against what was left of its face, James squeezed the trigger, covering both him and his ex-wife in gore as the dead man's head exploded. Pumping the slide, James put the barrel to the thing's back as it hit the floor and fired again, obliterating the tick-like monstrosity living inside.

Over! Damnit, this was supposed to be over!

Dianne looked ready to faint, so James stepped in, catching her with his free arm. He held her close, looking down into Dianne's face with a deep affection he thought he'd lost long ago. She blinked her eyes a couple of times and said in a weak voice, "James," and passed out.

It's going to be fine now, baby.

A deep growl rumbled from behind him and James turned to face it. A big St. Bernard stood between him and the doorway leading out of the apartment. Its eyes were glazed over, its fur, dirty and matted and reeked of the grave. Blue-green foam dripped from its massive jaws and fresh blood trickled from its nose. James Sanders was a sitting duck, as there was no way he could think of to lay Dianne on the floor and pump the shotgun's slide before the big dog bore down on them and tore them to pieces.

Their eyes locked; the determined eyes of a man calculating his odds, and the milky- white eyes of a creature that was no longer an animal —an entity of ancient origins had taken control of the animal's body. For the first time in many years, James Sanders felt tired; exhausted to the point of falling over. He was at his rope's end.

"I'm sorry, Di, so damn sorry," James said. Then to the dog, he spat: "Finish it you big fucker! *Do it!*"

The dog began inching forward, blue-green foam falling from its muzzle and sizzling as it hit the carpet, small wisps of smoke rising in its wake. The St. Bernard's growl deepened, and it steadied its body to leap. That's when Julie Fontaine seemed to appear from nowhere, James having forgotten all about her. She dropped onto the dog's back and plunged a large kitchen knife into its neck. The St. Bernard shook Julie free, the knife jutting from its neck, blood seeping from the wound. Landing on the floor in front of her couch, Julie threw her left arm up as a shield, closed her eyes, and turned her head away from the gnashing teeth, preparing for the worst as the big dog advanced on her.

James laid Dianne Townsend to the floor as quickly and gently as he could, gripped the shotgun in both hands, pumped the slide once more, and squeezed the trigger. The St. Bernard's head, what little was left of it, tore from its shoulders and hit the wall, leaving its massive body to hit the floor with a heavy thud, blood spewing from the stub of its neck.

"I need her," Julie's voice was weak and timid between hitching breathes. James looked over to her and she pointed to Dianne and spoke again. "I see now what I have to do, but I need her to protect me. You need to get to Ray. You need to hurry and go to him, explain to him what must be done."

"I can't involve you or Di any further," James said, lifting Dianne Townsend off the floor with his free arm. I'll go and handle the boys… It's family business."

"I'm sorry, Mr. Sanders," Julie protested, as she got to her feet, a little shakily, James noticed. "But we, me and her, are already involved. It has to be. You know that, don't you?" This was not a question.

James did know this and a tear-streaked down his cheek. He knew this as well as he knew he would die this night. "Let's go and get this over with, then." James tried to give Julie a reassuring smile, but only managed a thin mockery of one.

CHAPTER THIRTEEN

It had taken the girl and her lover by complete surprise, waiting until they were in the heat of their lovemaking to spring. They huddled together in human blanketing on an insignificant patch of grass along the river, not too far away from its birthing place. The seclusion of the area was perfect and the fact that the human couple had been copulating was a bonus, as the raised temperature in their bodies made the feeding easier, not to mention tastier. There had been no struggle from the couple, just a choked scream from the girl and a startled expletive from the boy, as it had taken a neck in each of its hands and squeezed, squeezed until their eyes had popped from their sockets. In death, their bowls and bladder had let go and it had deeply inhaled the scent of feces and urine, like a well-refined woman in ecstasy over the most exquisite of perfumes. But even after such a fine meal, it couldn't understand why it felt so much distress. The night was cool, the moon full and the mist surrounding it was sparse and thin. It should feel happy, jubilant at such a pleasant night, but…

It looked over at the nude corpses of the couple; the new births were feeding, suckling the fresh lifeblood and nutrients they needed in order to survive. Scattered around them were the hollowed-out hulls of several large rats. These new births would need larger hosts soon. After feeding this, well they would need a much larger host than a cat or small dog; they would have to seek out larger animals so that they could continue with their growth cycle. This worried it, too, as there were now six members of the human population in this settlement that posed a threat to their growth cycle, a threat to their existence. Of all the human emotions it had experienced since occupying this human body—though the brain was dead, it didn't erase the human ability to feel—sadness was what it felt now. It did not want to die, nor did it want its species eradicated. This world was so full of resources and the species of this world, especially the humans, reproduced at phenomenal rates, so there was always an abundant source of food. Why hadn't the master given the order to eliminate all those that pose a danger to them? Why must it wait to rid its species of their biggest threat?

One of the new births began to whine as it fell away from its meal, larger new births pushing it away and not allowing it to suckle. It reached over with its human hand and picked the hungry new birth from the wet grass and placed it on one of the girl's bare breasts to feed, making room for it by shoving the larger new births to the side. The little one sank its feeding stalks into the girl's flesh and immediately began to suckle. It was their way, the weak suffered and the strong thrived, but since attaining this body and its loathsome emotions, it did things that were beyond their natural order. For instance, forcing the other new births to allow the scrawny one to feed just now

—that was not its way or the way of its kind. Under normal circumstances, the little one would have perished if it could not fend for itself.

The new births were beginning to move away, off into the wooded land beyond. They had had their fill and were searching for new hosts, no doubt. It was as it should be, as it has been for millennia. It was by itself now, by the riverside, aside from the dead couple, and it knew that it was time to move on as well.

It stood with Donnie Atkins's legs, feeling something tear loose somewhere internally. It pulled up the dirty dress shirt and frowned with bloodless, cracked lips. The stitching had come loose. This body would not last much longer, and it hoped that it would at least hold together long enough for its clutch of new breeds to hatch. Then it could switch over to a new host-body for its own growing cycle to end. It reached down, grabbed a handful of hair on each corpse, and felt even more distress as the stitches along Donnie Atkins' arms began to tear-free. Regardless of this body's rapid decay, it would have to do in order to take the fresh kills away to its sleeping place. Their eyes were ruined, but that was of no concern, as the bodies were still suitable for habitation. *Soon*, it thought. Soon.

<hr>

The floodlight at the end of Judd Atkins's driveway flickered indiscriminately, a young bat circling around it in search of a meal. The rain had not yet started back up and a low, misty fog hovered above the ground like a ghostly snowfall. Judd, sitting on his back porch in his favorite chair, smoking a cigarette, and sipping from a newly opened can of beer, stared out across his dimly lit backyard with an agitated scowl contorting his face. He had come mighty damn close to snapping Dale's neck tonight; had thought about it as his no-account brother's neck was in his grip. And for what?

For a useless, drugged-out, whore-of -a-wife, that's what

Maria was Judd's sister-in-law, but that was as far as Judd cared for it to go. He had despised the prissy bitch back when Dale had dated her, outright loathed her when they were married. Judd had known the moment he first met Maria that she was different, how someday she would pose a threat. There had been others like her, those that could see through the veil of deception the Odomulites used to keep the people in the grove blinded to their presence, to their feeding from its populace. Judd had buried them all, except for Maria. She had always been sensitive to what was happening around her but had never made a move to act on what she was sensing. And she was Dale's wife. As much as Judd wanted her dead, it was Dale's place to kill her, but the boy never had the balls to do so.

However, Maria was not the direct threat she had once been, as a newer threat, a younger threat, was posed to bring it all down. Julie Fontaine, a descendant of one of Maple Grove's founding families, granted with the gift of seeing and with it, the power to send the Odomulites away, now stood in his way. Julie was stronger than Maria, Judd could feel it, like if he was standing bare-naked before the wrath of a category 5 hurricane. Presently, her abilities were just beginning to awaken, but she was like the batteries you got with new cell phones or with cordless power tools, she needed to be charged. Granted, there was no time for her to charge-up naturally— that would take years—but Maria was a good booster, that she was. It was up to Dale now, to make sure they would never meet. That was if Dale would grow a pair, take care of business, and kill his drugged-out wife.

From somewhere deep in the woods came a series of howls and barks, followed by yelps of pain. The new births taking new hosts, no doubt. This brought Judd to yet another concern: Earnest Sanders' boy Ray. Judd hadn't expected the boy to stay after his mother's funeral; Ray had always been somewhat aloof on matters of family and tradition. Judd figured Ray would have posted a "for sale" sign at the end of his drive, cut tail, and headed back down to Panama City. But he hadn't, and, in fact, had said he planned on *not* selling his house or land.

This was a problem in a big way. If Dale failed to kill Maria, by either incompetence or lost will, and the Fontaine girl and Ray Sanders were to meet, it would be catastrophic. As is it had been with Earnest and James Sanders, it was with Ray and Roy Sanders. The eldest held the key to the blood pact with the Odomulites in his blood and only Ray Sanders, with the assistance of Julie Fontaine—a freshly charged Julie Fontaine—could destroy a pact several decades in the making. And Judd hadn't spent his entire life serving *them* for Earnest's brat and the little Goth whore to render his lifelong servitude for nothing.

Judd flicked his cigarette butt over the porch railing and took one last sip of beer before crushing the empty can and dropping it into the empty five-gallon bucket next to his chair. The night's festivities were not over, it seemed. Judd was going to have to make a final visit to his old friend's riverside cabin and send all those interfering with his business to wherever the world of spirits would take them.

Goin' show them what happens when you cross old Judd, sure the hell am.

CHAPTER FOURTEEN

The vast expanses of the Sahara Desert could not have been any stiller and quieter than their house was when Dale returned home. Maria heard the downstairs door catch as he pushed it shut and heard him climb the stairs. Even with the thick carpeting, Dale couldn't hide the creak that rose from every other stair. She heard him creeping clumsily down the hall towards their room, heard the floor underneath the carpet release a gentle moan with each step he took. She heard the doorknob to their bedroom door turning, slow and easy, then a quiet click and he eased the door open. "Maria," he called in a whisper almost low enough that only a dog could hear. "Are you sleeping?"

She didn't answer. *Let him think you're still under from the drugs. Why pretend? Why let him think what isn't true? The dreams are why. You saw what your husband and that piece-of-shit-brother of his really were. He let Donnie die, and he'll let you die, too. This is crazy. Can you really let a few bad dreams lead you to believe that your husband is a sadistic monster? Remember the two boys in the car. Remember...*

Dale was inside their room now, over next to the closet by the sound of it, and then there was a minor squeak of hinges as he opened the closet door. Following this was the sounds of him rummaging through it, still trying not to make any noise. *What was he doing? Do I dare open my eyes? NO! Stay as you are.* Then the rummaging stopped. The only noise in the room was the whishing of the overhead fan and Dale's labored breathing. There was a grunt and some mumbling that she couldn't make out, then he was at it again. *What are you looking for?*

"Damn it," he hissed under his breath, and there was a thump as something hit the wall.

Silence. She had heard that you could feel it when someone was watching you. She had never truly believed it, but that wasn't the case now. Right now, she desperately believed it. Dale was staring at her, hitching in breath after breath in shallow gasps. She could imagine the look on his face, intense, angry, and depraved—she had seen that look there before, and she was willing to bet it was the same one there now. It was a trace of his father's madness, the only true legacy of Donald Atkins. Now he was moving again, he was to her left, next to the bed, kneeling. The stink of whiskey and stale cigarette smoke was as thick on him as the smell of permeated fruit locked up in a cellar. She fought from tensing up as his fingers traced along her arm, over her left breast and along her throat, as gentle a touch as that of a considerate lover. *What are you planning?* Her mind cried. *What are you going to do to me?"*

"Maria," Dale whispered as his hands found her breasts, pricking at her nipples through the thin silk fabric of her gown with his thumbs. He leaned close to her, his breath hot, rancid, a feverish evil incorporated each time he exhaled. "Wake up, baby."

He must have gotten boozed-up after he left Judd at the cabin, boozed-up enough to handle his business. She had witnessed their meeting, their discussion, or at least enough of it to know the truth before she woke this last time. And now she had to deal with the fact that her husband was plotting her murder. Dale was too afraid of Judd and too weak of a man to stand his ground. *If he loved you, he wouldn't be about to do what you know he is about to do now, would he?*

"Maria. Hey, honey, can you hear me?"

Pain and ecstasy rippled through her body as he pinched her nipples and she let out a moan and bit her lower lip. Why was her body turning against her? She burned with hatred for him, yet his touch was turning her into a lust-crazed teenager.

"That's it, baby," Dale whispered into her ear. "Feels good, don't it?"

No. Don't let him do this. Don't let him manipulate you. You know what he is. You know what he's up to. He's lowering your defenses…

Stroking and squeezing her left breast, nipple pinched between thumb and forefinger, Dale reached down between her thighs with his other hand and underneath her panties. Maria gripped onto both sides of the mattress. A husky, yearning desire escaped her throat and she rocked her hips against Dale's roving fingers. Resistance was the key, now, but these feelings, to be touched with such passion, such tenderness. He was her husband. He was the father of her children…

He's a bastard. Your oldest child is in prison and your youngest is dead, dead because of Dale. Now hubby dearest is trying to seduce you, to take your mind off… Off what? What exactly does he have in mind? To kill you, you know that, but how? And when?

"That's it, baby. Really get into it. You know you love it when I get you off." His breath was hot and moist, and he licked her left ear. "You know how much you love it."

"Stop…" Her voice was weak and scratchy, her throat was dry, but she managed a feeble attempt at resistance. "Please, stop."

"Stop?" Dale asked, mockingly jubilant. "But, baby, I can't stop and leave you *unfulfilled.*"

Maria opened her eyes. Dale hovered over her, eyes glazed, brimming with insanity. Sweat rolled from his brow and dripped down on her face. "Come on, baby. Just give a little. Enjoy it."

NO! "No." She whimpered. "Please, Dale, don't."

Dale took his hand from her breast and grabbed her throat, still using his other hand to molest her most private place and gave a slight squeeze. But she had to end this, end it before he was at the apex of complete control over her. The morphine had been Dale's leash around her neck, his way to control her by keeping her unconscious, and this seduction was his was way to keep her distracted. If not for the dreams, as unwanted and terrifying as they were, Maria would have fallen into his and Judd's plans as a dim blip on their twisted radar, just another name to scratch off the list. If she gave in now, she would die.

"No means yes and stop means go," Dale said and applied a little pressure around her throat. "Isn't that what you told me once when we were dating? I believe so."

Weak and forced: "That was different. That was a long time ago. I don't want to, Dale."

"No means yes and stop means go," he repeated, almost chanted.

"No…"

Dale took his hand away from down there and straddled her, both hands around her throat now. This was it. *This is where he takes care of his business. If you are going to do something, you had better do it now. Before this sick game goes too far. He's crazy, Maria, husband or not; he's too afraid of Judd and too far gone to realize he has a choice.* How? What was she supposed to do? Dale was stronger and now all his weight was on top of her, pinning her to the mattress. What *could* she do?

"Yes," Dale said and pressed his thumbs into the base of her neck. It was difficult to breathe, and the pain was excruciating. She tried to catch her breath but all she got for her trouble was a mouthful of Dale's sweat. Salty and sour, it rolled along her tongue and knotted her stomach. "Yes, yes yes yes yes."

Maria slapped feebly at his arms and back, but her strength had not fully returned from the numerous times Dale had drugged her and each slap was doing no more than brushing against him. His eyes grew larger, hungrier, and a homicidal smirk tainted his face. Dale was keeping the air away from her lungs with his strong, skinny hands and soon, she would fall into the deepest sleep of them all. It would be asleep from which she would never wake. Already her vision was beginning to blur, and the sounds around her grew distorted. Maria was dimly aware of Dale shaking her, violently thrusting her head repeatedly into the mattress as he throttled her and screaming what now seemed to be his mantra: "No means yes and stop means go."

Maria reached her arms out to either side of the bed, fingers searching for purchase of anything she could use in self-defense, a ballpoint pen; one of the thick hardcover books she so enjoyed; one of Dale's heavy beer mugs, anything at all. Dale wasn't a big man, but he was stout and as he leaned forward, adding what little weight he had with the effort of strength he was using to choke her, Maria was resolute in her decision to live. She flailed her arms with more vigor than before, hoping for, at the very least, a chance miracle. Her lungs were forest-fire-hot in her chest, starving for air and thirsting to breathe. Something slender and cool snagged in the fingers of her left hand. It was an electrical cord, to either the lamp or the clock radio, and she closed a fist around it. This would be an I-hope-this-works move and Maria knew it might be just as futile as her attempts at slapping him off her, but there were no other options swinging her way.

She looked one last time into his crazed eyes, then yanked whatever it was from the nightstand and swung it like a knight swinging a mace. For a second, she thought it wasn't going to work, that Dale would strangle her until she was blue, and then she heard an audible clunk as the clock radio smacked Dale just above his left eye. His grip on her throat loosened and then disappeared as he raised his hands to the sides of his head. Maria let go of the clock's power cord and shoved both hands into Dale's chest, pushing him off balance. He tumbled off the bed, onto the floor.

Maria inhaled fresh air into her lungs, coughed a little, and winced from the pain of her bruised throat. *Now run!* She swung her legs over the edge of the bed, stood up, and hit the floor as her legs, weak from lack of use, pins, and needles, they called it, buckled. From the other side of the bed, Dale groaned and cursed. *Damn hardheaded bastard.* In fear of him pouncing on her at any given moment, Maria began pulling herself along the floor on her belly, thankful that she had given in last year and let Dale replace their old carpet with the thick shag carpet that was there now. She had made it to the armchair in the corner; the one Dale sat in to keep his vigil over her and lifted herself about midways to its seat when Dale's slurred speech broke the silence.

"Damn, baby! Why would you hit me like that?"

Why would you try to choke me to death? Maria thought but did not say. It hurt to talk and, besides, she was too busy pounding fists into her legs, trying to coax some feeling back into them. Slowly the pins and needles sensation died away, leaving her with a few mild cramps, but nothing mind-numbingly painful and she could stand. Dale moaned again and one of his hands appeared over the edge of the bed. She had to hurry. He was conscious, and now that he had just been cracked over the head with an alarm clock, he was probably furious and in more of a killing mood than ever.

"Why, why, why? Why in the hell would you hit me?" Dale's other hand appeared over the edge of the bed and he rose to his feet. "Why?"

Hands behind her back, Maria edged towards the door, feeling her way along the wall and praying that Dale hadn't locked the door behind him. She didn't want to take her eyes off him. Not only was Dale stout, but he was also as quick as a rattlesnake when he had to be, and Maria was pretty sure that this was one of those moments when he felt he had to be. As it was, her legs were still about as consistent as a bowl of Jell-O and quick movement was not a guarantee but a fantasy. If Dale decided to rush at her, she was, for the lack of a better word, screwed. What he did next caught her completely by surprise. He started to cry and dropped to his knees, elbows resting on the bed, hands pressed before him as if in prayer.

"Hurry," he croaked. "Hurry and go, baby. Get as far away from the Grove as your feet can carry you, or you could drive." Dale laughed in good humor, a cry away from the lunatic he was only minutes before. "Yeah, I suppose you could get out of here a tad faster if you drove."

"Dale."

"Don't. Don't you dare." He looked up at her; his face streaked with tears, and let his hands fall to the bed. Regret, love, pity, fear, all bundled in one package and all delivered at once. She wanted to go to him, wanted to turn and run. Conflicted, she stood there, inches away from the door, about eight feet from where Dale knelt beside the bed. "Just go, don't argue with me, and for once in this marriage let me win. Please."

"Judd can't always—"

"Judd does what he wants. But it doesn't matter, not anymore. He belongs to *them*, has for a long, long, time now. And I'm beyond anything like hope. Just go. Before they dig at my mind enough to finish what I started."

"Dale! Maybe you—"

"GO!" Dale roared. "HURRY!"

Maria started to speak, to say something about how they could both leave, start over somewhere else and then realized (other than how much that line sounded like some cheesy romance novel) that it would be no good. Judd wouldn't let Dale go just as *they* would not let Judd go. She put her hand up to her bruised throat, vision hazy with tears then opened the door and slipped out into the hall, shutting the bedroom door behind her. She staggered down the hall like a drunk, moving closer to the stairs as fast as she was able, holding her emotions at bay by only the thinnest of margins, and trying not to bump into the wingbackchairs or the console tables between them. As she reached the head of the stairs, she looked back once to her bedroom, expecting to see Dale explode through the door like some mad jackal ready to rip her into pieces. But nothing of the sort happened, so she turned and went down the stairs.

After she had gone, Dale stood and turned to the nightstand on that side of the bed and opened the drawer all the way to the stop. There was only one item in the drawer, covered with an oily piece of terrycloth. *If all else fails, take the coward's way out.* A dry, colorless smile curved his lips and he snatched the terrycloth from the drawer and threw it aside. Now the item he wanted was in plain view, and he picked it up and reveled in its weight. The .357 was a birthday gift from Judd a few years back and Dale had treasured the big gun. Had even taught both of his sons how to shoot it. It was funny, really, a knee-slapping riot, how this gift from Judd was what would dissolve his older brother's hold over him.

"Run and don't look back, Maria. I love you." Dale shoved the barrel under his chin—no need to check and see if it was loaded, he kept it loaded in case of a break-in—and pulled the trigger.

The gunshot halted her where she was, one foot on the ceramic tile of her kitchen and the other poised on the planking of her back deck, a loud hollow blast that made her feel as insignificant as a speck of dust caught in the breeze. She wouldn't waste time crying, though, not now. Right now, she had to put a good distance between her and this wretched excuse of a town. Up North, all the way up to Kentucky. Her dad lived in Lexington, so she supposed she could stay with him until she was on her feet. But what would she tell him? How would she explain what had happened here, to her, to Dale, to Donnie, how would she explain it at all?

The cabin, Maria. Earnest Sanders' cabin. That's where you must go.

Again, she stopped. This time it was just as she cleared the last step on the deck and was moving along the gravel path leading around to the front of the house. That voice—it wasn't her inner voice, the one Maria associated with her thoughts. In fact, it wasn't a voice Maria knew at all.

The cabin, the voice insisted, rather impatient. *You have work to do.*

"Why?" Maria pleaded. "The gunshot. Someone is bound to have heard it and come a running to check things out. The police will—"

The woods. Take the woods through to the Sanders's place. Hurry before someone comes. No time to doddle.

"I…" but it was no use. She supposed that she had known this was coming, ever since Donnie had died and the dreams had started, some part of her had foreseen the outcome of all this madness. Just beyond the edge of her backyard, just past the concrete patio set and the badminton net, was a woodland path that ran about three miles and opened up on the Sanders's property. The moon was hiding somewhere, occasionally peeking out from behind a cloud. The thick mass of trees and vines before her were dark, and foreboding, a place of nightmares and crooked fables created to frighten children. It frightened her as well, but she stepped into the darkness, with nothing to guide her through the night-shrouded foliage but the voices in her head.

Ray was standing on the front porch and leaning on the railing when Roy pulled up and shifted the Nova into park. When Roy got to the porch, lugging a beat-up gym bag and a few plastic grocery bags from the Piggly Wiggly full of God knew what, Ray stepped around him and offered to help with the load. Roy handed over a few of the bags to Ray, and the two of them moved inside. Setting everything down on the couch, they stared down at some of the spilled contents with dread.

Earlier, after Ray had woken up, finding that Beth had not up and left—in fact, she, Roy and Amy were down in the kitchen finishing up with a breakfast Beth had cooked—Roy had pulled Ray to the side and had mentioned getting rid of the girls because there was something he and Ray needed to talk about. It was with great reluctance, mainly because he wasn't quite ready to say goodbye and wanted to spend a little more time with her, but he was also curious to what his cousin was in such an uproar about, that he approached Beth with an endless stream of lame excuses filling his head. She was standing on the back porch when he found her, gazing at the sky with its rose, orange and violet hues, an artist's rendering of a picture-perfect sunset born by the strokes of nature's careful, talented hand. Her hair, that brilliant auburn flare, rivaled this spectacular sunset before them, and flowed down past her shoulders, ending at her slender, oh so huggable waist. She was wearing a tiny pink halter and blue jean shorts that accented every curve of her well-toned body. It was at this moment that Ray realized, somewhat painfully, that he didn't love Beth as he once did—not so much as had lusted for her. Granted, a part of him felt for her as one would feel for an old childhood friend, but he was not in love with her.

"I love the sky after a storm," she said as he approached, not turning to greet him, still goggling at the sunset with a little girl's wonder. "The colors are always so beautiful. Peaceful, you know, like the skies in a fairy story."

"Yeah," Ray replied evenly. "It's quite a view."

Perhaps Beth had caught the uncertainty in his voice, the slight waver he was unable to keep out of it, or perhaps she had missed it altogether. Nevertheless, she turned to him with tentative eyes. Ray swallowed, tried to look away, but felt drawn by those deep emerald eyes that had captivated him so many years ago. He had missed her; more than just a little, but having her, to force a love that was not there, was as much evil as the dark disease that infected the Grove.

"Something's wrong. Isn't there?" She put her arms around his waist and lay her head on his chest. "You going to tell me?"

Ray returned the embrace with one arm around her waist and the other snaked around her shoulder, his open palm cupping the back of her head as he stroked her hair. "I…" he started but didn't know how to finish. *You don't know what you're doing. You don't have any excuses.*

"What is it, Ray? Is it me? I thought we… Last night, it was so nice. I missed you so much and I know, now. I know that what I did—"

"Shhh. None of that, okay? That was years ago, and I can't say that I don't share some fault. I didn't deal with everything too well, I acted like a jackass. But all that, that's not it, not at all. I missed you, too. I just need some time. Say a week, and it's nothing to do with you or us or last night. But if you give me this week, I will explain everything to you, I promise."

For a minute, Ray didn't think she was going to respond, that maybe she wasn't willing to accept his words or how he had laid them out. Then, in a forced voice: "You can have your week. I owe you that, I suppose. But I love you, Ray. I really do, just don't take too long. Don't leave me hangin'."

"I won't." He was trying to sound optimistic but heard the rueful way his words drifted around his ears, ambivalently pessimistic, dire.

Five minutes passed with no words between them, only the sound of the crickets and the toads, the toads being vehemently lively in the post-storm dampness. Above them came the tapping of the rain on the roof and the skies slowly began to darken. Only a small break in the weather then, he should have known. It was apt to rain for the next couple of days; Ray had checked the Weather Channel earlier and had expected it to start up again, but after seeing Beth and the sunset, he prayed for the rainy weather to be over. He kissed the top of her head and listened to the drops on the roof grow harder.

"You two might want to get on the road before it gets as bad out as it was this morning," Ray said, not wanting to let her go. "The roads are already as slick as owl shit, as dad used to put it. And they're only going to get worse."

Beth pulled away and looked up into his eyes, then leaned in and kissed him. After the kiss, she walked back over to the porch railing, staring at the dark gray beasts that had eaten the beautiful sunset she had so adored. "Amy!" she called. "You ready to go, girl?"

"Comin'," Amy called back and a few moments later she stepped out the front door, tucking her white tee with the heart on the front, announcing that bad girls needed love too, into a pair of blue jean shorts similar to Beth's. Roy, right behind her with a smile on his face as big as a billboard, was buttoning his pants.

"What?" Roy asked, catching the teasing, dirty-minded look that passed between Ray and Beth.

"Oh, nothing," Ray said lightheartedly, grinning like a mischievous twelve-year-old boy hiding under the bleachers and sneaking a peek at the cheerleaders' panties.

Beth giggled and threw a hand over her mouth to stifle it. Roy flushed a bit and looked over at Amy who only shrugged indifferently and winked at him.

"We're all adults, here, right?" Roy looked from face to face. "You guys are actin' like I'm the town virgin."

Ray went over and patted Roy on the back. "It's all right, dude. We're just fucking with ya. But you got to admit, it sure beats a porno mag and a bottle of Jergens, don't it?"

"That's just wrong," Amy said, guffawing so hard that she had to turn away from everyone to regain her composure. Beth burst into a volley of vivacious giggles; dried them up and grabbed onto the banister in order to subdue snippets of laughter.

"Man, why does everybody got to pick on me," Roy tried to mimic an expression of hurt, pouting out his lips and flashing eyes that plead sympathy, but what he came up with was the face of someone who had just chugged a mug of lemon juice.

"I'm sorry," Beth said courtly, then saw Roy's face and went into a howling, giggling fit.

"This isn't junior high," Roy said, curt and flat, but grinned despite his mock sullen mood.

Standing on the porch and waving as the girls drove off, a feeling of incipient terror settling in his gut, Ray looked at Roy. "What was so important? And please don't tell me—"

"It has to do with when we were kids, Ray. Something that happened then, something that I've tried to block out. But it keeps coming back, nagging me. Nagging the shit out of me. Do you remember, Ray, about what we saw in your basement?"

CHAPTER FIFTEEN

I t was 1998, a cool October breeze was blowing, and a bright afternoon sun sat snug against a mild blue sky. Exhaust trails from planes and jets crisscrossed here, there, and over yonder, and plump, lazy cumuli lounged. On the branches of the dogwoods congregated in the Sanders' front yard, blue jays sung in jubilant spurts and squirrels played their never-tiring game of tag along the edges of the woods and across the yard, occasionally chasing one another up into one of the dogwoods, upsetting the jays and causing a raucous series of angry screeches and screams. Earnest Sanders was out back of the family's two-story Victorian in his shed, bent over a small workbench in the corner, the sleeves of his flannel shirt pushed up to the elbows. He was working tirelessly to repair a handful of small engines: Sonny McLain's Briggs and Stratton, and two Hondas that belonged to David Morris over at the post office, plus one brand of engine he had never laid eyes on before and wasn't too sure he could do anything with. This one belonged to that lawyer, Matthew Groggins was his name, who had just moved to the Grove from up North; he knew Groggins and his family was from Vermont, but as to what part, he couldn't say.

In the kitchen, stirring sugar, and cream into a fresh cup of coffee, Elizabeth Sanders stood, her nightgown billowing around her ankles from the floor vent, looking out the window above the sink, enjoying the scenery of her back yard. One spot was the patch of land just to the left of Earnest's shed where her vegetable garden grew. Before long, winter would rush in; singing its bittersweet lullaby and her precious garden would sleep. There was plenty in the basement, though—she had spent the last four months canning all sorts of fruits and veggies, and if they should happen to run short, there was a grocery store just a few miles down the road, although she preferred the veggies she had raised herself to anything store-bought.

In the basement, hung from a nail by a weathered leather strap on a support beam in the east corner, a worn-out transistor radio coughed out *Sweet Child of Mine* by *Guns and Roses*. Overhead, banks of fluorescent lights issued a dim whiteness, a surreal glow that was tangent to the murky edges of the cellar. Directly underneath the fluorescents was a bulky wooden workbench with a scattering of tools on its surface. Mounted on its north end was a vice clamp, and firmly bolted down on the southern end was a bench grinder. Flush with the wall, which would be the west section of the basement, was another workbench. Unlike the other, this workstation was of steel construction and all the tools hung above in neat, organized rows on a pegboard. There was another vice clamp, this one welded on the southern corner, and just on the outside of the northern corner, set level and flush with the wall, was an oxyacetylene tank, the torch itself carefully coiled and hung on the pegboard next to the tank. The eastern portion of the basement served as storage for the Sanders family with three sets of steel racks that ran a little over half the length of the basement, starting near the stairs and ending just a few feet beyond Earnest's work area. Each rack was loaded with old toys and out of date appliances, "junk" was what Elizabeth Sanders coined it, with about a two-foot gap from one set of shelves to the next.

Far off in the southeastern corner of the basement, stood another set of shelve reserved for the storage of holiday decorations: Halloween, Thanksgiving, and Christmas. Ten-year-old Ray Sanders and his cousin, nine-year-old Roy Sanders, sat on the cool concrete, backs against the wall, paging through a stack of old comic books. Both boys, their youthful love of comics and cartoons based on such, were adorned in the tee-shirt of their favorite characters, Ray with his *X-men* and Roy with his *Fantastic 4*. They wore faded blue jeans and sneakers and both Ray, with his midnight black hair and Roy with his firehouse red hair, had close-cropped haircuts. In most basements, there would be light spilling in from the windows along the tops of the concrete walls, but not this one since black paint coated each window. "Keeps it cooler for when we have to store perishables," his dad had replied once when Ray had asked about it. He didn't know if it was cooler or not, all he knew was it made the lights overhead sort of spooky and if Roy hadn't insisted on coming down, he wouldn't have. He would rather read his comics up in his room.

"This sucks." Roy tossed an issue of *Spider-Man* back

into the pile, apparently growing bored, as young boys often do after sitting still for more than ten minutes at a stretch.

"You're the one who wanted to come down here," Ray said in his soft I'll-break-if-you-touch-me voice he had had back then. "Besides, what else is there to do?"

"Lots!" Ray chimed.

"Like what?"

"Like…" Roy considered this, looked thoughtful and excited, and then considered again. "Why not see if your dad will let us go down to the river? We could fish or, or maybe catch a snapper! That would be cool."

The idea of catching a snapping turtle, a little beastie that would surely end up making a snack of their fingers, was interesting enough, and the idea of fishing sounded even better, but he already knew what his dad would say. "Not without an adult, son. Maybe tomorrow, okay? Got a lot of stuff to work on right now to try to earn us some extra spending money. And until Omnifab stops all this layoff bullshit, I got to do what I can to make sure we got us some food on the table. You understand, don't you, son?"

And Ray would say that he did understand because he did. At any other time, his dad would jump at the opportunity to be sitting on the riverbank or out in his boat with his rod and reel in hand, maybe drinking a few beers, and telling his son all sorts of interesting stories. But since the layoff two months before, his dad had been real busy doing odds and ends jobs to bring in money for bills and groceries. So, yeah, Ray understood. At least there was a legitimate reason, not like Billy William's dad who never took Billy anywhere or even cared to. He overheard his dad tell his Uncle James that all Billy was to Larry Williams was a punching bag. For the longest time after that, Ray carried a picture in his head of poor Billy hanging up by his ankles on their back porch while his dad punched on him like Sylvester Stallone in one of those *Rocky* movies.

"My dad won't let us go down there without a grown-up, afraid we'll fall in the river and drown or something. And he's too busy working on getting us money to go down there."

Roy frowned and made a sound that was somewhere between a grunt and squeal. He began to fidget, stood up, and kicked over the stack of comics, scattering them over Ray's feet.

"Hey!" Ray snapped in surprise and mild frustration. "Why'd you do that for?"

"I dunno."

Looking at Roy, standing there like a wooden doll with an empty expression on his face, what one could only characterize as a blank stare, Ray sighed. He was annoyed with his cousin, true, especially since Roy seemed to be having another one of those tantrums that kept him in constant relations with a belt, but he was sort of bored himself. He just wished Roy wouldn't act like such a spaz when he didn't get his way; it was a real pain to deal with.

"We could ride our bikes," Ray suggested and stood up, pushing a few comics out of the way with his foot. "Dad made me a bike trail. It has hills and dirt mounds to jump and everything."

"I didn't even bring my bike," Roy complained.

"That's okay, I have two. You can ride my old one."

"Won't be the same," Roy replied stubbornly.

"It's the same kind," Ray persisted.

"Uh-uh." Roy shook his head. "Mine has those cool stunt pegs on the wheels, yours don't."

More than mildly frustrated now, Ray said, "You don't even know how to use those. And I've never seen you do any stunts on your bike. I've seen you fall off it, though."

"Hey!" Roy said with such suddenness, that Ray nearly slipped and fell trying to back away. "We could go and target shoot with your pellet gun! Jimmy Fontaine says if you shoot a can of Coca Cola with a pellet gun it'll explode!" Roy spread his hands wide apart. "BOOM! Just like that!"

Yet another way Roy could trigger the old irritation button was how he got overexcited about some things, like the target practice idea just now. And that always led to problems when the idea was shot down, usually another tantrum or a "cryin' fit" as his granddaddy called it. So, Ray braced and said, "I don't have any pellets, used them up shooting at cans."

"Oh," Roy said, disappointed. "That sucks."

"We could go upstairs and watch cartoons." Another suggestion and one Ray hoped would pry them from the basement. It smelled funny down here and he just wanted to get away from it. That and it felt rather... *It feels bad.* Yeah, bad was exactly how it felt, bad like the haunted houses or haunted trails the school set up and took you through on Halloween night. The high school kids dressed up in scary outfits and waited for you to come by, waited so they could jump out from some dark corner or shadow of a tree screaming, moaning, and lurching around. It all looked somewhat stupid when you knew what it was, but when you weren't expecting it, it gave you a good scare. And up until the point where they jumped out, you were almost completely in the dark and it felt *bad* with all the spooky noises. This felt like that now, only different—worse somehow.

"We watched cartoons the last time I came over. *B-o-r-i-n-g*. Boring."

"Well, what *do* you want to do?"

"I dunno," Roy said and walked over to the adjacent corner where another rack hosted a variety of Elizabeth Sanders' canned preserves.

It was dark in that corner where only a fraction of the fluorescent light dared to touch it as if the light itself were afraid of the darkness huddled up in that corner. Ray could see Roy or rather a gray, blotchy outline of Roy. His mom had taken some pictures last year at his birthday party, which they had held on the back porch, and some of those pictures she had taken near sundown when the light was poor. There was no flash on the camera, either, and his mom told him later that was why some of the pictures had gray ghosts in them. "I didn't put the flash on, and the lighting was bad, and now look at how some of these pictures turned out…ruined. Nothing but gray ghosts is what's in 'em," she had said and promised that the next time she wouldn't forget the flash. That's what Roy looked like now, a gray ghost from some old, botched Kodak photo.

"Hey! Come here!" Roy ordered. "Help me with the light."

Although not as bright as the fluorescent tubes that provided light throughout the rest of the basement, the small sixty-watt bulb over Roy's head was decent. Not bright enough to blind, but bright enough to leave those little yellow spots floating around if turned on when you were asleep or maybe just resting your eyes some. Ray shivered at the thought of falling asleep down here in the dark, with God knew what lurking in the shadows. It tripled his feeling that something bad was down here, something potentially dangerous.

Don't be a baby, Ray, it's just your basement. All's down here is junk.

But still…

"C'mon, Ray. I can't reach it by myself."

Ray started to protest about how he was only an inch taller and how was he supposed to reach the drawstring for the light, then nipped it before it left his mouth. Arguing with Roy was like arguing with the stump of a tree. Instead, he walked over next to his cousin, trying to ignore the gooseflesh on his arms, and tilted back his head to look at the light. He made a feeble hop to reach for the string and then shrugged his shoulders.

"That's the best you can do?"

"Why did you come over here anyway? All's here is peaches and apples and junk my mom put away in them jars."

"I dunno."

"Let's go upstairs," Ray said and started towards the stairs.

"No!" Roy grabbed a handful of Ray's shirt and pulled him back.

The collar of Ray's shirt tightened around his throat, choking him, and he stumbled backward, gaining his balance at the last moment. He turned to Roy who still had his hand knotted in Ray's shirt.

"Let go, dummy!" Ray shouted, his shirt twisted sideways from where he turned to face Roy and batted at his cousin's hand.

Roy let go of his grip and Ray shook his shirt to straighten it, although it remained partially twisted, then started for the stairs once more.

"Wait!"

"What?" Ray asked, irritated and a bit frightened. Not only was there a horrible smell down here, but there were also, at least Ray thought he could hear them, hushed, whispering sounds, like people talking real low, the way he and Roy would do on the nights Roy slept over so they wouldn't get caught staying up past bedtime, or "lights out" as his dad called it. But some of the words he was hearing—words *you* think *you're hearing*—he didn't understand. In fact, they didn't sound like words at all, or least not any words he had ever heard before. Gibberish is the word he was looking for, like baby sounds, not words, but gibberish.

"Help me push this. It's on wheels."

The radio. That's what you're hearing, you big dummy.

But it wasn't the radio. The radio wasn't playing anything.

I didn't shut it off. Roy had to have shut it off, but he passed it by without even a look. But he had to have shut it off because I didn't. When did he do it?

"C'mon, Ray, help me," Roy whined. Roy shoved against the shelves with his shoulder and there was thick clink as the glass jars rattled and bumped into one another.

"Why'd you turn off the radio?" Ray asked.

"What? I ain't touched the radio. You goin' to help me or not?"

"I don't think we should. I think we should—"

"Why you bein' such a wuss? There's something cool back behind there, can't you feel it?"

All Ray could feel was fear. Whatever may be behind his mother's rack of preserves, other than dust bunnies and dead mice, could *stay* back there, as far as he was concerned. The smell was worse yet, like spoiled milk and rotted meat, and it was making his stomach sick. And those noises, those hissed whispers, were louder, rebounding in his head like a pinball.

Open the gate. Hunger. Feed. Nourish. What did that mean? Those were the only words he could pick out of the babble and understand.

Another clink of glass. Roy panting like an exhausted dog. Whispered voices in unknown tongues. The slight, almost inaudible hum of the fluorescents. Sweat on his forehead, despite the cool, damp air in the basement.

"You should stop that before you break one of momma's jars," Ray croaked. Suddenly his throat felt dry, gritty as if he had swallowed a sheet of sandpaper. "She'd be pretty mad. Whoopin' mad."

"Not if you help me push. We won't break not a one."

Without even realizing he was doing it, Ray grabbed the rack and helped Roy roll it out away from the wall. One of the casters on the back end caught a rock, a rat turd, or something solid enough to keep it from rolling and it dragged, vibrating the shelves. The jars of preserved fruits and vegetables rattled fiercely, but none fell.

"Wow!" Roy said. Awed, dumbfounded, and intrigued, all the above. "You see that, Ray! *You see that!*"

He did see it; in fact, he wished he couldn't see it. Bright, greenish-blue light seeped from between the cinderblocks and quickly enveloped everything in its peculiar video-game glow. The hair on the back of his neck prickled. A sharp, vehement buzzing sent spiked agony through his head as if a thousand angry hornets were swarming around in there. He put a shaking hand to his nose and pulled it away smeared with blood. Welled tears began to spill over his cheeks. Then it was gone, no fading into nothingness, no slow dying drone, just gone.

"*Ray! What—*"

Roy was reaching out towards the wall with a deranged wonder in his eyes and somehow that seemed like the wrong thing to do. But Ray stood there, letting his cousin reach out to the unknown, still caught between belief and disbelief at what had just happened. What had just happened? He didn't know. His fear, combined with what his parents had tried to explain—somewhat unsuccessfully—about what was real and not real, that fine line between believe and make-believe was dissolving coherent thought.

"Don't..." Ray started, but his voice didn't reach above a hoarse whisper, and he was vaguely aware that he was trembling. Warm, sticky wetness trickled down his legs as his bladder let go and soaked through the front of his jeans. Somehow, this made him want to cry harder than the strange lights and noises; big boys were not *supposed* to pee their pants, not even when they were scared.

"Roy..." he tried again. "...Don't touch it."

But Roy was too far into it, *too* gone, to hear a word he said. The look on his face reminded Ray of one of those crazy terrorist men from one of those action movies his dad liked to watch, the ones his mom would fuss over if she found out his dad was letting him watch them. He was breathing hard, his fingers shaky and he was humming something under his breath that Ray couldn't make out.

"Stop it, Roy! Stop it!"

Something happened then. Something, something... What?

What had happened then? That part of the memory was still lost to him, trapped somewhere in his mind; locked away from him the way you would lock important documents or valuables in a safe. Ray stood on his front porch with the rain pattering the roof and the muggy afternoon sky tapering away into twilight, trying to recall a more vivid image of that day almost twenty years ago, when he was ten and Roy was nine. His dad had hurt his arm that day, Ray remembered the blood-soaked towel wrapped around his arm and there was something about a seal, something his dad spoke to Uncle James about over the phone.

CHAPTER SIXTEEN

Ray walked back inside and gawked at the items scattered on his couch from one end to the other. He had remembered some of it earlier, standing beside Roy on his front porch while the pouring rain fell in fat heavy drops. There was more to it, he knew that, a lot more, but he couldn't seem to bring the rest of the story into focus. *You were scared then and you're scared now, that's why. You pansy.* Yes, he was scared, and he didn't need the internal yammering of self-contempt to remind or belittle him about it. What he did need was to be in-the-know, as they used to say as kids. *Roy knows; he remembers it all.* Yes, perhaps he did, but just like with the growling severed head of Lady, Mrs. Johnson's beloved German Sheppard, he wasn't ready to face it, not yet.

What would it take?

Go away! He commanded the voice in his head. No answer to that question, none whatsoever, and it occurred to him in grim fashion that the constant recurrence of 'what would it take' was either a mockery of his cowardice as a child or a reminder of his inability to cope with the recent horrors on his return home as an adult. *Maybe though, it means you're crazy, crazy, crazy.* Yes, that too was an option, and not one that he hadn't already considered, either. But if he was crazy, then so was Roy. After all, they had both witnessed something a tad bit on the impossible side, hadn't they? A little something from beyond the grave.

Don't touch it, Roy.

Don't touch what? But that was a stupid question. The wall behind his mother's preserves that was what he hadn't wanted Roy to touch and Roy *had* touched it and released… *Damn it! Why can't I remember more of this shit? What the fuck was so bad? What was so goddamned bad?*

"You think this'll do it?" Roy asked. Slow, thick, frightened, he wasn't right out asking, but his voice hinged on him needing reassurance. In a way, they were both still the little boys of yesteryear…small, pale and shaking at the things bumping in the night: a frenzied scratching on a pane of glass in the darkest hours or maybe a creaking floorboard. Their adult minds told them that the scratching was the wind blowing a limb against the window and that the creaking floorboard was no more than the sound houses make when they settle. But still…

"Well," Roy persisted.

"It'll have to," Ray replied evenly. "It's just going to have to."

Ray picked up a large hunting knife from the couch and held it out in front of his face. Captivated by the way the light glinted off the stainless-steel blade, Ray fell backward in time; back through the years of memories stored and forgotten, backward into 1998, when the two of them had been too stupid to let well enough alone. *We were kids, doesn't that count? Doesn't that release us from at least a fraction of blame? Doesn't it?*

His dad had had a big hunting knife in his hand when he came to pull them away, but before that, Roy had touched the wall and the screams had come. How could he have not remembered this at once? It was so clear now; a live performance from the damned? The screams were coming from the dead people, the ones chained to the basement walls like prisoners in a dungeon, only they were not the lost souls from some old movie, hanging there flaking away from malnutrition. Someone or something had strung these poor bastards up and cut from asshole to appetite, as his dad would say, steaming ropes of intestines heaped in piles on the floor beneath their feet. Hearts still beating in the open cavity of their chests, eyes welling with tears of pain, crying for mercy, and screaming with throats that were nothing more than lumps of raw hamburger, those bodies hung writhing and squirming. How could he have forgotten such a horrendous nightmare? But it hadn't been a nightmare and there was...

"There was fog on the floor. All around us."

"Huh?" Roy, momentarily startled, then a look of remembrance and his pallor became that of a convalescent returning from a long, diffuse illness, such as cancer or AIDS—even though to Ray's knowledge there was no true cure of either.

"You remember?"

Roy nodded his head slowly and said. "And the bodies... On the floor, the wall...Christ, some were nailed to the ceiling or staked to it, or whatever. And those damn whining sounds! Jesus, Ray, it sounded like somebody was scratching a chalkboard with a garden rake. You remember what they looked like?"

It was Ray's turn to nod. Like the image of the condemned ones hung from his basement wall, he was baffled as to how he could possibly forget such hideous creatures, and even more confused at how easily he could remember them now as if they were popping into his head on cue. Like he hadn't forgotten them at all. "You said they looked like big, ole giant deer ticks," Ray said with a semi-crazy grin. "Only that wasn't quite right, was it? They had—"

"—Tentacles like an octopus," Roy finished. "But not exactly similar because they had only two pairs of tentacles, and those were coming out of their backs and reaching—"

"—for us." Ray shivered and shook it off. "There were little mouths on the end of them too, remember that? Little mouths full of teeth. And they kept smacking open and shut."

"How could we forget something like that?" Ray stiffened at hearing his own thoughts being voiced and listened as Roy went on, not seeming to notice Ray's unease. "I mean, how is it possible? That's not the kind of shit you forget. What episode of *Transformers* the dinobots appeared in or the name of some kid that transferred in for a few months then left out again, that shit you forget, but not this? Know what I mean?"

Ray dropped the knife on the couch. It bounced on the cushion and bumped against its twin with a clink. "I don't know," he answered honestly and unlatched a small leather case. From it, he removed a 9mm handgun and began to give it a thorough examination. "I couldn't begin to tell you why we forgot, I'm not a shrink."

"No, but you took a semester of Psychology. That makes you the closest thing to an expert we have right now." Roy unlatched another leather case, identical to the one Ray had opened, took out another 9mm, and gave the weapon a quick exam before putting it back into its case.

Hearty, effervescent laughter welled up, and Ray nearly choked on it. "*One* semester, that's it. And it was only for a few credits. You don't think any of that crap Mr. Ratcliff taught actually sunk in, do you?"

"You passed, so something must have."

"I passed thanks to Sally Anne Baker not knowing when to cover up during tests. Just looked right over her shoulder. Thanks to good, old Sally I was exempt from the exams on grades."

Ray was grinning big and wide, the grin of an adolescent that has just outwitted their parents for the first time and gotten away with it then saw the disheartened look on his cousin's face and the smile faltered, then fell flat. Even if he didn't know jack shit about Psychology—and he didn't, he hadn't lied about that—Roy still needed something to hold him together, some little hint of wisdom that would stave off a nervous breakdown.

Or maybe it was a trifle beyond need; he was clinging to the hope that Ray would have all the answers and lead them through this unscathed, clinging to it as tightly as the survivor of a ship lost at sea would to the floating debris left in its wake. What was he supposed to say? *You're the one who touched the damn wall! You tell me! Damn it! You tell me! You're the one who was curious, remember! My dad used that big hunting knife to slit open his arm because of you! Slit his arm open all the way up to the elbow and damn near to the bone. Had to have umpteen billion stitches because of you! Why did he do that, cut himself like that? For the seal? What seal? Oh, damn, why can't I remember?*

"I'm scared, Ray." There was a waver in Roy's voice

and not too surprisingly, his lips were quivering. He ran a hand through his long black hair and looked at Ray with eyes promising tears. "First that crazy shit in your back-yard, that's what got me started remembering, and now, now I don't exactly know what I'm saying. We're getting ready to go down in your basement with my dad's guns and do who knows what, and we don't even know if a gun will work, or even if there's anything down there to begin with."

Roy dropped his gaze to his shoes, a sheaf of hair like a funeral veil fell over his face, and he was silent for a long time. Suddenly, Ray was furious with himself for the blame he was placing on his cousin's shoulders. It was quiet blame, but nonetheless, he should have never let it enter his thoughts. He was about to say something comforting or at least something congenial enough to bring Roy around to a better mood when Roy's head rose, and slowly turned, the hair falling away from his face to reveal an expression of fear, guilt, rage, sorrow, a wild mixture of emotions laboring to be released.

He said, "They need you, Ray. For a sacrifice. Your blood. Only your blood can either create or dissolve the seal. And it's not *creating* a new seal they're interested in."

What the hell are you talking about? "Where'd that come from?" Ray asked. His complexion was now the color of ash and his heart was hammering in his chest.

Don't do it, Ray. Don't be the sacrifice. Don't let them get to you. It was the voice of the girl, the one in his dreams, the one with the pale skin and big, pleading eyes. *They* want *you to go down there, Ray. They* need *you to go down there.*

YOU WILL NOT LISTEN TO HER, RAY! SHE'S JUST A LITTLE WHORE! SHE WANTS TO HURT YOU! The he/she entity roared in his head and just as in his dream, Ray staggered back a few steps in surprise. Then, the girl's voice again: *I'm not trying to hurt you, Ray. I want to help.*

"–It just popped in there. I don't know—"

"What?"

"I said 'I don't know where that came from'. It just popped in my head. I don't feel so hot, dude. I think that maybe we should just leave it alone, you know. Let whatever's down there have the house. Shit. Let it have the whole goddamned town…I don't care. You and me can head on down to Florida. No worries."

"And your dad and Dianne?"

Roy sat down in the La-Z-Boy, propped his elbows on his knees, and as he dropped his face into his hands and that same black veil of hair drew around his head and hung there like the wings of a dead crow. To Ray, he looked ready to abandon the here and now in favor of some other saner environment, somewhere where severed dog's heads didn't growl and little tick-like creatures with tentacles didn't exist. Roy said he was scared, and Ray believed him one hundred percent, primarily because Ray was scared, too. He was more afraid now than he had ever been in his—well, no, not more than when he was ten; when he was ten that was when he had been the most afraid. But this ran a very close second.

"Roy–" but that was as far as he got. That's when the front door burst inward and James Sanders staggered through, blue chambray work shirt soaked in blood and encrusted with gore. His jeans were in tatters and there was a large cut on his forehead. He stood there, in the doorway, breathing hard and staring at his son and nephew with tired eyes; he looked to have survived some great battle, or maybe a missile barrage.

Roy's head snapped towards his father and his hands clasped together, elbows still resting on his knees. "Dad?

A long, red-rocked road winding through colonies of pines, oaks, elms, red maples and sparse dotting's of black gums lay before the blurry radiance of a cloud-shrouded moon like a bloody, infected wound. The usual calls and communications of the local nocturnal residents inhabiting this wood were nil. Not even the throaty dialogue of the toads was present. These small, bulky amphibians that had earlier found so much joy in the damp grass and the woodland substrate of pine needles and fallen leaves were now only silent, brooding shapes hidden away in their burrows.

A buoyant, chill wind soughed through the treetops, a brisk, natural melody that rose in a soft crescendo and then tapered off before repeating the tune in an endless series of encores. Then from underneath the wind's enchanting song, came the supple purr of a V-6 engine, preceded by two dreary eyes of light, bouncing and bobbing with every small rut the Datsun's tires happened upon. Dianne Townsend sat behind the wheel, piloting along the bumpy path with the windows up and the radio off, the concert of the wind and the Datsun's engine drowning beneath the waters of her pooling thoughts.

She felt faint and tired, wanting nothing more than to cuddle up under the warmth of her thick, goose down comforter and go back to sleep. But tonight's work was far from finished and she found herself wishing that she had left Maple Grove when she had had the chance, back when she was seventeen and her best friend, Betty

Douglas, tried to convince Dianne to run away with her to Nevada.

"What's in Nevada?" Dianne had asked, with a hearty bout of giggles. "Other than not a damn thing."

"*Vegas!*" Betty had replied enthusiastically. "Think about it, Dianne! The money we could make. Could be one of those showgirls, I hear they make good money!"

"Me?" Dianne had giggled again, unaware that her days of giggles, boys, and dreams would soon be at an end. "Get real."

"Please, Di," Betty sometimes called her Di, Dianne remembered with a fondness that sent a tear rolling down her cheek. "You got the legs for it, and don't tell me you don't."

"Maybe I got the legs for it, but I sure as hell ain't got the talent for it. I don't know a thing about choreography, and you know it."

There was more discussion, mostly pleas from Betty and an endless stream of pitches to try to sell Diane on the wonders of Las Vegas. Then they hugged, kissed each other on the cheek and Betty Douglas was taking reluctant steps down the Townsend front walk, out through the gate and climbing into the passenger side of her boyfriend's 1980 Ford pickup. A year later, almost to the day, Dianne's mother brought her the news of Betty's murder, an apparent mob-related incident that left her best friend's naked, scavenger-ravaged body lying to rot on the sunbaked desert floor. A wandering hermit had found the corpse, a man by the name of Gary Pritchett, who believed at first that he had found a desert treasure. The shiny object that had caused his mouth to salivate and his mind to turn towards a night of cheap booze and even cheaper whores, was, in fact, Betty Douglas's wrist-watch, complete with Betty Douglas's arm and attached to what remained of Betty Douglas, the pretty young brunette from Alabama with dreams of becoming a famous Las Vegas showgirl. Dianne had wept for her friend and had sworn to everyone that if she had been with her that Betty would still be alive, regardless of how many pointed out that if Dianne and Betty had been together, it could very well have been both of them sharing such a grizzly fate.

Nevertheless, Dianne believed they could have escaped from that horror and lived to this day happy and content, possibly sunbathing under a California sun and gossiping, growing old and free without any burdens. *That's bullshit, you know, and even as much shit that has happened between you and him, James Sanders was a good husband and Roy was—well, Roy was never the ideal son, but you loved him all the same. After all, you possibly could have died right there alongside Betty and would have never known the love that you and James had shared. Died as some dreamy schoolgirl with stars in her eyes and a knife in her throat.*

And you're being selfish, she scolded herself. She was not the only one in this mess and it wasn't fair for her to think otherwise. Her biggest fault, selfishness aside, or selfishness in her opinion, was her naive belief that everyone else involved in this particular turn of events was at fault. But there really was no fault. You couldn't blame Ray and Roy for what was happening no more than Dianne could be blamed for her friend's murder out in Nevada. What was the old saying? Shit happens. Yes, and shit was happening in big, steamy piles now, wasn't it?

The Datsun hit a bump, aggressively shaking the small car from the jolt. Beside her in the passenger seat, the girl grunted in her sleep and Dianne winced, the wound on her left shoulder singing a death metal chorus of pain. This was where one of those S.O.B.s had lanced her with its stinger, and now the substance, whatever it was, that the creatures used to paralyze their prey had worn off and every little bump and shake felt like a set of teeth clamping down on her shoulder.

There was a curve up ahead and Dianne slowed the car down and got ready to ease the brakes. She knew that curve well. There was an uneven dip and an even deeper set of ruts, and the Datsun came close to dragging its bottom on the raised middle strip of the road every time she drove through here and if you hit the curve *too* fast and *too* hard, it would drag and scrape and shake like the devil. Her wound bothered her, but the girl was at the forefront of her mind. The poor thing had been through enough excitement already, and there was no telling what was yet in store; Dianne didn't want to scare or excite her unnecessarily.

Five minutes later, Dianne parked at the edge of the Sanders' driveway, the little Datsun idling softly, thankful for the rest. Parked out front next to Ray's Tahoe was James's blue Dodge Ram. James had beaten them here, which was no wonder considering how heavy a foot her ex-husband had. He was inside, convincing or doing his damndest to convince the boys of what they must do. She looked over at the girl who seemed almost comatose; balled up in the passenger seat; knees against her chest; head down. Dianne felt bad for the girl, Julie was her name, Julie Fontaine, and wished that she didn't have to suffer through this nightmare. But Elizabeth had said there was something special about her, and when Dianne had woken from the dream, she had found Julie's address scrawled on a piece of notepaper stuck to her refrigerator by an apple-shaped magnet.

I hope you're right, Ellie, Dianne thought and eased the Datsun forward, in the direction of Earnest Sanders' riverside cabin. The wind whipped and moaned, and the moon poked nonchalantly out from beneath a cloud, a silent, considering observer of the events unfolding in the world of man.

CHAPTER SEVENTEEN

Had this all really happened or was it a dream? It sure felt like a dream but at the same time, it had felt *so* real. A waking dream? She wasn't sure.

There were screams, shouts, and gunshots. A loud, metallic rattling in her kitchen, clinks, clanks, bangs, and bongs, it had sounded like every pot and pan she owned was tossing around, a battlefield scattered not with corpses but with kitchen utensils. Before all of that, though, before the chaos, the atmosphere in her apartment was serene. Not family movie night serene, but the tranquility of dozing under her big, fluffy *Peanuts* comforter with classic rock pouring from her stereo was bliss, nevertheless. In all honesty, it was the best sleep she'd had in weeks or the best sleep she'd had since Donnie died. Around the time he died, the nightmares had started. But they weren't quite nightmares, were they? Odd dreams, something akin to a significantly hellish acid trip is what they were, but close enough. She didn't even remember exactly what it was that had stirred her from her sleep.

Yes, you do, a cold, hard, traitorous inner voice assured her. *You are just like the other one in that you are too afraid to admit what's happening, afraid of seeing what a rational, civilized world chooses to ignore.*

Where did that last thought come from? Other one?

You know you have to remember, and not just tonight, either, or the last few weeks. Dig all the way in, girl. Remember what secrets you hold, the ones not even your parents knew of. Remember? What was it that made you different as a girl, so special? What was it? Dig, dig, and dig. The other kids knew you were different. They didn't know the how or why, but they sensed it, feared it, teased you about it. But it is that difference that you have to rely on; that difference that will make a difference.

I'm not different, her mind spoke up in defiance. *I never was.*

Now her dream world woke around her, filled with images that were wholly memory. Her apartment; plain, white walls tacked with posters and a few family photos. Faded blue carpet with a big spaghetti stain just under the lip of the couch, which was her best attempt to hide it. A wobbly entertainment center, a used gift from her brother in Huntsville, a cheap wafer board construct he picked up years before at some retail store or the other. A forty-five-inch Sony flat screen T.V. set at its center, an inexpensive off-brand DVD player set atop it. On the left set of shelves was an unimpressive collection of movies, about fifteen or twenty in total. On the right was a grander collection of, statues—wizards and dragons mostly—with a few fairies and elves for diversity. The crown of this collection was of a wizard in a long, red, jeweled robe standing on a mountain's peak and facing off against a menacing red dragon designed to appear as if it was hovering, wings spread wide, neck craned low, its head on the level with the wizard. This had been a birthday gift from her baby sister some years back.

"Julie. Do you understand your gift now?"

"I don't have a gift. I'm just me, so will you please leave me alone."

"You reconstructed that room of your apartment perfectly."

"It's a memory. Memory in a dream. Please just go away. Please!"

"For others, maybe, but they cannot perceive quite like this. Tell me something, Julie. How many dreams have you had that were this real?"

Julie stumbled over this question in her mind, flipping it over like a hotcake on a griddle, giving it every ounce of attention her deflated state of mind could offer. She had had a good many realistic dreams as of late. But before that? Before Donnie's death. Had there been others?

"I don't know. I don't want to know." Tears coursed down her cheeks and she tried to turn away from these images, quiet now, but she knew what was about to happen, what she was about to relive, and she didn't want to see or hear any of it again. She closed her eyes.

When she opened her eyes, Donnie was there. His strong, calloused hands, prominent veins appearing just behind the knuckles and snaking around under his fore-arms, ending an inch or so before the crease of his elbows, were on her shoulders. He was dressed as he was the day, she met him, Abercrombie tee, blue jeans, and a well-worn pair of Nike high top sneakers. His hair a bright, Ron-Howard-red, cut short and combed back, the crease in his hair left by his Atlanta Braves ball cap visible from where he had taken it off and tossed it in the cab of his pickup. Dotting his arms, underneath the tan and fine wisps of hair, were the ghosts of boyhood freckles and his eyes… That was where the resemblance of her first sighting of Donnie Atkins ended. They were still that deep jade green she had loved looking into, but they were missing that dangerous glint that had turned her on to Donnie from the moment he casually asked her out, without a trace of shyness in his voice. The change was so unlike Donnie, so out of character for him, that Julie tensed up and tried to pull away, but he held on, firm and unflinching.

His eyes were kind. *That* was what kept throwing her. Like shoes tumbling in a dryer, her heart thumped. Click, click, thump. Click, click, thump. This wasn't Donnie Atkins, the bad-tempered, although passionate, young man she was dating up until he was run down by Sonny McLain. Old Sonny driving his big rig way too damn fast down a town road posted with a twenty-five mile per hour speed limit. This was a Donnie as unfamiliar to her as a beggar on the street.

"We all make mistakes," he said, pulling her into an embrace. *"We make mistakes and have to live or die with the consequences. I made my share, more than my share if we were to get right down to it, and the biggest mistake I could have made never happened. The night I died I wanted to hurt you, was going to hurt you, and that would have been the biggest mistake out of a career of mistakes. I was going to hurt you because you had made me mad, and it was my fault. I was, well not stupid, but uninformed. Being alive, in a physical form with all its trials and errors is a privilege, a right that too many shun and spit on. You're alive, Julie, and you have a gift that can help so many others. Don't ignore it; don't run from what it is that you must do. My mother shares your talents, but it's*

not her calling, it's yours. Her role in this, sadly, does not end well...

Standing here in Donnie's arms, face pressed against his chest, the smell of Axe body spray wafting under her nose, Julie Fontaine had never been so confused in her life. The man holding her looked like Donnie, sounded like Donnie, but spoke softer, kinder, and with a distinct increase in vocabulary. This, like the gentle light in his eyes, was not like the Donnie Atkins she knew at all, he of clipped, hurried sentences. *Am I imagining this? Dreaming up the man I wished Donnie had of been?*

"I'm not dreamt up, Julie. There is a change when you pass over, but that's not important, you'll see for yourself someday. What is important is that you face up to the twisted reality that my family helped to create so long ago by two men like you, two men that abused their gifts.

She was about to ask what he meant when the world began to shake. Lifting her head from his chest, she watched as her brother's beat up, second-hand entertainment center spat her movies, statues, and T.V. onto the floor. Dragons, wizards, elves, and fairies shattered, and the television screen exploded. Her movies hit the floor and spread out like a dropped deck of cards. Julie shut her eyes and then opened them again in a squint and grunted. Her mind was pushing something away. Her neighbor, James Sanders, Roy's dad, had come over to help, had saved Dianne Townsend from a busted-up Doug Feldman. When did Dianne Townsend show up? And the St. Bernard, she stabbed it, but when did that happen?

Then it was dark, all except a dull lime green glow. Julie vaguely remembered climbing into Dianne Townsend's little matchbox of a car and curling up and falling into a frightened, depressed sleep. The glow was the Datsun's dash lights and Julie again closed her eyes. Donnie was gone. The living room of her apartment was gone. The madness that had happened there was over. All that remained was the dark and mocking laughter of *them*.

The clouds and moon were at it again, their little game of hide and seek. Thanks to the cloud cover, there was nary a star in the sky and the wind was tugging at Judd's clothes something fierce. The rain wasn't quite finished, not yet—he could smell it on the breeze, feel it in every whipping current. And from the looks of things up above, it was going to be a whopper of a downpour, maybe twice that of what had fallen earlier.

Judd took a long drag of his cigarette, burning it to the filter and flicking away the butt, exhaling in a plume of smoke like a mushroom cloud rolling from between his chapped lips. Things were going sour on him, as sour as a glass of milk left out in the sun. Dale was dead, blew his own goddamned head off, *they* had told him so. *They* had told him how the woman had been too much for Dale to handle. Judd wasn't surprised at this; the boy had always been the frail sort. Anyone who couldn't control their kids and wife and keep them in line with the role of the husband and father (which was the dominant role in family living, as far as Judd was concerned), deserved to have their brains drying on the walls and carpet of their own house.

But it wasn't just Dale's failure that had him upset. If it was just that, he could ignore it. The problem now was the woman, his late brother's wife, Maria, and the

Fontaine girl from town. Both were having the dreams, but the dreams alone were not enough to pose a threat. After all, there was only so much a disembodied spirit could do. However, the Fontaine girl was unique; had some special talent that scared the bejesus out of *them*. And Maria held yet another secret—something more than the talent she shared with the girl— something neither *they* nor Judd could pick up on. Nevertheless, it was a threat and Judd feared that if those two women got together, it would play hell on the plan. All of this, and he had yet to deal with the Sanders clan. Never in his wildest dreams had he even considered Ray Sanders as a problem, and when the boy had moved away Judd thought that was the end of it. He didn't expect Ray to stick around after Elizabeth's funeral at all. Instead, he expected the boy to cut out and hotfoot it back to Florida. Without Ray, his cousin Roy would have been easy pickings.

Ain't doin' you much good standin' here thinking about it, Judd thought as a strong gust whipped around the eaves of his house, causing a few lose shingles to flap around in scratchy thuds. On the west corner of the house, the wind caught hold of a stack of tin sheets, clattering and shrieking through them, sounding like some bizarre metal animal protesting its last in dying agony.

Judd turned and went inside, letting the screen door slam behind him. It caught a piece of the wind, swung open, and then slammed shut again. He strode down the hall, a tall, husky man in faded torn overalls and checked shirt, yet no heavy clunks or clops issued forth; he moved along like a wraith in smooth, silent strides. Down the hall he went, snatching the keys to his Ford from the coffee table and his father's old double-barrel shotgun from where it leaned against the couch as he passed through.

There would be plenty of shells in a box behind the Ford's seat; enough to take care of what he had to do.

Once behind the wheel, slamming the door shut and firing up the engine in one smooth stroke, Judd took a moment to contemplate, to focus on what lay in wait for him over the next couple of hours. The two women would be first—they posed the biggest threat—and then he'd do the Sanders boys and use their blood to open a few locked doors. He'd have to be quick and as quiet as an old field mouse in case one, if not all, of them, had decided to bring along protection. Judd supposed he could park at the end of the road leading up to the Sanders' place; there was a thicket of trees where he could stash the Ford to keep it hidden from any passing traffic. Being dark and late, Judd didn't figure anyone would notice, and given the bottom looked about ready to drop out of the storm at any minute, not many folks in the Grove were apt to be running the roads.

Lighting a cigarette and dropping the Ford into drive, Judd pulled out of his driveway and nosed the old Ford towards town just as the first drops of rain speckled his windshield.

She could see neither moon nor sky; the overhead foliage formed a formidable canopy against it. It was as dark as a hell-bound soul, but somehow, amazingly somehow, she could see where she was and where she was going. Since leaving her house, her trek through the woods had been an easy one, as if the sun was burning high above. No, it wasn't exactly like the sun, not really. It was more like walking beneath the lights at the park, not as bright, but enough to see by, even though the nearest streetlamp was on the other end of about five acres of trees and brush.

But why am I in the woods to begin with, when my husband is lying dead in our bedroom? Why am *I out here?*

To end it, that strange voice blurted in her mind, quick, clipped, and final.

"Have to end it," Maria whispered underneath the drowning roar of the river off to her left. A drop of rain splashed down on her forehead and a few moments later, the woods around her came alive with heavy thuds as more raindrops collided with the tree leaves.

CHAPTER EIGHTEEN

Dianne had awoken from her dream that was not a dream—where dead friends sat down to have coffee and send you on ominous missions—and had found Julie Fontaine's address scribbled down in Elizabeth Sanders's smooth script on a piece of notepaper. The note had been stuck to the freezer half of the refrigerator with an apple-shaped magnet. Dianne had yanked it down, the magnet flying away to somewhere, landing and skidding to nonexistence beyond Dianne's line of sight, vanishing into that void where all objects below the range of significance disappear. Not that she noticed this; her attention was on the wrinkled piece of paper in her trembling hand and the words written on it. Even as she had gotten out of bed and trundled down the hallway in a sleep-leaden haze, Dianne had hoped, had prayed, that a dream was all she'd had. A creepy dream, of an old friend, speaking nonsense, but one look at her refrigerator had dissolved that in a hurry.

The first thing to strike her as she had gone over the

girl's name and address were not weird dreams with dead friends or some town girl with uncanny abilities, but that James was there. Not with the girl, but he and Roy shared an apartment at River View in the same building, right next door to her, in fact. That's when Dianne had crumpled the note into a ball, dropped it to the floor, and got dressed.

All sorts of thoughts had come to her on her drive to the River View apartments, none of them she could remember, except for one: for James Sanders to be asleep. Thinking back on it now, it had been a lucky thing for both her and the girl that he had not. If James Sanders had been asleep, Dianne and Julie would not have escaped the grizzly fate they no doubt would have suffered as an entrée for the monstrosities that had stormed Julie's cozy abode.

Dianne brought the Datsun to a stop at the end of the red-rocked road, holding back a shocked gasp at what the headlights high beams fell upon. The unkempt, overgrown strip of field before her couldn't possibly be the peaceful riverside paradise she had enjoyed on so many occasions. She, James, Earnest, and Elizabeth, had shared good times here while the river rushed along and bonfires popped and crackled, their flames licking the air. This was all wrong. The grass was almost higher than the Datsun's hood and the river, well she couldn't see the river, not even the pale reflection of the moon in its maddening rush for cover shone on the surface of the water, nor did the Datsun's high beams.

Hand steadied to key off the ignition, (a mercy that would shut out the ruin of the onetime-Eden caught in the headlights) Dianne glimpsed Julie shifting around in the passenger seat.

She ain't sleeping so much as she's knocked out. Can you blame her? Honestly? After seeing a corpse walk, could you really, truly, blame her? The girl is lucky to have any of her marbles left rolling around at all. And it had her by the throat, breathing its rotting breath in her face. How does that not *turn you into a nutcase?*

Soon she would have to wake the girl, as much she didn't want to, so they could saunter up to Earnest's old shack and do whatever they had to do there. What kind of trials was yet to be posed? What sorts of beasts were lurking in the high grass?

They would make it halfway to the cabin; *they* would let them get that far at least when the grass around them would start to rustle. At first, Dianne would assure Julie that it was nothing but the wind. Wasn't that how it was always explained? A loud bang against the side of the house on a stormy night, just the wind, ungodly moans, wails and whistles after the telling of a scary story, nothing but the wind. The wind was always the most logical culprit, but not this time. No, this time it would be the corpses—she didn't want to think of them as zombies, couldn't think of them as zombies, not when she knew what was curled up inside and pulling the strings. How would it go down? Would they leap up from the brush and pounce, or would they remain in hiding waiting to grab a hold of an ankle and pull her down? She hoped it would be the latter. At least the grass, as thick as it was, would spare her from seeing as one of *them* burst from dead human flesh, slimy limbs like entrails flailing around like out-of-control fire hoses, and dirty little mouths, filled with dirty, sharp little teeth, clamping around her throat.

Dianne's eyes popped open and she whirled her head in every direction it would turn to make sure no one was watching her, as if she had done something, she was ashamed of, like breaking wind in a public place. She had dozed off. Impossible after tonight's interlude? Not really. She was exhausted. For how long, was a better question? It was still dark out, so she couldn't have been out for an extensive amount of time, but that wasn't of much consolation.

She depressed a button on the side of her watch and the tiny screen lit up bright blue. Ten after two, so she had been out maybe ten minutes.

Still, it wasn't quite time yet. She leaned her head back against the seat. Maybe not a good idea considering how tired she was, but her neck needed a rest. Suddenly, her head felt as heavy as an anvil about the size one would see in old Warner Brother's cartoons. Her eyes batted. Once. Twice.

Numbing pain shot up and down her left shoulder and her eyes popped open again. Fresh blood rose from her wound and the makeshift tee-shirt bandage darkened into a deeper shade of scarlet. Dianne dropped her hand into her lap, unconsciously wiping the blood on her hand onto her jeans; her shoulder was throbbing like mad now, her wound reopened and upset. At least she was wide-awake.

The wound was good and deep, too. The bastard had stuck it to her right and proper. By tomorrow afternoon her shoulder would be stiff and about as flexible as a sheet of plywood. Dianne had managed to keep the Fontaine girl from getting her throat torn open, that was the mythical brighter side of the things, wasn't it? If James hadn't come in when he did…

…You wouldn't be sitting here, and neither would she.

Several of Julie's neighbors were stirring when Dianne had approached the girl's apartment, no doubt from the girl's screams, but not a single one of them looked like they wanted to be very neighborly and offer up any help, not when it sounded like someone was being murdered. To most of them, it sounded like a domestic issue and beyond the anonymous call to the cops; most people wouldn't risk any involvement in such a matter, especially when the violence was apt to fall back on them. Their role was observation more than anything else, and if possible, *silent observation.* Dianne had stepped around them, the murmured gossip and wagging, pointing fingers all in the background, playing a minor part in this tragedy. Someone had shouted at her, asking her if she was crazy. She was, probably, but Dianne had ignored this and as she had stepped inside and found the door to the apartment lying on the hood of someone's car, smoldering, Dianne had wanted to scream right along with her. Though it had turned to her, she had known the thing that had pinned Julie Fontaine against the wall with a bloody, lacerated hand wrapped around the girl's throat, was hideous. Worse yet, was that she had known what it was and what it wanted.

Most of what had happened from that point on was still unclear because of the poison injected into her from the thing's stinger. That was how she saw it, anyway, as a stinger; if there was a scientific name for what it was called, she didn't know what it was. What she did remember was rushing in to help the girl, trying to pull the damned thing away from her. That was when it had whirled around, giving Dianne a brief look at to whom the body had belonged before the new tenant had moved in. It was, or what was left of, Doug Feldman, a local boy who made meager living selling marijuana to the local potheads. Now, he was no more than a marionette. His long, greasy black hair, a mess of dried, clotted blood with loose chunks of his scalp that lay tangled in it like fish in a net, was limp around his shoulders. Several cuts had ringed his face, slivers of glass occupied most of them to Dianne's disgust, and his right eye had been a mass of congealed blood. He had smiled and Dianne had seen that most of Doug's teeth were missing or broken, jutting from torn gums like rocks jutting from some wasted landscape. It had mumbled something through split lips and broken teeth, a garbled message in a language she didn't understand, and white-hot pain had shot through her in torrents. She remembered looking down at the slick umbilical-like membrane that connected her to it, but not much else. Someone had shouted—a man, probably James—and someone had screamed, a girl, probably Julie, and then everything had faded away.

She had only been aware of being alive when James was putting them into the Datsun, shaking her, and calling her name over and over. She had opened her eyes and James had pulled her close, kissing her neck, his warm tears drying on her face.

"Take this," she had said and pushed him away, shoving Elizabeth's tarnished dolphin pendant into one of his open palms. "It was Liz's. She wants Ray to have it. It's—"

"–Her talisman," he had finished. "I know. It always was."

She tried to say something else, but James ushered her behind the wheel of the Datsun and shut the door. "No time, baby. You have to get the girl away from here."

Behind them, shouts and confused clatter rang out. James stood there, a big gash on his forehead and his clothes in tatters, and Dianne wondered just what he had gone through to save them. "I love you, Di, never forget that. Now get out of here. We need to have all of this behind us before the cops blow up the show."

With that, he turned and walked to his truck, no long *Casablanca* ending brimming with romance and mystery, just cut and dry. And she had driven out here where the girl was supposed to do something, something special.

Dianne was reaching over to wake the girl when the drivers' side door was jerked open.

⸺⊷⊶⊷⸺

"I guess you boys would like to know what's going on." James Sanders scrutinized the items on Ray's coffee table closely as he stripped away his gore-splattered work shirt. Underneath it was a plain white tee. He didn't know whether to laugh, cringe, or cry. Two 9mm handguns, two hunting knives, a couple of crucifixes, two necklaces made from cloves of garlic, a bible, and five vials of what James guessed was supposed to be holy water. The guns and knives would be useful, the rest utterly useless.

"I'm sort of curious," Ray admitted.

"Ditto," Roy agreed.

"I'll start with a little history lesson, boys, then I'll get to what happened tonight," James said as he nodded at the wadded shirt, he'd discarded on the coffee table. "Deal?"

"Sounds good to me," Ray said and would have been relieved if not for the severity of their situation. "How about you, Roy my Boy?"

Roy nodded slowly, almost carefully, and answered, "That's fine."

"This is going to take a minute or two, and probably you boys won't believe a whole lot of it." James took a sip of his coffee, setting the cup down on the end table beside the recliner, and itching with regret for not having told this tale sooner. Ray and Roy were sitting on the couch, their monster hunting supplies between them. Ray was leaning forward in anticipation and Roy was just rocking back and forth in a big bundle of nerves.

"Belief is a very narrow subject at this point," Ray commented bleakly.

James nodded and in an unknowing imitation of his son, he dropped his elbows on his knees and clasped his hands together. "We should have told you back when Earnest refurbished the seal—should have told you then and been done with it."

James thought Ray would say something at the mention of his father's name, possibly bombard him with questions, but he remained silent and intent with staring eyes urging James to continue.

"This goes back some years," James started, reaching a hand into his right pants pocket taking out a pack of cigarettes and a lighter. After lighting his cigarette and with the first puff of smoke circling his head like clouds around a mountaintop, James went on. "In the years between 1820 and 1860, Maple Grove wasn't much more than a river camp with a few little shanty cabins thrown here and there along the river. For the most part, it was just a group of fifty or more people tired of traveling, and by 1930, there was a good hundred and fifty people here, the majority being coal miners and coal miner's families. I suppose that's where the troubles came from."

James, taking another sip of coffee and sitting there with the cup in his hands, his thumb, absently stroking the mug's handle, the cigarette hanging from between his lips threatening to go to ash, sighed heavily. The skin on his forehead pulled tautly and his eyes were lost in recollection of his father telling the same story to him as a boy.

"In 1820, five families stopped here, settled here. These were Maple Grove's founding fathers, you could call them, but I wish to God they had kept right on going along their trail and left the Grove behind. The five families were Sanders, Atkins, Townsend, Fontaine, and Burrows, and they settled down along the river, claiming little patches of land, and building their cabins and shacks, making babies and tending their fields. Everything seemed normal and peaceful, just an ordinary group of settlers that had finally found a piece of ground to call their own after months, maybe years, of traveling around the countryside.

"Maybe it would have been best for them to have kept right on along, made a camp for the night and packed up and moved along the next day. Maybe a few of them wanted to, but for the most part, they were tired of moving along, and something about the Grove seemed to be calling to them, begging them to stay. And their mistake was in answering that call, listening to what the caller had to say. I don't want to say they were under some kind of hypnosis, but, in a way, that was very much what it was, and once it dug into their heads, they couldn't ignore it, so they stayed."

"What kind of hypnosis?" Ray asked.

"I'm getting to that," James favored Ray with a look that told him not to be so damn impatient and finished the last of his coffee. He went to set the empty mug on the coffee table, but Roy leaned forward and took it from his hands before he was able.

"More coffee, dad?" he asked.

"That'd be fine," James said and crushed out his smoke in a dolphin-shaped ashtray. "But don't be wasting any time; we haven't got much of that left to waste."

Roy jumped up and left the room. He returned five minutes later with a coffee mug, little tendrils of steam rising and curling into the air over the rim; he handed it to his father. James accepted the mug, took the ever-cautious first sip—lest you scorch your mouth and throat, the first sip of hot coffee is always cautious—and set the steaming mug on the table in front of him.

"Thank you, son," James regarded Roy with a tired, but appreciative smile.

"No prob."

James nodded and continued with his story. "Everything was going fine up until the summer of 1854. I mean there were a few bad winters in between, but most of these folks had migrated to the Grove from up North. They had seen far worse winter weather than a hard frost on the ground or a light dusting of snow, so they handled the cold days well. But the summer of '54 is when that unknown voice in everyone's head made an appearance.

"It was Louis Sanders, your great, great, great grandfather, and Elias Atkins, old Judd's great, great grandfather, who started messing around with shit they should have left well enough alone when they dug the Sanders family well. The well is filled in now, has been for sixty years or more, but until around 1947, or maybe it was 1948, water was pumped up from that dirty hole in the earth. The water was clean, or at least it *looked* clean and didn't have a stink to it, but it was dirty all the same."

"Dirty with what?" Roy asked. He wasn't nervously rocking anymore but lounged back with one arm slung over the arm of the couch and rapping his fingers restlessly.

"Parasites."

"Parasites?" Ray asked. "You mean like fleas and ticks?"

James shook his head and lit another cigarette. "No. Internal parasites, but not like any I've heard of, not even today. These nasty little bastards can get into a person, animal, or whatever and grow until the host body becomes too cramped, and then it moves on. In the case of people, the parasite would grow until the body was beyond its needs, lay its eggs and shed itself free of the flesh, go into some weird cocoon and come out as a completely different creature, one that doesn't need to survive as a parasite, but one that can function on its own. Unfortunately, its favorite food just happens to be people."

"*Aw shit!*" Roy said, alarmed. "I've had about three glasses of water since I've been here." His eyes widened and he looked at James with horror so deep it was almost comical. "How long have I got? Please say you can flush them out." He turned his horror-stricken face to Ray. "Laxatives. You've got to have some laxatives here somewhere. Please say you do? I don't want to end up as a pile of cast-off skin with tick eggs in me."

"Calm down. The town's water is pumped in from elsewhere. No, I have a feeling the buggers got out from somewhere else."

He gave the boys a cursory glance. Neither of them was saying much, outside of Roy's frantic tirade just now, but there were plenty of questions on their faces. He went on. "The biggest problem *they* had, *they* or *them* or *it*, is how we had always referred to *them*, never really gave them a name. Never been anyone in either of the families with much of an imagination. Well, except…" He paused, took a sip of his coffee, considered, and then continued. "They couldn't maintain live hosts for long periods. Your grandfather was the one who figured out why, or least he was the one with the best guess at it.

"Will power. He figured living people had too much in the way of brains, free will and shit like that and it prevented them from keeping live hosts. The fuckers have a sort of telepathy or something like that, and they are not stupid, no matter what they look like. They make you see things that aren't there, make you hear things that aren't there."

"Well, damn, if that's the case," Ray interrupted. "Shouldn't they be everywhere? I can understand some of what I've seen, the dreams, and the dead rat that was a dog's head a few weeks later, but if they need dead hosts, there's a whole graveyard full."

"The corpses have to be fresh, they last longer that way." James shuddered, possibly, at how morbid that last had sounded coming out of his mouth and possibly because he could feel them, could sense them. They were close. "Like the one I killed tonight, at the Fontaine girl's apartment, the one sent to stop her, I imagine. Once they get inside, they repair, well, more like they patch up whatever was damaged in the kill. This lasts them until they are either ready to move on to the next host, or in people until they can lay their eggs and go into their cocoons. In either case, they are vulnerable until the monstrosity they become hatches. That's why they need a common human presence to protect their nests. Dianne is taking the girl to the Atkins's nest as we speak, to wait on us."

James put his cigarette out next to the last one and took notice of the wall clock near the front door. He had to hurry.

"In the short of things, these creatures were more supernatural, I suppose that's the best word for it than alien, which was the original thoughts on the matter. What your grandfather had learned, or hoped he had learned, was that if you sealed the human cohorts away, then the parasites went into a sort of hibernation. But the seals had to be refurbished ever so often with fresh blood to keep *them* locked away."

"You mean there's an old wrinkled up escapee from the *Creep show* in my basement." Ray's eyes lit up, the realization of his uncle's macabre history lesson dawning on him; it was like a slap in the face with a shovel made of iron. "Oh, damn!"

"Yup. Your great grandfather, my grandfather, George Sanders, is sealed away in a concrete room underneath the basement, more like a subbasement. Likewise, with Leonard Atkins, Judd's granddaddy, only he was buried in a concrete room down on the riverbank—"

"Where dad built his cabin," Ray finished. It wasn't a question.

James sighed. "Yeah. Where Earnest built his cabin. Judd was supposed to be in charge of keeping that seal refreshed, but he's always had a mean streak in him and over the last fifteen, twenty years, or so, he's not been holding a full sack of marbles. Not that he ever was too sane, to begin with."

James stopped suddenly, his face went pale, and he looked ready to keel over. Tiny beads of sweat stood out on his forehead and then his color was back, bright splotches of red spread across until he was wearing a mask as bright as fresh-spilled blood.

"Dad?" Roy asked concerned, frightened. "You okay?"

"That son-of-a-bitch. *That stupid son-of-a-bitch!* It's Judd. He's the one done gone and opened up the seal, he's the one that probably stirred them up in '98 when you boys went down there. *Son-of-bitch!*"

"So, if old Judd's the guardian of freakville, why isn't he here?" Roy asked.

James looked at his son and shook his head. "Because this isn't his nest to protect, but if he gets to the cabin before the Fontaine girl, then we're royally fucked. If those cocoons hatch..." He gave his head another frustrated shake. "*Shit* We've got to hurry, boys. Because you don't want to see one of those fuckers hatch, I swear to *God*, you don't want to see that."

"What do you want us to do?" Ray asked as he stood up.

"Grab those pistols and knives and leave the other shit behind. We have to break the family seal."

CHAPTER NINETEEN

Judd knelt in the wet leaves and pine needles and put one calloused hand to the ground before him, fingers splayed. To anyone passing by he would appear to be a man stopping for a rest and trying to catch his breath before moving on, but there were no passersby here, not on this night and not in this dense thicket of wood. He looked in all directions, a silver strip of moonlight, all which shone above, lit on his face. Eyes dark and shinning with insanity, mouth pulled down in a grimace that could be of pain but was of a slow rising fury, Judd watched in intense silence as the ground below his palm began to glow a bright, crimson hue. The ground thrummed softly like some wayward minstrel playing a long-lost ballad. After a moment, the glow was gone and Judd stood, not bothering to dust away the leaves sticking to his clothes. He lifted the shotgun from against the oak in which it was propped, situated the .22 caliber rifle that he carried slung across his back and started walking forward, mindful not to step on downed limbs or anything else that would give him away.

For a minute there, he thought he had lost the cunt's trail, she who had murdered his baby brother and who now threatened to ruin what by all rights was as sacred to him as the Holy Church and Christ, the Son of the Father. The cunt and all the other cunts wanted to hurt *them*, to cripple *them*, to see *them* broken and dead. That just could not be, not now or ever.

Find her, Judd. Shoot her dead or drown her in the river, but don't let her near the girl.

The rain had ceased again and in that, he was thankful. Even with his little gift from *them*, it was difficult to track in the rain and given the moisture that had already seeped into the ground from the previous fall, it was difficult enough with no need for the added burden of further precipitation. Oh, the sky was apt to open again at any minute, the moon swept away by banks of unseen clouds, but for now, he would accept this small grace and treat it the best he could. To look this gift horse in the mouth would be foolish. But he would catch up to Maria, rain or no rain, and that would be that.

Judd canted his face towards the moon, now partially hidden in the abysmal sky and smiled. His crooked teeth, yellowed like jaundice, jutted from his gums in uneven rows and gleamed despite their dullness. The hot, iron smell of blood was close now, and soon he would be bathing in it.

It slumbered uneasily in its nest. The human interlopers were here, somewhere above. He could smell them, could hear their weak hearts beating in their chests, and yet the master still made no plans. The master was sure the protector would defend them, but it thought that not likely to happen. The girl was strong. And the boy would be here soon, he of the old bitch's womb and seed of the family that had betrayed their trust. Yet, the master slept and did nothing.

Two of the others were dead. It had sensed their passing, had felt when he of the traitorous family had murdered them, had felt the cold barrel of the man's gun and then a sharp, burning agony and an ebbing life force. Yet, the master slumbered. How could he when their species was on the verge of extinction? Only ten clutches of eggs remained, none of them ready for the stage of hatching, and there were but two younglings sealed away in their protective cocoons, their final growth cycle only just began.

Yet, the master slumbered.

It opened its eyes, the eyes of a boy now a month dead. These eyes were beyond sight, but it could see through them, nonetheless. The nest, a concrete box ten feet beneath the ground and about as big as the lower level of Ray Sanders's house, was nothing more than a dank, dusty crypt for the long-deceased Leonard Atkins. In the far corners, tucked away in nests made of grass, twigs and discarded clothing, were clutches of eggs and on the opposite wall was a rusty old bed. Atop the moldering mattress lay what remained of Leonard. He was no more than a mummy, but his essence still lingered, and his body housed an entity of great presence. They had tried to preserve the body as best they could over the years, but they were no gods, no matter how much of the old power they possessed and could only do so much. The master that inhabited the man that once was the protector of this nest would never reach a final growth cycle, having chosen to remain as it was for the sake of their kind, but now it did nothing but sleep. Aware of the danger, yet it ignored its children.

Turning to the two gel sacks, the gelatinous cocoons glowing with crimson-hued luminance and attached to the concrete wall at the foot of Leonard's bed, the Odumulite that now inhabited the late Donnie Atkins felt another of those discomforting human emotions and knew not what it meant. It was a heavy, sinking feeling—like having weights tied to one's ankles and being tossed into a deep body of water—and it hated being open to such things, to such *regret* It longed to lay its own clutch and reach its own final cycle of growth, but with these feelings (It didn't understand sorrow or fear, but felt both of these now) that now ravaged and fought against its better instincts, it knew that it may never attain that final, warming sanction. To become one of the great ones that would roam, hunt, and build. The ones destined to walk the earth as gods would walk the heavens.

With these thoughts, it felt a new human emotion, one so powerful and dark that it seemed to burn from within like the fires of hell.

This emotion was hatred.

Maria saw the car's lights cutting a path through the overgrown grass as she cleared the woods' edge. She thought she could make out two forms, one slouched over the seat, and one sitting bolt upright in the driver's seat, but chalked it up to imagination. The rain had ceased again, not before it had managed to soak her through, and the moon was a faint glow in the sky. Not enough light shone for her to be sure of anything she saw. *They* were here. *How do you know that? What if it's just a couple of teenagers up to some heavy petting? What then? How silly will you look approaching them? How* strange *would you appear to them, showing up out in the outskirts of town in the middle of the night, soaking wet and looking half-mad? You would surely scare them and possibly get yourself shot.* Many folks in the Grove carried firearms in their vehicles, it was just a way of life out here in the country, and if not a gun, they would surely have a knife or some other type of blade or maybe even a bat or some other blunt object.

There's a gun, tucked away behind the drivers' side seat and wrapped neatly in a patchwork quilt. This is no couple out for some heavy petting or anything sexual. These were two women, one of moderate age, the other just a girl. And they are waiting for you. The girl needs you to help her, to complete a ritual... No, not a ritual, something like, but her mind couldn't touch on what it was. How is it possible to know any of this?

Grabbing the sides of her head, tugging painfully at her hair, Maria dropped to her knees. She was mildly aware of her nightgown, once a fine silk garment from JC Penny, now dirt-stained, torn. Dale had surprised her with the gown on her birthday last year and she thought it the nicest gift ever because she loved the way it felt pressed against her skin as she slept. Donnie was alive then, and Dale too, and they had been happy, or so she'd thought. Her oldest, still locked up for some stupid crime or the other, never far from her mind–that was depressing, but she'd had her youngest son and her husband to make things easier.

Tears streaked over her cheeks, slicing their way through the grime that had caked to her face on the trek through the woods, spilled over her chin and dropped unnoticed to her soiled nightgown. She cried for family, now lost to her in the void known as forever, but she also cried in fear of something even dearer, her sanity. Here she was a grown woman, a respected woman in a quiet, respectful town, and she was fit for a white coat, the kind with straps and buckles to keep you from harming yourself and others. There were voices in her head, voices that were not her own, and that was scary. That she was listening to those voices, doing as they instructed, was scarier still. And with all this, she was here on her knees in the damp grass under the obsidian eye of night, crying and fretting to approach the people the voices told her that she must.

I... was all her mind could manage before the other voice broke in.

No time for second thoughts. It's beyond time for that. Move forward, like the wind across an open plain, but do not turn back. Do not let your foolish emotions best you, not now, not when everything is near to be done.

Maria's feet were carrying her away from where she had knelt and wept, but don't ask her when she had stood and wandered away from the edge of the trees, she was no more aware of that than she was of her purpose in this gross spectacle of illogic. She was walking towards the Datsun, its headlights ceaselessly illuminating the high grass before it with dim light. Inside, Dianne Townsend was recalling what there was to remember about her encounters at Julie Fontaine's apartment and was readying to lean over and shake the girl awake.

Before Maria's eyes, the moderately sized Datsun seemed enormous, *majestic,* appearing to grow with every hurried, unsteady step. Maria skirted the rear of the car, and her earlier thoughts of surprised gun-toting lovers unheeded approached the driver's door. She knew better than that, no matter how much her mind refused to see, but, still, the thought of opening the driver's door to be greeted by the cold barrel of a gun or the hard, razor-edged blade of a knife… Her hands were trembling, and tears pooled in the corners of her eyes. Reaching out, she took a deep, steadying breath and jerked open the door.

⸻ ❖ ⸻

Dianne recoiled from the filthy, ghoul-looking thing that had jerked open her door. Long, dark, matted, and dirty hair reaching to its shoulders filled Dianne's vision. It wore a filthy nightgown, made of silk or rayon; there was so much mud, and grime spattered across it that Dianne couldn't determine which. The woman, for that, was surely what she was, now that Dianne's eyes were in synch with her mind, was either dark-skinned or her arms and legs were coated with the same muck that sullied her sleepwear.

"Need…you," the woman croaked and put a wet, muddy hand on Dianne's shoulder. Dianne flinched from her touch, scooting on her rear until her back bumped into the center console.

"Wha…whaz…goin…" Julie mumbled incoherently beside her.

"Need you," the woman repeated, out of breath and choking on the words. "I need you to help."

Slipping an arm between the seats, Dianne fumbled with her unseeing hand until she happened upon the quilt. Bundled as it was, and wedged between the backseat and driver's seat, the shotgun would be troublesome to unwrap and swing up. But she had to try…

You ain't thinking too clear, girl. That gun is all wrapped up, and even if it wasn't, how do you expect to pull it out from back there and use it before the woman gets at you?

It was an easy answer, but an answer that seemed to triple her heartbeat and quadruple her terror. She couldn't.

Judd cleared the last copse of pines just as the moon exited the clouds once more. The land sloped away, giving way to the moonlit field along the riverbank. Shapes were forming under that pale light. In the distance was Earnest's cabin, the Townsend woman's beat-to-shit little car, a little closer, and the conniving cunts were in the middle.

Judd propped the shotgun against a nearby pine and slung the .22 around. With a predator's smile, he brought the rifle up, braced the stock to his shoulder and took aim at the nearest fleeing shape.

"You cunts forgot all about old Judd," he murmured under his breath. "Yup."

CHAPTER TWENTY

They say silence is golden. Who are 'they'? Who are they to say? It probably doesn't matter, but there were apparently enough of them saying it for the phrase to kick around in Ray Sanders' head while he watched his uncle staring down the hallway into the kitchen, his deceased brother's shotgun snug in the crook of one arm with the barrel pointing at the floor. A look of dread was on his face, a face that bordered on terror and expected death. Not a word was spoken among the three of them and the silence wasn't golden at all. The silence was leaden. He could hear their breathing, slow and heavy, and he could hear the wall clock ticking, but even worse, he heard the twinkling of wind chimes. The chimes were distant, muffled, but he heard them just the same and it was driving him mad. Why didn't his uncle just go already? Go and get this crazy shit over with so life could go back to the normal clusterfuck that he had grown used to? Outside, the wind brushed the eaves and shutters and there was more than a rattle as some of the shutters banged against the house, some with such force that Ray thought they might break off altogether, it grew much stronger or slam right through the wall. He jumped and out of the corner of his eye, he saw Roy doing the same. They were scared, the three of them, fearing a death that was near at hand and apt to be excruciating.

"Oh yeah," his uncle broke the silence in 'an-on-second-thought' tone and reached into his shirt pocket. "Almost forgot."

He tossed something to Ray, something on a chain. Ray caught it in his free hand, the one not holding the 9mm, and turned it over, gawking at it like his uncle had just thrown him the Holy Grail and the commotion in his head, threatening his sanity, began to quiet. It was his mother's pendant—a tarnished silver pendant in the shape of a dolphin—the one she always wore around her neck for as far back as Ray could remember. The one she was wearing on the day they buried her. His Aunt Dianne had handed it to James Sanders after he had saved her and Julie Fontaine from *them* as *they* had tried to kill the two women in Julie's apartment. His uncle had explained what had happened before he arrived at the Sanders' home, how he had struggled with the corpse of Doug Feldman before shoving the barrel of his shotgun between the thing's eyes and blowing its head off. Ray looked over at his uncle and there was an expression on his face: sorrow, surprise, awe, all the above and his uncle gave him a knowing nod.

"Her talisman," Ray whispered. He wasn't aware, not completely, of what that meant, but he slipped it in the right front pocket of his jeans—it was too small to slip around his neck, and he feared losing it if he put it around his arm or wrist.

"Her talisman," his uncle repeated, and Ray heard the

chimes again, though not so muffled this time. They were in his head and sounded as if caught in gale-force winds.

The three men were walking now, wearing the silence like a shroud with their heavy strides echoing around them: deep, plodding thumps on hardwood. Ahead, the hardwood floor gave way to green linoleum, an odd image, but the kitchen had belonged to his mother and she wanted linoleum in there, God knows why. Like the floors throughout the house, the linoleum had a layer of wax coating it, his mother's work and done not long before she passed, Ray figured. The wax caught the light thrown from the overhead lamp, amplified it, and gave the worn linoleum a deeper, glossier, green shine. Ray hadn't noticed this, not since returning home or even before leaving it and it almost seemed *too* bright. *Bright enough to sear the eyes right out of my head*, he thought. The hallway, the kitchen, everything seemed to swoon around him, and he was scarcely aware that he was falling. His knees had buckled, and he was falling.

A hand gripped Ray's right arm tight enough, it seemed, to rip it out of the socket, then another hand gripped his left, lifting and balancing him, but he was still swooning. That reflection of deep green glimmering from the kitchen was still too brilliant to bear.

Don't go down there, Ray, they want you to go down there. They want you to be the sacrifice. Don't be their sacrifice. The girl's voice, Julie Fontaine's voice—some girl from school he had never even spoken the first word to—trying to warn him. They had called her a skank. They had called her a whore. And at one time wasn't he a part of *them?* Those shouts and whispers of skank and whore blurting from between his stupid adolescent lips, aimed and shot like a sniper's bullet at an innocent girl's heart. Fear, as powerful and debilitating as it was, was no match for the shame rising in his chest. This girl, a girl he had helped to condemn in the ignorance of his youth, had come to him via some sort of spiritual thorough way or maybe it was a *dream way* and tried to warn him of some malevolent danger.

She holds you no grudge, son, his mother's voice came, tender, warm, whispering in his ear. *You ask yourself what it would take. What it would take, son is to take the girl's advice and stand at her side. The evil that's here, she can't get rid of it by herself. I gave you my gift, my only true gift. Take it now and help that girl.*

"You okay, dude?" Roy's voice sounded distorted as if he was speaking through a thick sheet of glass.

The basement is death. It almost had you once and it would have at you again. It wants you here and away from the cabin, away from the real threat. Your uncle means well, bless him, but there's nothing down there but a burned-out orb, a pile of bones, and death waiting for you to release it.

"I'm fine," he lied. "I'm sorry I lost it, haven't been sleeping all that well." His uncle and cousin were looking at him doubtfully. "I'm *all right.* You guys can let up, now. I can stand on my own."

Roy's grip disappeared but his uncle's hold remained as tight as a crocodile's jaws. He was looking at Ray, his stony eyes still doubtful, but also concerned. "Uncle James. I'm fine. You can let go."

With some reluctance, his uncle did let go of his arm, but not his doubt. "Just take a few deep breaths," he said. "Get yourself together. If you pass out down there, they'll take you and I can't promise I'm quick enough to save you. You understand?"

Ray nodded.

Death. The basement is death.

"We have to go to the cabin," he blurted, as his uncle and cousin began to walk away. In his mind, he saw the hideous creatures that awaited them in the dark, with their grotesque, oversized, pulsing, tick-like bodies and ever-hungry tentacles. He could see the human remains of those passed from this world, dangling from the walls with their insides strewn at their feet and their agonized wails; the way they writhed against their restraints and those lost, wandering eyes. But there was something even worse behind the seal, something deadlier than the tentacle-flailing little beasties. It was one of the evolved. A monster so terrifying, Ray believed just to look at it would turn him inside out, just as its *Ginsu* sharp claws would fillet him in a minute flat.

James Sanders stopped in the archway that connected hallway to kitchen. "After our business in the basement, we'll haul balls down there. But—"

"The basement is death," the words tumbled out of his mouth, as cold as ice cubes. "They want us to go down there, to keep us away from the girl… To keep us away from Julie. She's the key, but she needs us, needs *me* to help her. To send them back she needs me."

"What?" Roy asked and not without a hint of irritation. "What girl? Julie who?"

"Julie Fontaine," Ray answered. "She's the key."

"The skank that used to polish Donne Atkins pole. What she going to do? Bang them to death. *Jesus, Ray.* What the fu—"

"Don't talk about her like that!" Ray grabbed Roy's shoulders, the tips of his fingers digging into the soft flesh below the shirt and Roy winced. "She's just as human as any of us standing here, no, more than that, she's…"

There was a clamp around his wrists and his uncle

removed his hands from Roy's already bruising shoulders. "Easy, now. Who told you this?"

"Mom. She says the orb is burned out and that the basement is death. She wants us to go to the cabin. I don't know what I'm supposed to do but it's pretty important."

"How do you know it was your mother who spoke to you? How do you know it's not one of *their* head tricks? It could be, you know. The orb holds something special to them, possibly their existence in this world depends on the damned thing. If we destroy—"

"No," Ray shook his head and looked his uncle in the eyes. "It was mom, no doubts. The orb is dead, I guess that's what she meant by burned out, but… There's something else waiting for us to break the seal. I think it's one of those you were talking about, one of those that walk on two legs like a man. One of the *evolved*, don't know how I know, I just felt it."

"All right," James agreed and took the shotgun from the corner where he had propped it. Once again, it settled in the crook of his arm, the barrel aimed at hardwood. "We'll go out the back."

As they crossed the kitchen, James Sanders' hand reaching for the back door, it happened. At first, Ray associated what he was hearing with Bobby, the Rat Terrier they'd had when he was around ten or eleven. Bobby loved the kitchen and had a doggy bed in the laundry room off in the far corner, just past the basement door. Hearing the click-click-click-click on the linoleum sounded to Ray the way Bobby's claws used to click on the floor as he had raced from the laundry room to greet Ray after school. But Bobby died in 2000, so what was this?

James was the quickest to react, swinging the barrel of the shotgun up and popping the slide as one of the tick-like creatures leaped onto the kitchen table, sending empty beer cans and glass dishes in all directions. Underneath the shattering dishes was a high-pitched screech, like fingernails on a chalkboard. James Sanders squeezed the trigger. The shotgun roared in his uncle's hands. Metal pellets tore the creature apart, ripping through its body and throwing it backward in a spray of internal organs and a purple goop Ray thought might have been the thing's blood. However, before disappearing from view, he'd had a brief glimpse at its tentacles, those deadly arms with the hungry mouths attached on the ends.

They were stretching, reaching, my God. Even in death, the son-of-a-bitch wanted to feed.

There was another gunshot and a startled, hurt cry.

"Roy!" Anger, concern, and fear-filled his uncle's voice and Ray turned to see Roy staggering backward and swatting his gun at a black and red throbbing mass clinging to his chest, tiny segmented legs scrambling for purchase.

As Ray watched, frozen and white-faced, one of the thing's tentacles whipped out and stuck to the side of Roy's neck. There was a sickening sucking sound and Roy screamed. Dropping his gun to the floor and trying to pry the thing loose by clawing at it wildly, Roy backed against the wall with bright rivulets of blood trickling down his neck below where the tentacle had latched on.

"Ray! Shoot the fucker!" Roy begged, his voice muffled by the weight of the thing's body pressing against his face.

"*Shoot it, Ray,*" his uncle bellowed.

"*You* shoot it!" Ray snapped. But before James Sanders could respond, Ray knew the truth of it. If his uncle were to take a shot at the creature, he'd take a substantial portion of Roy's face with it. Scatterguns were useless in some scenarios.

"I—" James Sanders started, and Ray lifted the 9mm, once as light as air in his hand and now as heavy a burden as any there had ever been. He held the gun in a two-handed grip, the way his father had taught him, and sighted down the barrel, not at the thing's head with its deep red eyes and chattering mandibles, but at the point where the tentacles connected with its body. There was no snide remark or catchy phrase before he squeezed back on the trigger, only a smile that held just the slightest hint of dementia. Ray took his shot.

The crack of the 9mm wasn't as deafening as the shotgun, but it wasn't anywhere near a whisper, either. The slug found its mark, severing the tentacle from the thing's body and spraying its purple blood on the walls and floor (not to mention coating Roy in a fair amount of it). The tentacle hung from Roy's neck a moment longer, swishing the air like a pendulum, then fell to the floor in a jerky spasm. The creature shrieked and shivered but did not give up its hold, even as the fat sack that made up over half of its body was deflating, its strange purple blood flowing from its wound like a burst water main.

"Jesus!" Roy screamed, struggling harder than ever to pry it loose. *"Jesus GOD!"*

Several bright crimson dots appeared on his cousin's shirt where the thing's tiny barbed legs began to burrow into flesh and one of the remaining tentacles rose even with Roy's face, a small, slimy spear-like object slowly sliding from the mouth at the end, what Dianne Townsend would have identified as the thing's stinger. Watching as Roy's eyes grew wide with terror, Ray first took aim, and then squeezed off another round, disintegrating the threatening stinger and tentacle before it could inject Roy with its paralyzing agents.

From behind him, the shotgun roared once more, followed by another of those high-pitched shrieks. *It's as if they know that we changed our minds about the basement and are pissed off about it*

Finally, the thing on Roy's chest and face called it quits, giving one last attempt to raise its last two tentacles. A fierce spasm rocked its oddly shaped body that reminded Ray so much of a giant tick, and it fell to the floor at Roy's feet, jerking and squealing.

"You all right?" Ray asked, taking a few steps toward Roy in case he needed a boost.

Another roar from the shotgun, a shriek, and what sounded to Ray like every piece of glassware in the kitchen shattering to points unknown.

"We got to go, boys! *Now!*"

Roy gave the dying creature at his feet a look of deep contempt and kicked it. The thing squealed, and then it was no more. "I'm cool," he asserted and picked up the gun he'd dropped. "Let's go."

Giving the large, bloody raw spot on his cousin's neck a despairing glance, Ray followed, swiveling his head around as he moved, searching for signs of *them.*

A dismal thought occurred to him. *If everything down there's sealed up, how did they get out?* Then, just as dismal and not without its share of terror, he thought, *they didn't escape the seal. Not these. They came in after mom died or after I moved in and nested up. They were waiting for me to come down, all this time, waiting for me in the dark.*

Ray shivered and then shuffled out the kitchen door, but not before hearing and seeing two more of the creatures trying to squeeze through the hole in the basement door and sending more splinters to the floor as the hole widened to accommodate them. Without knowing he was going to do it until he was doing it, Ray reached in and locked the door before pulling it shut behind him. He didn't think it would matter one way or the other—if they wanted out, they would get out. At least the locked door might buy them some time.

"Holy shit!"

Startled out of his current train of thought and his heart already doing double-takes from the excitement in the kitchen, Ray spun around, raising the 9mm as he did so. *Seeing is believing* he had often heard from various sources, but he couldn't bring himself to believe what he was seeing, having seen too much of the bizarre already. So how could he *not* believe what he was seeing? In part, he figured this was because he still wanted to think like a rational adult, and this was too much like a scene from a Stephen King novel to be a rational, real thing. On the other hand, he was afraid to believe, afraid what other horrors were lurking on the edge of the dark, horrors that were just as real.

"This is a bitch and half," Roy shouted as the kitchen door rocked in its frame behind them. The little freaks were trying to knock it down. But those few beasties left behind were the least of their problems. The congregation of animals and livestock occupying his backyard was the forefront of their problems now.

"I was afraid of this," James Sanders said and reached into his pocket for fresh shells.

There were cows, coyotes, cats and dogs, some as God made them, others with those hideous tentacles extruding from their sides and flailing around. Next to his dad's workshop stood a couple of horses and a mule trotting around in circles. The horses were snorting, the mule was braying, and all of them had yellowish foam around their mouths. Some of the cows, six in all, and emaciated to the point that their ribs were visible underneath their taut, dying skin, were shaking their heads violently as if shooing off flies. Those were Mr. Livington's prized Holsteins, the ones he was so quick to brag on when they took a first-place ribbon at the town fair.

Near the north corner of the house was a group of boar and sow hogs, none of them emaciated—yet —but a few of the sows had those tentacles waving around and the big boars were exposing their tusks and making some God-awful squealing sound deep in their throats. The coyotes and stray cats sat directly in front of them, making not a sound, but staring at the humans with a sort of malicious glint in their eyes. The cats were the eeriest, sitting on their haunches, tails swishing restlessly and purring so loudly that it felt like they were transmitting that grating, vibrating sound straight into his brain.

"Do we have enough bullets, you think?" Roy inquired. He was taking in hard, raspy breaths and his complexion was sallow. Ray wondered if the creature had passed on some type of infection after all.

"Our best bet is to shoot on the run," James answered, as the beasties inside the house slammed against the kitchen door again, causing him to flinch and tighten his grip on the shotgun.

How long before those bastards figure they should be trying the windows instead of the door?

"Or maybe a slow walk until we can get past the yard and down the path." This time James didn't sound all that convinced; it sounded more like he was grasping at straws. "We shoot anything that gets in front of us. You boys understand? *Anything.*"

"And if they come at us when we move?" Ray asked.

"Shoot on the run."

"Roy isn't going to be doing much walking or running," Ray gave his uncle a sideways glance. "Look at him. He's two nods from passing out."

"I'm fine," Roy babbled, raising the muzzle of the 9mm to his sweat-soaked brow, miming a salute. "Mom's down there." He pointed the handgun in the direction of the woods south of the house. "Got to get her out of harm's way. Got to be men. Right, Rayford?"

"Right, Roy my boy," Ray replied with a tear on his cheek. Whatever disease or poison *they* carried was in his cousin's bloodstream now and it was killing him. *This isn't how it happens with other people. With other people, it just numbs them up, but Roy is a Sanders. His is the blood of betrayal. How do I know that?*

The small window over the kitchen sink exploded outward, shards of glass raining over the floorboards and following that was a hollow thud. Roy reacted first this time, sick or not, lining the 9mm up with the thing's face as it sat there preparing to reach out with its tentacles. In the windowsill of the busted window, another of the creatures sat, whining and chattering and Ray aimed over his cousin's shoulder. They fired simultaneously. Ray's shot was as clean as a cleaver, decapitating the creature and sending it back into the house with a sickening plop as it landed in the sink. Roy's shot took his target between its mandibles and exited through the large sack on its rear, decorating the side of the house with its insides and its weird purple blood sprayed all the way to the porch railings.

For good or ill, those two shots, still ringing painfully in their ears, set to motion all that was to follow.

"Run!" James cried.

They did as bid; giving the dying thing Roy had shot a

wide arc. As the three of them turned the corner a muscled Rottweiler ran to greet them, snarling and snapping its jaws, strings of saliva and yellow foam flying from its mouth. James Sanders wasted no words or risked a break in stride. One quick pump of the slide and a quick squeeze of the trigger and the shotgun bellowed its rage, taking the top of the Rottweiler's head off in a spray of bone, fur, and brains. The big dog didn't stop right away but ran on past the three men a few feet before colliding with the porch railing and falling over.

About a third of the way along the side porch, a plump, gray tomcat with two bloody sockets where its eyes would normally be located, leaped from the porch railing and struck Ray full-on in the chest. It buried its sharp needle teeth in just below his neckline while its claws ripped through the thin cotton tee and flesh alike. The pain was sharp and hot, and the cat dug in even deeper with both its teeth and its claws. Ray, bouncing off the side of the house, was reaching up to pull the cat free when Roy grabbed it by the throat, pulled it away (with a startled yelp of pain from Ray), and spat on it. The cat struggled against his cousin's grip and growled deep.

"Hold still, you fucker."

There was a wet tearing sound and a tentacle burst from the cat's side. Ray thought the cat might have screamed at that moment but couldn't be sure. The tentacle whipped out at the hand holding its host and Roy flung the cat away. It landed in a sprawl on its back and that's how he shot it, blowing the possessed feline in two.

"Fuck with me," Roy said with a cough.

"Look at that shit," Ray pointed at the top half of the cat, crawling towards them, trailing its gore behind it. "What the fuck?" Ray finished it off with one shot that appeared to disintegrate the pitiful thing.

How long will it take for me to get sick like Roy? Ray wondered as fresh blood trickled down his stomach. He dared not look down, afraid that if he did, he might see his insides strewn around his feet like the hapless victims from his dreams. *It's not that bad and you know it.* But still.

"Rayford, you may want to pray that you can squeeze the hell out of that trigger," Roy's voice trembled on the last part. Looking back the way they'd come, Ray saw the path blocked by two coyotes and a mangy pit bull. Swinging his head back around, he saw that two Rottweiler's, one massive boar hog and what appeared to be a naked teenage boy blocked the path in front of them. Along the railings, more house cats perched and the yard beyond was crowded with the larger animals, the horses, cows, and one deranged- looking mule.

"If this isn't the deepest goddamned hole I've ever been in," James Sanders' face was grave in the haunted moonlight.

"Ditto," Ray agreed, took aim at the nearest cat and pulled the trigger.

CHAPTER TWENTY-ONE

"She's here to help. Don't be afraid."

Julie's voice startled her, and Dianne almost went for the shotgun anyway.

"Please. I need you," the dirty woman begged. "*Please.*"

"Stand back, then, and let me get out," Dianne directed the dirty woman. The woman did as instructed, and Dianne wiggled out of the Datsun, her shoulder burned with fresh fire as she did so.

"Thank you," the woman cried, fresh tears streaking her dirty cheeks. "My name's—"

"I know who you are," Dianne cut her off. "Maria Atkins. And you should know me, sugar." Out the corner of her eye, Dianne saw Julie moving around the front of the car to join them. "We've lived in the same town our whole lives, so you should."

Maria stared at her a moment with a puzzled expression, then her eyes lit up and a smile touched her dirt-crusted lips. "Dianne Townsend!" She sounded ecstatic; as if Dianne was a long-lost friend, she was seeing for the first time in several years. She then threw her arms around Dianne's neck and hugged her so tight Dianne felt like the last bit of toothpaste squeezed from the tube; she could almost feel her feet curling up to help the process along. "I don't think I've ever been happier to see anyone, not like this, anyway." Maria stood back, tugged at her nightgown, sobbing, "I'm a filthy mess."

"We're all a mess right now," Julie put in. "But we don't have much time left. The guardian of the seal will be here soon. Do you know what I'm talking about, Mrs. Atkins? You do, don't you?" Julie stepped forward and took Maria's hands into hers. As their skin touched, a warm tingle rushed over them and for a moment, a bright golden glow encompassed the two women.

Maria nodded and Dianne stood looking at them with her own puzzled expression. Julie must have noticed because she said, "The families thought they were the ones to figure it out. But not really, the knowledge of the seal was passed down from the Odomulites, or as they were known in ancient times, *Antiquus percatus*, or ancient sins. Back when the Odomulites were attempting live hosts, this must have been. Just like transferring data from one computer to another." Julie let go of Maria's hands and faced Dianne directly.

Dianne lifted an eyebrow, unsure what the girl meant. She knew the old stories of the seals, but she never knew exactly how the knowledge of creating them came about, and she suspected that her ex-husband was just as blank on the subject as she was. Scarier yet, was how this girl knew. *It must be part of what makes her so damn special.*

"I really can't explain everything, not even to myself, and don't have the time for it. It's freaky how I know this, but somehow… It's just there. What I can say is this, for every planet in the Universe there are three levels of existence." Julie stopped, appeared to be considering what she'd said, and then went on. "A top, a bottom, and middle. For Earth, the bottom is the spirit world, the middle is… Well…The one we live in now and the top is something of a chaotic wasteland.

"For the most part, creatures that die there come here and are born again as animals or people or even trees, and then after passing on in this world, they move on to the spirit world. However, some are so vile that they are not allowed to stop and be reborn but are sent directly to a part of the spirit world called *Wandering Plains*. Odomulites are an example of this."

"Then how is it they're here now, darlin'?" asked Dianne, flatly. "How is it they've been here all these years stirring up trouble?"

"Because sometimes they get stuck here. I don't know how, or I don't understand how it happens, I just know that sometimes they get stuck here."

"Anything else useful we should know?"

"You have to protect us on our way to silence the orb and open the gate."

"You and Maria?"

"No. I'm not sure. Maria is like me, but not like me, I can't explain it. All I know… Or rather picked up on, is that her strength is to become my strength and that I must enter the nest with one other, but not her. I'm confused."

Frowning, Dianne reached in behind the seat, grabbed the shotgun, and began freeing it from the quilt. "Then, I guess we'd better get started. Maybe we can get it figured out before *they* kill us."

Above them, the moon was full and fat, finally free from the bondage of clouds, and shone down in dreamy, pale light. The three women turned away from the car and began walking in the direction of the cabin, Dianne cradling her ex-husband's Browning 12 gauge in her arms, Maria and Julie walking behind her, defenseless. At that moment, James Sanders killed his first Odomulite for the night and though the dense foliage between them and the main house muffled the shot, Dianne heard it and snapped her head back towards the red-rocked path. It could have come from anywhere, that mild explosion, but she knew better than that. Either James or one of the boys had made it, which meant their trouble was just starting.

One of them was tugging at her sleeve and Dianne turned back to see which one it was. Maria stared back at her with blank eyes and an expression of total fear. "Was that a gunshot?" she asked in a timid mouse of a voice.

"What do you think, hon? You raised two boys and a husband. I'm sure you've heard that sound before. Don't they like to hunt?"

Maria looked stung and fresh tears appeared at the corner of her eyes. For a moment, Dianne wasn't sure what that stung look was about and then it hit her. *Her family's gone. All but that no account son that's locked up and for all Dianne knew that one was dead too. But her husband...* Yeah, him too. Something to do with this business, Dianne assumed, but Dale Atkins was just as dead as his youngest son, of that she had no doubt.

"Maria...I'm sorry, dear. Sometimes I just don't think."

Maria nodded, wiping a dirty hand at her tears and sniffling.

"We have to hurry," Julie interrupted.

"Yea. The sooner, the better." Dianne once again took the lead.

They were fifteen feet from the cabin's front door when the whip-crack of a low caliber rifle rang out, and Julie went down in the tall grass with a grunt. The shooter was much closer than what Dianne had been hearing through the trees and before she could make a move to check on the girl, another shot took Maria Atkins between her shoulder blades. There was a splattering of something dark that Dianne knew was blood, and Maria toppled forward with nary a sound.

Better find something to hide behind, she thought, as something hot zipped beside her head. She registered later that there had been a third shot fired and the hot, zipping object had been a bullet meant for her. In the distance, more gunshots erupted from the direction of the main house, and Dianne darted into the trees behind the cabin as, yet another shot whined behind her, biting into the cabin's side and splaying off a few splinters. She hit the underbrush hard, driving the stock of the Browning painfully into her right hip. She wanted to cry out but bit down on her lip instead, the salty, iron taste of her own blood filling her mouth. With some effort, Dianne got to her hands and knees and crawled as close as she dared to where the trees ended.

There was no sign of movement from where Julie or Maria went down, but she thought she heard someone whimpering, so at least one of them was alive. Turning her head in the direction in which she believed the shots were fired, she saw a big man with a mane of white hair and wearing overalls. He was taking little, searching steps down the slope leading to the clearing, a rifle held out before him.

The guardian of the nest had arrived, and Dianne didn't need a hell of a lot of light to recognize it was Judd Atkins.

Two young men limped along a red-rocked path under a swath of silvery moonlight, arms around one another for support. Their clothes were tattered and ripped, and wherever their skin was exposed were cakes of congealing blood. They both had a 9mm handgun tucked into the waistband of their jeans and both were crying. The younger of the two had just lost a father, the older, an uncle. James Sanders went down fighting, as cliché as that sounded, but he did, and in the end, when the big Winchester was nothing more than a club, he swung it as a club. The sight that burned into Ray Sanders's memory, however, was of a big Rottweiler ripping his uncle's throat out, even as James Sanders drove the blade of his big hunting knife up between its ribs. So, cliché or no, his uncle went down fighting.

Roy coughed and vomited a mouthful of blood onto the red rock beneath his feet. He was holding his side and grimacing with every step. His complexion was now as pale as the posters of *Dracula* Ray had hung in his room as a child, and a single line of blood trickled from the corner of his mouth. His breathing was more than raspy now. Now it sounded like a vacuum cleaner with a penny stuck inside. As for Ray, he had his own aches and pains, namely a big gash on the calve of his left leg where one of the boar hogs had clipped him with a tusk, not to mention several scratches and cuts from the animals he'd shot his way through. His back burned where the naked kid had clawed him, trying to grab hold of him. Roy had ended that poor bastard's misery with a single shot to the face.

"Hold up, dude," Roy said abruptly, spitting out more blood in the process.

Ray stopped and looked at his cousin. Roy was smiling, but Ray wished to God that he wasn't, for all he could see of his cousin's smile was blood, which looked as black as soot in the moonlight.

"You know what?" Roy asked in a voice that was a hundred miles away.

"What, cuz?" Ray answered, trying not to sound choked up. Roy was dying, there was no way around it, and he hated it.

"I just wanted you to know that I love you, Ray, like a brother, you know? I just want you to know that, okay. You're my best friend." Roy tried to laugh, probably at how lame he'd sounded just then—like one of those commercials for Hallmark greeting cards he enjoyed ragging on—but vomited another mouthful of blood, instead. "Sit me… down."

Ray found an oak that would semi-hide Roy from the road and they limped to it. He leaned his cousin against the backside of the tree and knelt in front of him, his vision hazy from the tears building up in his eyes. This wasn't fair. No goddamn way was it fair for Roy to die, not when he was in the prime of his life; not when the two of them had so many old times yet to catch up on.

"We did something to be proud of," Roy said, taking one of Ray's hands and squeezing it. This time he did laugh, and although it was a weak, phlegmy sound, it was better than puking blood. "I think we killed the entire cast of *Animal Planet* in the process, though."

Forcing a smile, Ray squeezed his cousin's hand back and said. "I don't think that what we killed constituted as being animals anymore. I think we saved them. Put them out of whatever pain they may have been suffering."

"Yea," Roy agreed, with a dreamy smile curling his lips. It was a sweet smile, an innocent smile and it reminded Ray of how his cousin was as a boy, how they both were. Always living day-to-day, no worries, no burdens, no cares in the world, just living in that highly overrated state of boyhood known as adolescence. His eyes felt as they'd been doused in gasoline, his tears like drops of napalm, and his body like a nuclear warhead on the verge of implosion. He looked away from Roy and wiped his tears away with the filthy wadding of his tee-shirt.

"Hey, Ray." Roy coughed so harshly trying to speak those two words that Ray thought he would choke before being able to finish whatever it was, he was trying to say. "You really believe Julie is something, don't you? Think that she might be able to do these fuckers in?"

"Yeah, I believe she can," Ray assured him.

Roy thought about it, flashed another ghastly smile, and nodded. "Well, I hope she shoves it right up their asses…no lube, either. Corn hole them mothers dry just like they have been doing our family all these years." He stopped, coughed up a clot of blood roughly the size of a golf ball and then lay with his back against the oak with tears in his eyes. "Fuckers," he spat at last, wheezing the word out as if he was breathing through a sieve. And with that, Roy Sanders said no more.

The awful wheezing and coughing were gone, but so was the wisecracking, smiling jester that had been his best friend. A brief image of Roy popped up in Ray's mind, one of an eight-year-old Roy Sanders in the crook of an old maple tree in his backyard, naked but for a pair of dirty Underoos and a cape made from a bath towel, clothespinned around his neck. There was a big, crooked *Superman* S insignia scribbled across his bony chest in red permanent marker and a sloppy, green *Joker's* smile shaded around his mouth.

Then another image of Roy, a much older Roy, showing up at the Maple Grove High School prom in a burgundy zoot suit. Complete with a matching fedora and dragon-headed cane and, of course, the burgundy tie with the navy-blue pinstripes that ended the night flying from the antenna of Roy's old Nova (along with Denise Jensen's panties) like a flag. That was also the night Roy had taken a joyride in Chester Owens' payloader, riding right up Main Street and through the front window of the Ace Hardware, still dressed in his prom attire and laughing the insane laughter only teenage boys drunk on whiskey and life seem able to produce.

Ray pulled Roy into an embrace, his dead cousin's head resting against his own chest with his still-alive heart pounding inside it, and wept. He sat that way for a good five minutes or more, shivering in the cold presence of death; his tears, warm on his cheeks, spilling over and soaking Roy's hair. Everything they had been through over the years, for it to end this way was almost blasphemy against the natural order of things, yet he realized that was a selfish and ignorant thought as soon as he thought it. This *was* the natural order of things. People live; people die. That's how life works; even if that person's death was supernatural rather than natural, that was how life worked. Fair? Of course not. Nothing was ever fair when faced with losing someone we cared about, but natural, yes. Life is a circle after all.

Leaning Roy back against the oak as gently as his shaking, trembling arms would allow, Ray slipped the remaining 9mm from his cousin's waistband and stood up. Stepping back onto the red-rocked path, he cast a glance back to where he left Roy and it hurt his heart. It hurt to have to leave him there like a broken and castaway toy. It hurt having to face that Roy was gone. Then he thought of Beth and her cute little friend Amy and felt a smile tugging at the corners of his mouth. That big, goofy grin on Roy's face when he and Amy stepped out onto the porch, the way he blushed a few moments later.

At least you enjoyed life up until…Well, all the way until the last. Wish I could say the same for myself. Then aloud, Ray said, "After this is over, cuz, I think I'll have to be more like you. Now you stay put, I'll be back in a few."

Just then, there was the crack of a rifle and Ray followed the sound, a pistol in both hands.

Julie heard the rifle report twice more. There was a thud and a rustle of grass after the first one, and she knew the shooter had shot another of her companions. As to which one, she was too afraid to risk a peek. She tried to rise a little on her side, hoping this minor bit of movement wouldn't draw the shooter's attention, and pain flared up and down her left side, releasing a fresh gush of warm, sticky wetness in the process. She had no way to stop the blood from flowing and wondered if that even mattered, now that she knew what had to be done and that the bleeding and the pain would end soon enough.

"I'll be damned if you cunts almost made me work a little." It was the voice of the shooter, loud and spiteful. Julie recognized that voice. It was a local voice, a town voice, but beyond that, she could not say for sure to whom it belonged.

"I'll tell you what, though," the shooter continued to bellow. "You ladies picked the wrong pot to go stirring around in. Done gone and got yourselves knee-deep in one hoss of a shit pile. But don't fret none too hard, old Judd's going to take care of everything."

I can't die here. Not on the outside. Julie began to

crawl, ignoring the jeering, disdainful man that had shot her, using her fingers like hooks to dig into the moist soil and pull herself along. She would not die, lying here on her belly with the pungent smell of wet grass and decay burning her nostrils. She would not let that happen.

An explosion of dirt and grass less than an inch from her face, and she bit her lip hard enough for it to bleed when a small chip of rock stung the corner of her eye.

"If that don't beat all. You cunts just don't give up. Should've put one in your back like I did the other bitch. Oh, well, ain't much in the way of fixing that problem, now is there?"

Julie heard the grass whispering as Judd neared. He wasn't in an all-out sprint, but he was moving at a decent jog. *"Fuck!"* she mouthed under her breath and sped up her crawl, the muscles in her arms protesting against such unheard-of exercise and the place where Judd had shot her protesting against any movement, unheard of or otherwise. Another crack of the rifle and another explosion of dirt erupted two inches to her left. *He's playing with me. Could have already shot me, could have taken my head off with the last one but he's playing now. Doesn't think he can lose.*

"Got a lot of heart girl, I'll give you that. But you're too ignorant to know when heart just ain't enough. You done lost, girl, yup, and I think I'll see to it that you understand exactly what that means." Judd squeezed off another shot.

The images of all that followed after he left Roy by the side of the road would haunt Ray in his dreams for the rest of his miserable life. Coming upon his father's old cabin alongside the edge of darkness, a creepy yellow moon hung above, and a mystic orange glow radiated from the cabin, giving the world around it a campfire glow. Hearing Julie scream as one of Judd's rounds bore in just below her right knee, fanning blades of grass in scarlet tears. Dianne Townsend rushed out of the woods and pumped off a shot, but not before Judd had put a bullet in her high up around her collarbone.

Watching in pure horror as Maria Atkins rose from the depths of the untended grass in a lunatic frenzy, bleeding from a nasty wound between her shoulder blades, and sunk her teeth into one of Judd's calves as if she were biting into nothing more than a piece of fruit, Judd's blood streaming down her face. The way the heartless old bastard didn't show the first sign of pain, neither from Maria's teeth nor from the handful of buckshot that had grazed his side, he just put the barrel of the .22 to Maria's head and pulled the trigger.

Ray remembered firing both 9mms in unison, not taking aim, but shooting in much the same frenzy that had overcome Maria Atkins at the end of her life. At least two of the slugs caught Judd and spun him around and Ray had caught a glimpse of a crimson-eyed, slack-jawed monster with rows of needle-sharp teeth. Ray realized that it was only Judd, tobacco-stained teeth, blank uncaring eyes and a slather of drool on the corner of his mouth, and he was aiming at Ray, one-step away from putting all the images out of Ray's head forever.

It was Dianne who saved him and possibly the entire

town, shoving the barrel of her 12-gauge pump into Judd's flabby, exposed backside and squeezing the trigger, screaming like mad the whole time. Judd toppled forward in a spray of gore. Not quite cut in two from the blast but close enough. Ray stepped over to where Judd twitched and jerked and pressed the 9mms into Judd's eyes. He fired both guns, staining the grass with the old man's brains.

"You all right, Auntie Di?" It was the way he had always referred to her as a child.

"I'm not going to lie, this hurts like a son-of-a-bitch. James? Roy?"

Ray shook his head, new tears forming on his cheeks. "I… There was nothing…"

Putting a blood-smeared finger to Ray's lips as he knelt beside her, Dianne hushed him. "Don't. We'll have time for that later. We'll mourn, but first, we have us one more chore to be done with."

The blood on that finger, Judd's blood, revolted Ray but he didn't budge. She was right, but he didn't think he could go any further into this nightmare, didn't want to go any further. He just wanted to go back to Florida, maybe take Beth along, and forget that Maple Grove existed.

"Go help her," Dianne nodded at Julie, who had continued to crawl despite her injuries and had pulled herself halfway up the cabin steps. "She needs you more than I do, I think."

Taking her right hand into his, Ray refused to budge, refused to leave another person he loved behind.

"I'll be fine," Dianne assured him as if she'd read his mind. And maybe she could, after all, he'd seen since returning home to bury his mother, would a little something like mind reading be all that hard to swallow?

"You're hurt," Ray protested but she gave him such a

stern do-as-I-say look that Ray flinched. For a second, he'd thought he saw his mother sitting there in the grass, covered from head to toe in blood and gore. Ray looked over at her again and it was his aunt, her lips drawing in a thin, determined line, her body hunched from exhaustion.

Hesitantly, letting go of her hand, Ray handed his Aunt Dianne one of the 9mms and the last magazine. "If any of those things should, you know—"

"I doubt I'll be any better with this one than I was with the other, but I'll give her a go. Now go, boy. Do whatever it is that girl needs you to do."

Ray leaned forward and kissed his aunt on the forehead, regardless of the blood-smeared there. "I love you, Auntie Di."

"I know. Now get."

She watched him go, watched until that weird orange light around the cabin seemed to swallow both him and the girl, and gave a little prayer. Already her body felt weak, too much of her own blood had spilled from it, and she wondered if she might be about to become a citizen of what Julie called the spirit world.

Well, old girl, might be you see that for yourself soon. Can't be all that bad. Ain't got nothing left here no ways.

Ray slipped an arm around Julie's waist, avoiding the large maroon patches on her side the best he could and lifted her to her feet. For a moment, their eyes met, and he felt a love for this young woman that he couldn't understand. She was special, and so much more than that word could justify. The presence around her was almost…

…Holy.

Before she could protest, Ray took a small folding knife from his pocket and cut two strips off his tee-shirt. Using these strips as makeshift bandages, he tied off Julie's wounds, getting them as tight as possible to stop the flow of blood. During this procedure, she winced once. She was holding her pain quite well and for that, Ray admired her even more.

"You ready?" he asked.

"Yes," she responded and curled an arm around his shoulders for support. "Are you?"

"No time like the present. Isn't that what they say?"

"Whoever *they* are, I suppose they do," Julie answered with a grin.

"You tried to warn me about all this, didn't you? In a dream?"

"And you listened."

"Thank you."

Julie kissed him on the cheek. "I'm glad you didn't sacrifice yourself to the evolved one, Ray Sanders. I'm really glad."

"I'm sorry," Ray blathered and looked away.

"For what?" Julie, bewildered by Ray's apology, stared at him.

"For being an asshole back in high school, for being one of those pricks that made fun of you…I was stupid. No. I was selfish and hurtful and—"

Hushing him with a finger to his lips, much the same as Dianne had, Julie leaned forward and kissed the corner of his mouth. "I never blamed you for any of it. And if you feel you need to atone… What we are about to do will take care of that."

Ray said nothing, could say nothing. There was nothing left for him to say, case closed.

"Once we step behind the seal, you'll have to use your gun on whatever's waiting for us while I open the gate."

He reached out for the door and Julie stopped him. "Aren't we forgetting something?"

"Wha…?" he started to ask, then stole a hand into his pants pocket instead, pulling out his mother's dolphin pendant…her talisman. His eyes grew in astonishment as he held it out before them. Watching, feeling as slack-jawed as he had envisioned Judd Atkins to be only minutes earlier, the tarnish on both chain and dolphin disappeared and the dolphin changed. Right before their eyes, it changed, warping and mangling itself into a tiny hexagonal shape with a capital S at its center. It began to glow red hot, which should have caused the hot metal to sear his flesh, but instead filled him with an inner warmth that reminded Ray of a thousand spring mornings on the bank of this very river, dozing in the sun.

"Now you can open it," Julie said. "I think now we're ready. Maria lent me her strength."

Standing in the clearing just beyond the porch with her hands clasped in front of her was the transparent visage of a woman of Hispanic descent. She was dressed in a white nightgown, her long, curly raven black hair draping over her shoulders, and she was smiling.

"My power is hers," the spirit of Maria Atkins said. "As your father's is yours, Ray. Now go. The both of you. Go and end this madness." Then, she was no more.

Ray, heeding Maria's words, swung open the door and a kaleidoscope of colors washed over them. Greens, reds, yellows, blues, all shades, all tones. It was like walking into a tunnel with tie-dyed walls, walls that glowed as bright as all creation. Ray leaned over, kissed the corner of Julie's mouth, and they stepped through.

First appearances are not always what they seem, as Ray Sanders figured out upon stepping through the doorway of swirling light. Once past the initial barrier, the warm, inviting colors began to darken, melding into morbid parodies of their former luminescence. Scenes of grotesque mutilations wavered in and out of their view. One such horror was of an old sallow-faced man in faded slacks and a bloodstained checked shirt plucking out the eyes of a small child with a rusty buck knife. The old man was gaping at the child with hungry bloodshot eyes and his mouth hung open, revealing the rotted stubs of his teeth and a swollen, lolling tongue. Julie shivered and dropped her head against Ray's shoulder as they limped along. Ray, without the luxury of being able to hide his face, found himself forced to watch the scene carry out in detail. He felt his stomach give a lurch, but he held it back.

That's what they want. That's why you're seeing what you're seeing. What was it Uncle James said about how they could make you see things, things to mess with your mind?

Up ahead, a malnourished dog was tearing into something with its teeth. Whatever that something was, it had a wet, fleshy sound to it and the smell that arose from it was a rotting meat smell, the smell of something that had died in the woods and lain undiscovered for several weeks. The dog snapped its head at them as they hobbled past it, baring its teeth in a throaty snarl. Over half the dog's face was a mass of raw, infected tissue and the eye on that side of its face was nothing more than a paste mashed into a rotting black socket. Ray had the 9mm in his hand, not aware that he had pulled it from his waistband and was ready to shoot if the rotting corpse of a dog made a move towards them. A lot of good that had appeared to have done him… once they were out of the dog's territorial zone, the two humans ceased to exist to it, and it went right back to its grizzly meal. What bothered Ray was, he didn't even think the gun would have hurt the dog to begin with, not even a scratch. Ray put the gun away.

"We're close," Julie said, raising her head just a hair before again sinking it against Ray's shoulder.

"How can you tell?"

She didn't answer.

As they continued along, the light surrounding them grew dim until eventually, it was nothing more than a thin, white, wavering line above their heads, like a fluorescent tube. Without the rainbow-light show, Ray was able to get a good look at their surroundings, which seemed to be nothing more exotic than a concrete tunnel. On the walls hung what appeared to be hundreds of framed portraits, each portrait containing some long-deceased member of the Atkins family tree, Ray figured. The oddity about each picture was how the people in them seemed to be whispering—no, no *seemed to be* to it, they *were* whispering.

Traitor, Backstabber, Fool, be damned were a few of the hushed, papery jeers he could make out, the rest nothing more than gibberish.

"Don't be afraid," Julie said and raised her head. "That's what they want."

"I'm good. No fear here."

"You're trembling. You don't have to pretend to not be afraid. You don't have to stop *being* afraid. Just take a deep breath and do your best to control your fear."

Ray gave her a halfhearted smile and followed her advice, exhaling in short, shaky breaths. He was more than just afraid he was terrified. It was by sheer will that he was still moving with all those horrid pictures doing a slideshow around them. Rapes, murders, child degradations, tortures, the human mind wasn't designed to sustain such horrors. On their right was a mixed group of white and black youths wearing athletic sweat suits forcing a homeless man to swallow his own feces. This inhumane act was playing out so vividly, Ray recognized where it was taking place. Just behind the visitor's side bleachers at the Maple Grove High football field. Apparently, the kids in the Grove had adopted a new half-time activity, but the bleachers were empty and the sun above was a dim orange ball. Apparently, this was an after-school activity. Julie began to retch.

"Don't you dare. I held it in, so can you."

She did, but Ray was worried about her, nonetheless. She was pale and there was a sheen of sweat on her brow. Ray wanted to contribute this to the amount of blood Julie lost before he had tied off her wounds, but it was more than that—it was this place. Something about it was making her sick, poisoning her as it had poisoned Roy. If they didn't hurry, Julie may be dead before she could even make an attempt at opening the gate.

A sudden series of raucous cackles, like those of some deranged witch from a fantasy tale, caused such a start in Ray that he nearly let go of Julie and beat his feet back in the other direction. One of her hands went to his chest, balling up what little there was left of his tee-shirt and the arm around his shoulder tightened. Their eyes met again, and again Ray believed he loved her. Whatever was inside of her was strong. Those eyes... not an ounce of fear shone in them. She had hidden her face and retched, almost vomited, but not once since they stepped through the doorway of light had she shown any signs of being afraid, disgusted, but never afraid.

A cold, steely set of fingers crept around his elbow and Ray jerked away, speeding up their limping stride and not looking back. He didn't want to know what touched him. He was still afraid no matter what Julie said; he couldn't help it.

"*There,*" Julie declared and pointed out an old wooden door at the end of the hall. "They're behind it. Can you feel them?"

Ray didn't know if he could feel them or not—maybe a slight buzzing in his head—but the insane picture show in his head had stopped. "Well, no time like the present." He scooped Julie up in his arms, being careful of her injured knee, and carried her to the door. Letting her legs go to touch the floor, he did as gently as when he had picked her up. He put a hand on the doorknob, and then paused.

"What?" She was as anxious as he was to get this over with.

"Before I swing this bad boy open, is there anything else to know?"

"Good luck?" she shrugged.

"Well, instill me with confidence, why don't you?" Ray said sarcastically.

"I'd say break a leg but that always sounded like a curse to me."

"Well, then," Ray smiled. "Good luck it is."

With this, Ray threw open the door and they hobbled through it.

The room they entered was a dank chamber that

smelled like the combination of mold, urine, rot, and human feces. That scant sliver of white light appeared to have followed them from the adjoining corridor and now was nothing but a small hovering circle. Ray took the room in with a child's curiosity, noting the creepy layout with enough detail to keep himself from dropping Julie and doing what he'd nearly done in the corridor—leave. On the far left wall was an antique wooden-framed bed (rotted through by the looks of it, and Ray wondered how it was still standing, let alone supporting anything at all) made up with dirty, moldering sheets and a quilt that was nothing but moth food. Of course, Ray doubted it was moths eating away at that county-day-fair relic. On top of the quilt was a living mummy, or maybe living was just the wrong description, more like a mummy on life support. Ray was looking at what was left of Leonard Atkins. The skin was dry and taut against the skeleton underneath. Ray and Julie moved in for a closer look.

Christ! How in the name of God is this possible?

Leonard Atkins, still wearing a pair of ancient trousers, lay on his rotting bed bare-chested, well *bare* was a nice way to envision it, mummy or not. Truth was, his chest was open from his collarbone all the way down to his waistline. Inside this dried-out husk that was, once upon a time, a man, were healthy, active internal organs. *My God! The fucker's heart is still beating,* Ray thought with another lurch in his stomach. He pulled the 9mm and Julie stayed his hand.

"Why are you stopping me? That's... That's..." He looked at her with pleading eyes. "*That's not natural.*"

She said nothing but pointed towards the wall at the foot of the bed. Halfway up were what Ray would describe as giant mud dauber nests, and so he would think of them as such for the rest of his life. Although they were not what you would call opaque, they had a rhythmic flashing from deep crimson to the same color of orange as that which had surrounded the cabin, and between each sequence of flashes, Ray could see the outline of something inside, something man-sized.

"The evolved," Julie murmured in his ear. "If you kill the master you may cause premature birth."

"Then what do we do?"

"Take me over there." Julie pointed to an object on the opposite side of the room. "Take me to the orb."

That side of the room was like a dismal black hole, and Ray could barely see anything there at all, much less if it was one of the orbs he'd heard about, but he took her to it anyway. And luck be damned, the circle of light shifted with them, illuminating that far corner of the room in semi-brilliant light. *Now, if the damn thing had come equipped with an air freshener things would be just peachy.* That dank piss and shit smell were burning his nose.

Against the wall was an old wooden table, probably had been Leonard's night table in the days of yore, and atop it was a volleyball-sized glass sphere mounted to four brass legs of intricate design, like some fancy thing you'd see in the homes of wealthy investors intent on impressing the world with their possessions. "Sort of looks like a crystal ball, like the kind fortune-tellers use."

"This is what holds them in our world. It's their anchor," Julie said.

"Right," Ray nodded and looked around. Piles of oblong, off-white shapes occupied the corners on this side of the room. *Eggs*, he thought. *This is a nest, remember? But if this is a nest... Where's mama?*

"Help me, Ray. Help me kneel down in front of it."

"Your leg…" Ray started, and she waved him off.

"I have to. No pain, no gain as my dad likes to say." Ray noticed something then, something far worse than the images out in the corridor. There were tears on Julie's cheeks, and he was not so stupid as to think of those as tears of physical pain. No, she was crying for another reason altogether.

She has to die, Ray. His mother's voice. *In order to open the gate to the spirit world, the one that opens it must sacrifice their soul.*

Ray's eyes widened and his grip on Julie tightened, tight enough to hurt her and she grunted.

"What is it? What's wrong?"

"Nothing," he replied and helped her to kneel before the orb. He wanted to stop her, wanted to yell at the top of his lungs that it was not worth it, but he knew in his heart it was the only way. Julie winced and moaned as her injured knee was forced to bend and she bit her lip when pressure was applied to it in order to kneel, but she did not cry out. Fresh rivulets of blood oozed from Ray's makeshift bandage around her knee and again, she waved him off as he tried to lift her back to feet.

"*No,*" she said. "*I have to do this, and you have to protect me while I do it.* It's the only way, Ray, please understand."

Ray straightened up and wiped the tears away from his eyes as she turned and put her hands on the orb. No sooner had she touched its clear, smooth surface than it roared to life in an awesome display of the same tie-dyed colors as the door of light. The bright, hovering circle of white above them dimmed at once, and the colors of the orb danced around the room like out-of-control party lights. Joining the wild, warm hues were the voices of *them*, thousands upon thousands of voices crying out in vehement rage.

NO! They cried. LEAVE US!

He shook his head, trying to shake the voices out, but they remained.

MURDERING BASTARDS! WE ONLY WANT TO LIVE! SPARE OUR YOUNG!

"Yet, you'd use us like cattle," Ray snapped.

"Ignore them. They want you to lose focus."

BASTARD! They roared.

The concrete wall directly behind the orb began to shake and a small pinpoint of crimson light appeared in its center, growing brighter and brighter as it grew in circumference.

"It's working, Ray!" Julie's voice, however, was weakening and Ray could see veins poking up along her arms and neck, could see the cords of her neck standing out like the roots of some ancient tree, and her face was soaked in sweat. "Keep it away, don't let it interfere!"

For a moment, Ray had no idea what she meant. They were alone in this dungeon of a room and whatever normally resided here had vacated the premises, and then he heard it speak, not in his head, but in actual, vocalized words.

"*Bitch!*" it snarled in a tone of bitter hatred and Ray whirled to face it, the 9mm held out before him in the same two-handed grip he'd utilized in his kitchen. Dangling from the barrel was his mother's pendant, no longer a hexagon, but a dolphin with its tiny red eyes glowing in a deep shade of crimson.

"*My house! My house!*"

Standing before him was Donnie Atkins, or at least what was left of Donnie Atkins, anyway. "Damn."

"Keep it away!" Julie repeated.

"Just keep your mind on what you're doing, sweet pea, and for the love of God, don't turn around." Ray didn't want her to see her ex like this. Donnie had been a prick and Ray seriously wondered why a girl as pretty as Julie had dated the guy, but she had seen something in Donnie and she *had* dated him, might have even loved him. For her to see him like this was out of the question.

"Trespasser! Traitor! My house. GET OUT!"

"Not by the hair of my chinny, chin, chin!" Ray shouted back.

Behind Ray, the crimson circle grew larger and from somewhere in its depths rose the screams of a million lost souls. The thing that had at one time been Donnie Atkins bellowed in rage, and four large tentacles erupted from its back, giving the thing an odd and slightly morbid resemblance to *Doctor Octopus* from the Spider-man comics. Ray squeezed the trigger and the creature charged, ignoring the round that literally obliterated its left arm from the elbow down, and collided with Ray. Two of those tentacles buried sharp little teeth into Ray's torso. The thing screamed again and brought the remaining two tentacles around to clamp down on Ray's shoulders.

Crying out a string of obscenities that did nothing to ease the pain, Ray took a haggard breath and fought to hold on to both his stomach and consciousness. The thing's breath, a fetid smell like spoiled milk and rotten eggs, rolled over his face in wave after gagging wave. The pain was subsiding, but that was a bad thing and Ray knew it. The fucker was pumping him full of the same toxins that had killed Roy.

"My house!" it screamed.

"It's working, Ray! Keep it away!"

Oh, I'm doing a bang-up job in that department, Ray thought.

"My house! Bitch! GET OUT!"

Leonard! Ray thought suddenly. *May cause premature birth, but what if…?*

Ray raised his arm the best he could. The toxins were doing their job, numbing him and every movement he made felt like moving around in a swimming pool. Leveling the sights of the 9mm with the blur that was Leonard Atkins' skull, he squeezed the trigger. The old man's head exploded like a melon and the thing holding Ray let go, staggering backward and shrieking. On the wall, the flashing cocoons cracked open and spilled out human-shaped globs to the floor, two of the evolved in mid-evolution, Ray supposed. Their bodies were black and scaly, reptilian in appearance, but their hands and faces were all-too human. Both were female and both appeared to be no older than sixteen or seventeen. They looked up at Ray with reptilian eyes and showed their teeth, rows of sharp, black spikes, and hissed.

"My House!" the thing screamed once more and Ray emptied the magazine, blowing off sections of Donnie Atkins' corpse until all that remained was the upper body, minus the head—Ray's second two shots had blown it to a nub.

The Odomulite inside broke free, writhing on the concrete and squealing. It jerked, shivered, and died.

"Ray! You have to leave. *Now!*"

He turned toward Julie and the circle on the wall was now a full-blown portal, or gate, or whatever the hell it was. To Ray, it looked like the inside view of the anus when seen from one of those little camera's proctologists rammed up your ass. Whatever it was, it was alive and protruding from its sides were rows on top of rows of gray decaying arms, reaching and stretching, fingers opening and closing.

"GO, RAY!"

Ray turned, dropping the now useless 9mm handgun to the floor, and grabbed the doorknob in both hands, but before he could turn it, the world grew bright with searing white light, and then went dark.

The ending of this tale isn't as dramatic as it is fast. All over Maple Grove, the parasitical creatures known as Odomulites began their unwanted trip to the spirit world, the gate to the spirit world pulling them through it. In some instances, they pulled free of living animal hosts and left behind ruined carcasses. Scientists would soon swarm the town to research and document the strange phenomenon. In the basement of Ray Sanders' house, the concrete room sealing away its evil secrets exploded and the only true evolved Odomulite was pulled to the gate and sent screaming as the reapers lining this tunnel between worlds ripped it apart, limb from limb. It screamed and fought against their digging fingers to no avail.

As for the house, it went up in flames and burned, destroying family history and evidence alike.

Down on the bank of the Locust Fork River, Dianne Townsend watched in awe as the gate sucked in the beasts that had haunted her town for as long as she could remember through the cabin door. To disappear, she prayed, forever. As the sun rose in the sky, signaling a new day, the cabin finally went dark, and, as if a sign that the gate had finally closed forever, it crumpled to the ground. In the distance, she heard the first sirens winding their way up the Sanders driveway and she smiled. She would mourn for those she lost this night, she would remember them always, and they always would be her fondest memory.

I hope you boys thought to send a meat wagon, she thought and passed out.

As for Ray Sanders, his tale will continue. Not now, as this portion of his tale is over, but sometime in the future the world will need him once more, and a new tale will begin.

Panama City, Florida
April 8, 2008

West Jefferson, Alabama
October 22, 2016

ABOUT THE AUTHOR

James Watts was born in Birmingham, Alabama in March of 1976. Growing up in the small town of West Jefferson, Alabama, Watts spent his days lost in his vivid imagination. At age 10, he discovered the Hardy Boys mystery series and fell in love with reading. By Age 12 the discovery of Stephen King's The Stand gave life to his need to write, to tell stories that he hoped the world would love. It would take twenty years of rejections and working low paying jobs, and going through two divorces, before he would see the publication of his horror novel Them. James Watts currently resides in West Jefferson, Alabama and has one 21 year old son, Bailey Watts.

https://authorjameswatts.home.blog
https://www.facebook.com/pg/Southernhorrorwriter/
about/